WITHDRAWN FROM STOCK

TWISTED
26

By Janet Evanovich

The Stephanie Plum novels

One For The Money
Two For The Dough
Three To Get Deadly
Four To Score
High Five
Hot Six
Seven Up
Hard Eight
To The Nines
Ten Big Ones
Eleven On Top
Twelve Sharp
Lean Mean Thirteen
Fearless Fourteen
Finger Lickin' Fifteen
Sizzling Sixteen
Smokin' Seventeen
Explosive Eighteen
Notorious Nineteen
Takedown Twenty
Top Secret Twenty-One
Tricky Twenty-Two
Turbo Twenty-Three
Hardcore Twenty-Four
Look Alive Twenty-Five
Twisted Twenty-Six

JANET
EVANOVICH

TWISTED
26

REVIEW

Copyright © 2019 Evanovich, Inc.

The right of Janet Evanovich to be identified as the Author of
the Work has been asserted by her in accordance with the
Copyright, Designs and Patents Act 1988.

First published in Great Britain in 2019 by
HEADLINE REVIEW
An imprint of HEADLINE PUBLISHING GROUP

1

Apart from any use permitted under UK copyright law, this
publication may only be reproduced, stored, or transmitted, in
any form, or by any means, with prior permission in writing of
the publishers or, in the case of reprographic production, in
accordance with the terms of licences issued by the
Copyright Licensing Agency.

All characters in this publication are fictitious and any resemblance
to real persons, living or dead, is purely coincidental.

Cataloguing in Publication Data is available from the British Library

ISBN 978 1 4722 4612 7 (Hardback)
ISBN 978 1 4722 4614 1 (Trade Paperback)

Printed and bound in Great Britain by Clays Ltd, Elcograf S.p.A.

Headline's policy is to use papers that are natural, renewable and recyclable
products and made from wood grown in well-managed forests and other
controlled sources. The logging and manufacturing processes are expected
to conform to the environmental regulations of the country of origin.

HEADLINE PUBLISHING GROUP
An Hachette UK Company
Carmelite House
50 Victoria Embankment
London EC4Y 0DZ

www.headline.co.uk
www.hachette.co.uk

TWISTED
26

CHAPTER ONE

SOME MEN ENTER a woman's life and screw it up forever. Jimmy Rosolli did this to my Grandma Mazur. Not forever, but for an afternoon last week when he married her in the casino at Atlantis and dropped dead forty-five minutes later.

So far as I know, the trip to the Bahamas was a last-minute decision, and the marriage was even more unplanned. I guess they were just a couple of wild-and-crazy seniors having a moment.

My name is Stephanie Plum. I'm five seven with shoulder-length brown hair that curls whether I want it to or not. I've inherited a good metabolism from my mother's Hungarian side of the family, so I can eat cheeseburgers and Häagen-Dazs and still button my jeans. The hair and a bunch of rude hand gestures I get from my father's Italian ancestry.

I work for my cousin Vinnie as a bail bonds enforcement agent. It's a crappy job, but it's not as bad as my present job of escorting Grandma to Jimmy's viewing at Stiva's funeral home.

"What do you think of my outfit?" Grandma asked. "I got a black dress for the funeral, but it's not my best color, so I thought I'd lighten things up for the viewing. It's going to be a doozy. All the bigwigs from the mob and the K of C will be there."

Grandma was wearing a simple pale green dress that made her complexion look like she'd been embalmed right along with Jimmy. Grandma was in her mid-seventies and didn't look a day over ninety. She had the posture and energy of a twenty-year-old marine, but gravity had taken its toll. She carried slack skin over lean muscle and spindle bone and was in many respects the human version of a soup chicken. The day before her ill-fated trip with Jimmy Rosolli she'd decided to shake things up at the hair salon and had gone with a short punk cut and flame red hair. If you knew Grandma you wouldn't be surprised at this, and in fact, I thought it suited her.

"I saw the Queen of England wearing a dress just like this," Grandma said. "She had a hat on that matched the dress, but I couldn't find one of those."

Grandma came to live with my parents when Grandpa Mazur ate his last pork chop, sucked in the last drag on his Marlboro, and went to heaven to keep his eye on Jesus. It's been a bunch of years now. So far, my father hasn't killed Grandma—only because we took his guns away and we never leave sharp knives lying out in the open.

My parents live in Trenton, New Jersey, in a small two-story house in a pleasant lower middle-class neighborhood called the

Burg. My mom has always been a homemaker. My dad is retired from the post office.

"It's too bad your mother is in bed with a bad back," Grandma said to me. "It's not every day that her stepfather is laid to rest."

"He was only her stepfather for forty-five minutes," I said.

"Still, this is an important occasion for me. I get to stand at the head of the casket and be the grieving widow. There's lots of women out there who would kill to be Jimmy's widow."

I had doubts about the source of my mother's back pain. She self-diagnosed on Google and was self-medicating with bourbon. I was pretty sure the pain had more to do with my grandmother being my mother's worst nightmare than with my mother having a potentially herniated disk.

"We better get a move on," Grandma said. "I don't want to be late. They said I could get a private viewing before they let all the other people in. You're lucky to come along with me on account of you get to go to the private viewing, too."

I was escorting Grandma because my mother had threatened to never again make another pineapple upside-down cake if I didn't stick to Grandma like glue. Then she sweetened the deal with the promise of lifetime unlimited laundry service, which included folding and ironing.

Stiva's funeral home is no longer owned by Stiva. It's changed hands several times and has been given a bunch of different names, but everyone still calls it Stiva's. It's a large white colonial-type house with black shutters, a wide front porch, a utilitarian brick addition in the rear, and garages behind the addition. I parked in the small lot designated VIP PARKING and followed Grandma to the side door.

Grandma knows every inch of Stiva's by heart. Ladies of a certain age use Stiva's as a social center. Grandma and her girlfriends are there four nights out of seven, whether they know the deceased or not. Two of the remaining nights are reserved for bingo at the firehouse. I suppose it could be worse. I mean, it's not like they're frequenting strip clubs or crack houses.

Mervin Klack, the current owner and funeral director of Stiva's, met us at the door.

"Mrs. Rosolli," he said, "my sincere condolences."

Grandma turned to look behind her before remembering that she was Mrs. Rosolli.

"Thank you," Grandma said. "Where's he at? You got him in Slumber Room Number One, don't you?"

"Of course," Klack said. "Nothing but the best for Mr. Rosolli."

"And he's in the mahogany casket with the satin lining?"

"Yes," Klack said. "I think you'll be pleased when you see him. He's wearing the tie you picked out, and he looks very dapper."

Grandma hurried down the corridor, past the refreshment kitchen, to the foyer with the center hall table and massive floral display. The double doors that led to the front porch were closed, but I could hear noise from the crowd that had gathered on the other side.

Slumber Room Number One was the largest of the viewing rooms. It was reserved for lodge members and the occasional decapitation that was sure to draw a crowd. Grandma marched down the center aisle, past the rows of empty folding chairs, and went straight to the casket at the far end of the room. She looked at Jimmy and nodded her approval.

"Yep, he looks good, all right," she said. "He's got good color to his cheeks." She looked around, checking out the flowers. "We got a good amount of flowers, too. Jimmy was real popular."

Good amount couldn't begin to describe the flowers. They were overwhelming. They were crammed in everywhere. My nose was clogged with the scent of carnations, and my eyes were burning.

"Okay," Grandma said to Klack. "I'm satisfied. Open the doors and let's get started."

I heard the front doors bang open and the mourners surge forward. Three old ladies dressed in black were the first to charge down the center aisle. I recognized all three. They were Jimmy's sisters. Angie, Tootie, and Rose. Tootie was using a walker hooked up to a travel pack of oxygen, but she was keeping up with the other two. Jimmy's daughter was close behind. And Jimmy's two ex-wives were behind her.

Angie stopped at the casket and looked down at her brother. Her lips were pressed tight together. Her eyes were narrowed. "Stupid man," she said. She glared at Grandma. "Slut."

"I'm no slut," Grandma said. "I'm a married widow woman."

"You took advantage of my brother's weakness," Angie said.

5

"He could never stay away from the women. And he always went after the young chickies."

Grandma perked up at being lumped in with the young chickies.

"He had no business getting married at his age," Rose said to Grandma. "And look at you, all dressed up like you're going to a party. Where's your respect? A decent widow woman would be in black."

"A lot you know," Grandma said. "The Queen of England has a dress just like this."

"I bet it cost you a pretty penny," Rose said. "No doubt bought with my brother's money."

"I bought it with my own money," Grandma said. "I haven't got your brother's money yet. I'm waiting for the lawyers to give it all to me."

The six women dressed in black sucked in air.

Angie leaned in and got a grip on the casket. "You'll never get his money. You don't deserve his money. I'll see you dead and buried before you get his money. That money goes to the family, not to some gold-digging whore."

Grandma went squinty-eyed on Angie. "Get your hands off my honey's casket, you frump crone."

"I'll put my hands where I want them," Angie said. "I'll put them around your scrawny turkey neck and squeeze the life out of you."

"We'll see about that," Grandma said, and the lid to the casket slammed down on Angie's fingers.

Mervin Klack jumped in and wrenched the lid up. "Ladies!"

Angie wobbled away from the casket. "She broke my fingers! They're all broke."

"It was an accident," Grandma said. "The lid just let go. It was an act of God."

"You did it on purpose!" Angie said.

"You can't prove that," Grandma said. "And anyway, you're going to have to move along. You're holding up the line."

Klack half-dragged Angie away, promising medical aid and cookies, and the rest of the women followed.

Harry Dugan moved forward.

"Howdy," Grandma said to Harry. "Nice of you to show up here for Jimmy."

"My condolences," Harry said, standing at a safe distance, careful not to put his hands on the casket.

Klack had everyone cleared out and the front doors locked by nine o'clock. I exited the side door first and looked around to make sure no one was waiting to ambush Grandma. When I gave the all-clear signal, she scurried to the car with me. We jumped in and locked the doors.

"That was a beauty of a viewing," Grandma said. "Capacity crowd. The funeral is going to be something."

The funeral was going to be a freaking disaster.

"It's Wednesday," I said. "Why are you waiting until Saturday for the funeral?"

"I couldn't get all the arrangements made any sooner. And

Betty Hauck is getting buried tomorrow. Not that she's any competition, but Klack had the big flower car already promised to Betty. And mostly it was that I had to find a place for the wake. Your mother didn't want it at the house, and it wouldn't have been big enough anyway. Lucky, I remembered Jimmy owned the Mole Hole. They said it would be an honor to hold his wake there Saturday morning."

The Mole Hole was a strip club that was famous for its massive Angus beef burgers and its cheap drinks. The drinks were cheap because they were all watered down, and half the time the booze was bootleg. Jimmy and his geriatric cronies met in the back room to play cards, plan the occasional whacking, and take naps in their La-Z-Boy recliners.

"You don't seem very upset about Jimmy," I said to Grandma.

"You get to be my age and you have relations with an old codger, you got to expect these things are going to happen. It's not like he's the first man who kicked the bucket on me. I have to admit it was a shock when it happened, and the first couple hours were rough. I went through a lot of Kleenex. But then I got to thinking it was a pretty good way to go. He hit the jackpot on one of the poker machines. One minute he was real happy and the next minute . . . dead. Death don't get much better than that."

There was a stretch of silence in the car while we took it all in.

"I want to go at bingo," Grandma finally said.

I put the car in gear and drove Grandma home. I idled at the curb until she was safe inside, and then I returned to Hamilton Avenue and drove to my apartment building.

I live in a clunky, three-story, no-frills apartment building about fifteen minutes from my parents' house. My one-bedroom apartment is on the second floor and faces the parking lot at the back of the building. I have a hamster named Rex as a roommate, and a boyfriend named Joe Morelli who does an occasional sleepover. Most of my furniture was handed off to me by my relatives, and since they wouldn't give their furniture away if it was any good, my decorating style and color palette is shabby *blah*.

I parked in the lot and looked up at my windows. Lights were on. This meant one of the two men in my life was upstairs, waiting for me. Morelli had a key, and the other guy, Ranger, didn't need a key. Nothing stopped Ranger, least of all a door lock.

I entered the lobby, sighed at the OUT OF ORDER sign taped to the elevator door, and trudged up the stairs. I let myself into my apartment and called out a *Hello*.

Morelli answered from the living room. "I've got pizza, and there's beer in the fridge. Hockey is on. Pre-season."

I grabbed a beer and joined Morelli and his dog, Bob, on the couch.

Morelli is a Trenton PD cop working plainclothes in crimes against persons. Mostly he pulls homicides and gang-related shootings and stabbings. He's a good cop and an equally excellent boyfriend . . . most of the time. His hair is black and wavy. His eyes are brown and sexy. His body is perfectly put together.

Bob is big and shaggy and sort of orange.

"I thought you could use a diversion after the viewing," Morelli said. "How bad was it?"

"I don't know where to begin. I suppose the highlight was when the lid to the casket let go and smashed Angie Rosolli's fingers."

"It just fell down on its own?"

"Grandma said it was an act of God. I wouldn't mind having a police escort for the funeral. It's on Saturday."

"I've already got it on my calendar. I figure if I'm there, I'll have a head start at solving whatever homicides go down."

"I don't think you have to worry about Angie. I'm pretty sure she's got a broken trigger finger."

"Angie is the least of it. There are rumblings that something was lost besides Jimmy's life, and there's a lot of panic and finger-pointing going on by the La-Z-Boys. Jimmy was known as the Keeper of the Keys. And the keys seem to be missing."

"This is a big deal?"

"Apparently," Morelli said.

"How hard would it be to find keys? Did they look in his house?"

"My source tells me they looked everywhere. Jimmy's house, his office, his car, and the box he was flown home in."

"Jeez."

"I'm thinking sooner or later the search committee is going

to get to your grandmother." Morelli looked over at the pizza box on the coffee table. "Do you want that last piece?"

"Yes."

"What would it take for you to give it up?"

"Make a suggestion."

Morelli smiled.

"I know what that smile means," I said. "And it's not going to get you that last piece of pizza. That smile is a promise of something I'll get no matter who eats the pizza."

"Okay," Morelli said. "*You* make a suggestion."

I had nothing. My mother was already doing my laundry. Morelli couldn't afford to buy me a new car. And at some time in the very near future Morelli was going to get me naked and make me happy. I suppose I had one or two requests I might make regarding the road to my happiness, but it felt awkward to say them out loud in front of the pizza.

Bob jumped off the couch, stuck his head in the pizza box, and ate the last piece.

"Problem solved," Morelli said, sliding his arm around me, cuddling me close to him. "Now let's discuss dessert."

CHAPTER TWO

MORELLI AND BOB left my apartment at sunup. I dragged myself out of bed a couple hours later. Unlike Morelli, I'm not required to attend early morning briefings. Plus, Morelli looks forward to a day of fighting crime. Me not so much.

I took a fast shower, got dressed in my usual uniform of sneakers, jeans, and a girly T-shirt, and ambled into the kitchen. Morelli has a big dog for a roommate and I have Rex. I love Bob, but I think I made the better pet selection. I don't have to walk Rex, and he has very small poop. I filled Rex's water bottle, gave him some hamster food, dropped a couple Froot Loops into his dish, and he was good for the day.

I grabbed a handful of Froot Loops for myself, and shrugged into a black sweatshirt. It was the end of September, and the morning was cool. I hung my messenger bag on my shoulder, locked my apartment door behind me, and trudged off to my car. Fifteen minutes later I was at the bail bonds office.

Connie is the office manager, and she's also a niece to the

late Jimmy Rosolli. She's a little older than me, a little shorter, a little more voluptuous, and 50 percent more Italian.

"Omigod," Connie said when I walked through the door. "I can't believe I missed the viewing last night. I knew it would be a mob scene, so I stayed home. Big mistake. Everyone's talking about it. Did Grandma really break Angie's fingers? Angie has her hands so bandaged up they look like basketballs. Louise Felati sent me a picture."

"Angie had a grip on the casket, and the lid let go and fell down on her fingers," I said. "It was an act of God."

Lula was sitting on one of the two uncomfortable plastic chairs that had been placed in front of Connie's desk. Lula is a plus-sized woman whose bounty runneth over in a size 8 minidress. The bounty would still be running over in a size 12 minidress, but Lula managed to pour it all into an 8. She's a former 'ho who kept her wardrobe but changed her profession. She works for Vinnie now and mostly does whatever she feels like doing. Usually she hangs with me. I suspected she was sitting in the uncomfortable chair, rather than the faux leather couch against the wall, because the chair was closer to the box of donuts on Connie's desk.

"No doubt it was an act of God," Lula said. "God works in mysterious ways. You never know when bad juju is gonna catch up to you. Lucky I only got good juju. That's on account of I live a righteous life."

"You were a hooker," Connie said.

"Yeah, but I was a damn good hooker," Lula said. "I gave people their money's worth. I never scrimped on anything. Everybody knew you come to Lula, and she gets the job done."

I took a donut from the box and went to the coffee machine at the back of the office. "Did anything new come in for me this morning? I'm running low on scumbags I have to find."

"I have two guys who didn't show for court yesterday," Connie said. "Tyrone Brown and Travis Wisneski."

"Hold on," Lula said. "We got a guy named Travis living in Trenton? That's just not right. You got to live in Tennessee or Kentucky with a name like Travis. What did he do?"

"Robbed a liquor store."

"What did he take?" Lula asked. "Liquor or money?"

"Money. At gunpoint."

"That's too bad," Lula said. "If it was liquor you could understand he just needed a drink."

I returned with my coffee. "What about Tyrone Brown?"

"Mrs. Schmidt said she caught Tyrone having relations with her dog."

I choked on my coffee. "That's horrible."

"What kind of dog?" Lula asked.

Connie paged through the police report. "It was a black Lab."

"That's a good-size dog," Lula said. "I'd need more information before I pass judgment on that. Like was it consensual. There's dogs out there that might say okay to that sort of thing for a doggie treat. I knew a few of them when I was working my former profession."

"When Tyrone was done with the dog, he had relations with Mrs. Schmidt," Connie said, "and it definitely was not consensual."

"I don't like that," Lula said. "Rape isn't something I take lightly. And I wouldn't be surprised if he had some drugs in him on account of not many men could perform like that. Most men would need a nap or a bowl of chili in between. Maybe some ribs or chicken wings."

I gagged down the donut, took the two new file folders from Connie, and shoved them into my messenger bag.

"Looks like you're getting ready to saddle up," Lula said. "Guess I'll tag along. Not every day we got a dog fornicator to bring in."

Tyrone Brown lived in a two-bedroom bungalow in North Trenton. A Brown's Plumbing van was parked in the driveway. A man left the house and approached the van just as we pulled up.

"This guy looks like the file picture," Lula said. "Skinny fifty-two-year-old guy with a scraggly brown ponytail."

I parked and walked up to the van. "Tyrone Brown?" I asked.

"Yeah, so?" he said.

"I represent your bail bondsman. You missed your trial date, and I need to help you reschedule."

"Sure," he said. "Reschedule me."

"We'll have to go to the courthouse," I said. "It will only take a couple minutes."

"I haven't got a couple minutes. Do it without me. I got a job."

I moved between him and the open door on the van. "Unfortunately, it doesn't work like that."

"Look, lady, I'm not going with you. Get out of my way. The whole thing is bogus anyway."

"We heard you did the deed with the dog," Lula said.

"The dog and the old lady came on to me. What was I supposed to do? I didn't want to be rude."

"It says in the police report that it was nonconsensual," Lula said.

Brown gave a derisive snort of laughter. "That's what they all say."

"Hunh," Lula said. "I don't like that answer. You got a nasty attitude."

Brown gave Lula the finger. "Nasty this, bitch."

"Okay," Lula said to me. "Do you want to give him a couple thousand volts with your stun gun or do you want me to shoot him?"

I clapped a cuff on his right wrist and reached to secure the second wrist.

"Whoa," he said, jumping away. "What's this about? I don't go for the kinky handcuff S&M stuff."

"This isn't kinky," Lula said. "This is police protocol."

"Are you police?" he asked.

"Sort of," Lula said. "We're like faux police."

I got the other cuff on him, wrestled him into the back seat of my car, and drove him to the police station. We turned him in, and I got my body receipt.

"That's a job well done," Lula said when we were back in my car. "I bet there's a lot of dogs resting easier knowing that guy is off the streets."

I squelched a grimace and pulled out of the lot into traffic. "There has to be more to life than this."

"Like what?"

"I don't know. I want something else. Something different. Something better."

"You need a cat," Lula said.

"A cat?"

"Yeah. I read an article online about how people are getting therapy cats on account of cats are good companions. We could go to the shelter and pick one out for you."

"That's a big responsibility. I don't think I'm ready for a cat."

"Well, your life can't be all that bad if you don't want a cat."

"A cat isn't going to fix my job."

"What's wrong with your job? You got a lot of personal freedom on this job. And some weeks we even make a living wage."

"We work in a cesspool. We hunt down creepy people. I'm tired of creepy people. I want a job with normal people. I want to work with people who use deodorant and don't eat out of dumpsters."

"I hope you're not referring to me," Lula said. "I'd be real insulted if I thought you were referring to me."

"I'm talking about the people we drag back to jail."

"Okay, I get that. They aren't always attractive."

"And I'm stuck in a rut. I'm fifty-six years old and I'm still doing the same stupid stuff."

"Say what? You're how old? How can you be fifty-six?"

I looked over at Lula. "Did I say I was fifty-six?"

"Yeah, and we know that's wrong because that would mean I'm a middle-age lady, and I'm not ready for that shit. Your mama is fifty-six. Not that fifty-six is so bad since fifty-six is now the new thirty-six."

"Well I *feel* like I'm seventy."

"That's the new fifty," Lula said.

"My life isn't going anywhere. It's same old, same old. It's stagnant."

"I see where you might feel like that sometimes. There's not much upward mobility in bounty-hunting, unless you're Ranger. But that's just your day job. You got any other stagnation problems?"

"My relationships are stagnant."

"Now we're getting somewhere," Lula said. "We're back to the cat issue. You got a problem with commitment. You've always had that problem. Only thing you can commit to is a three-ounce hamster. You got two hot men in your life that have been on hold forever."

Lula was right, but I was only half of the problem. Both the men in my life were committed to me at some level, but they'd made it clear that marriage wasn't on the table. Okay with me. I'd tried marriage, and it was a disaster. Still, it felt like my life was standing still when it should be moving forward. I mean, where do you go in a relationship after you've got the fantastic sex mastered and you're comfortable sharing a bathroom?

"You gotta shake it up," Lula said. "Get a new hairdo and some funner clothes. And we got Travis Wisneski in our future. He could turn out to be scary instead of just creepy, being that he's up for armed robbery."

"Tell me about him."

Lula pulled his file out of my messenger bag. "It says here he lives in one of those little row houses on the edge of the Burg. He's thirty-four years old. Unemployed. And I hate to tell you this, but I'm guessing from his picture he doesn't use deodorant. I'm not sure where he dines. Guess it could be a dumpster."

"Okay," I said. "Let's do this."

"My feeling is that you have a job and you do it as best you can," Lula said. "Doesn't matter if you like your job. You do it as best you can."

I agreed, but the unfortunate reality was that sometimes our best was lacking.

I cut across town and found the row houses. Travis lived in the middle of the row in a house indistinguishable from the rest. Paint peeling off the clapboard. Shades drawn on the two front windows. Bleak.

"Are we following standard procedure for an armed suspect?" Lula asked.

"We don't have a standard procedure," I said. "And we don't know that he's armed."

"Yeah, but we know he's got a gun."

"Lots of people have a gun. You have a gun. I have a gun."

"In theory, you got a gun," Lula said, "but I'm guessing you don't have it with you. I'm guessing your gun is home in your cookie jar, and it don't even have bullets in it. There's your problem again. You can't commit to having a gun."

"I don't like guns."

"I like my gun. Her name is Suzy."

"You named your gun?"

"Doesn't your gun have a name?"

"Smith and Wesson."

"That don't count," Lula said. "You got a poor nameless gun. I bet you don't even take proper care of your gun. When was the last time you cleaned it?"

"I put it in the dishwasher after Elliot Flug threw up on it."

"I never saw anything like it," Lula said. "Projectile vomiting. All over you and your gun. It was like something from a horror movie where after someone's head rotates they spew. Next time we go after a felon having a stomach virus we don't get so close."

Something to remember. I parked and cut the engine. "Let's see if Travis is home."

Lula and I walked up to the door and knocked. No answer.

"Hey!" Lula yelled. "Open this here door. I got Girl Scout Cookies."

There was the sound of locks being released, the door opened, and a woman looked out at us. She was somewhere in her thirties. Brown hair that was parted in the middle and needed conditioning. Thin, with tattoos covering her arms. Nose ring. Cigarette hanging out of her mouth.

"Where's the cookies?" she asked.

"It was sort of a fib," Lula said. "We just wanted you to open the door."

A guy who looked like the Travis file photo came up behind the woman and draped an arm around her. "What's up?" he asked.

"They haven't got any cookies," the woman said.

"Travis Wisneski?" I asked.

"Yeah," he said. "So, what?"

I introduced myself and told him he needed to get rescheduled for court.

"How about you kiss my ass," he said. "And then how about you and your fat friend go away and leave me and my old lady alone."

"Excuse me?" Lula said, leaning forward, in Wisneski's face. "Fat? Did you just refer to me as fat?"

"Yeah," he said. "You're fat."

Lula sucker punched him in the face, kneed him in his jollies, and he fell to the floor like a sack of sand.

"I'm a big, beautiful lady," Lula said. "I got class and style and all that shit. Don't you ever forget it."

Wisneski was bleeding from his nose and curled into a fetal position. I cuffed him, and Lula and I dragged him out of his house.

"He's gonna bleed all over your car," Lula said. "And on top of that he looks like he could be diseased, if you know what I mean."

"I've told you a hundred times not to punch the FTA in the face. They always bleed like this."

"I know," Lula said. "I wasn't thinking. I got carried away." She looked back at Travis's insignificant other. "Could we get a towel here? We got a bleeder."

The woman took a drag on her cigarette, stepped inside the house, and closed and locked the door.

"Don't think she's gonna be any help," Lula said.

We stood over Travis for a couple minutes, and the bleeding eventually slowed to a trickle. I got two pairs of disposable gloves from a box in the trunk of my car, and we pulled them on.

"Where do you want him?" Lula asked. "My vote is to put him in the trunk, but that's just me."

"We can't put him in the trunk. We only put dead guys in the trunk."

Lula grabbed the back of his shirt, I went for his feet, and he kicked out at me. He narrowed his eyes and growled.

"I hate when they growl," Lula said. "Freaks me out. It's like we got rabies in front of us."

I pulled my stun gun out of my pocket and tagged Travis on his arm. His eyes glazed over, and his entire body went flaccid. We wrestled him into the back of my car, and I took off for the police station.

"He smells bad back there," Lula said. "I think he pooped himself."

22

CHAPTER THREE

CONNIE WAS AT HER DESK, touching up her nail polish, when we walked into the office twenty minutes later.

"We're hot today," Lula told Connie. "It's not even lunchtime, and we got both our FTAs. We got body receipts and everything."

Connie leaned forward and sniffed. "What's that smell?"

"Travis had an accident after Stephanie stunned him," Lula said. "And he didn't even smell that good *before* the accident. I guess we picked up some of the stench."

"I'm done," I said to Connie. "I'm going home. I'm going to take a shower and review my options."

"One of your options should be magenta extensions," Lula said. "My girl Lateesha at the Royale Hair Salon can give you some with little sparkle stars in them. And you could get your nails done to match."

I stripped in my kitchen, shoved my clothes into a trash bag, and closed the bag with a twisty tie. I apologized to Rex for the smell and padded into the bathroom. I showered and shampooed my hair . . . twice.

23

You can tell the level of my insecurity by the amount of eye makeup I put on. I hide behind mascara. Today was a double application. No doubt compensating for my lack of magenta extensions. Not to mention that the clean clothes I put on were almost exact replicas of the clothes that were bagged in the kitchen.

"Stephanie, Stephanie, Stephanie," I said. "How did you get so boring?" I feared the answer was that I'd always been a little boring . . . and now I was moving into the *loser* category.

I called Morelli and asked him if he thought I was a loser.

"No," he said. "Not yet."

"Not yet? What does that mean?"

"I don't know. I was distracted. I'm at a crime scene. Some guy got electrocuted and sort of exploded. We're trying to find all the pieces. It would be great if you could walk Bob for me. This could take a while."

"Sure."

I disconnected and called Ranger. He'd been my mentor when I started working for Vinnie. He's former Special Forces and has moved up the food chain from bounty hunter to owner of Rangeman, an elite security firm. He's about the same height as Morelli, and Morelli is a smidgen over six feet tall. Morelli's coloring is classic Mediterranean, and Ranger's is Latino. There's a little more bulk to Ranger's muscle, but it's hidden behind perfectly tailored clothes. The clothes are always black. It's easy to lose Ranger in deep shadow.

"Do you think I'm a loser?" I asked Ranger.

"Babe," Ranger said. And he hung up.

Hard to tell exactly what *Babe* meant in this instance, but it didn't do anything to elevate my mood. I grabbed a can of spray deodorizer from under my sink, added the clothes bag from the kitchen to my already full laundry basket, and headed out. I'd left the windows open on my car, hoping it would air. As an added precaution I sprayed the deodorizer around the entire inside. I put the laundry basket in the trunk, and let the spray settle for a couple minutes before I got behind the wheel.

I drove with the windows open, and by the time I parked in front of my parents' house, my shoulder-length hair had frizzed out into a giant puffball.

I pulled my hair into a ponytail, secured it with an elastic scrunchy, and retrieved my laundry basket. Grandma met me at the front door.

"How's Mom feeling?" I asked. "Is her back any better?"

"She's in the kitchen. Says she feels fine. Just gets a twinge now and then."

My father was in front of the television in the living room, eating a sandwich off a tray table. He drives a cab part-time, but mostly I think he fibs about working and goes to his lodge to play cards and watch television.

I skirted around my father, careful not to get between him and the television, and took my laundry to my mom.

"I'm getting lunch together," she said. "Can you stay?"

"Sure."

"We're a little late with lunch because I got delayed at the bakery," Grandma said. "I went to get fresh rolls, and everyone wanted to talk about the viewing and how it's a shame I was widowed so soon." Grandma brought the rolls to the table. "I had no idea I'd be such a celebrity."

My mother was at the refrigerator, pulling out food for lunch. Egg salad, coleslaw, half a meatloaf. She looked over at me and cocked her head at Grandma. "She put on makeup and wore the queen's dress to go shopping."

"I always try to look nice," Grandma said. "And besides, I even got asked for my autograph."

My mother set the food on the table. "Marjorie Jean asked you to sign the receipt for the credit card."

"I saw how she was looking at it," Grandma said. "Like she was thinking of getting a copy to keep for herself."

I set my basket and messenger bag on the floor. "If your back is still bothering you, I can do my own laundry," I said.

"I'm okay, and a deal is a deal," she said. "I hope you have something to be ironed. I need to iron."

Ironing is my mom's safe place. When Grandma and I burned down the funeral home my mom ironed the same shirt for four hours.

I made a meatloaf sandwich and helped myself to coleslaw. "The clothes in the plastic bag might be a little smelly," I said to my mom. "I had to stun a guy this morning, and he had an accident."

"What kind of accident?" Grandma asked. "Did he hurt himself?"

"It was a bathroom accident," I said. "Except without a bathroom."

My mother white knuckled her fork and instinctively glanced at the cabinet where she kept her whiskey stash.

"You have an exciting life," Grandma said to me. "I wish I had a job like you. The best I got is bingo tonight. It's pretty good but it's not like chasing down scumbags."

My mom sat up straight. "You're not going to bingo tonight, are you?"

"Sure, I'm going to bingo. It's Thursday. I always go on Thursday. People are going to be expecting me to be there."

"That's not a good idea," my mother said. "Stephanie, tell your grandmother it isn't a good idea. What if Jimmy's sisters are there?"

"Angie won't be there," Grandma said. "She can't hold the bingo dauber with those big bandages on her hands."

"There are two other sisters," my mother said. "And a daughter. And ex-wives."

"I haven't got anything against them," Grandma said.

"They think you're a gold digger," my mom said. "They're worried you're going to get Jimmy's money. There are rumors going around that there's a contract out on you."

"Half the people in the Burg have contracts on them," Grandma said. "Nothing ever happens because all the mob hit men are in their eighties and have macular degeneration and clogged-up arteries. It's not a job for those millennials. Too much work. Too messy. And you gotta learn a lot of skills. I

27

hear the big thing now for the young folks is having a marijuana farm or being one of those hedge funders."

There was the sound of glass breaking in the living room, followed by my father knocking over his tray table.

"What the Sam Hill!" my father yelled.

I ran into the room and saw that the front window was shattered, and there was a bottle rolling around on the living room rug. It had a burning rag stuck into the top. I snatched the bottle and threw it back out the broken window. The bottle hit the side of my car parked at the curb and exploded. In an instant the car was engulfed in flames, and black smoke billowed into the sky.

My mom and grandmother had followed me into the living room and were standing next to my dad.

"Molotov cocktail," I said. "We were lucky the bottle didn't break when it hit the floor."

"Quick thinking," Grandma said. "You got a good arm. I couldn't have reached the car."

It was a surprise to me too. I'd thrown the bottle in a blind panic. Hitting my car was just one more indication that my life was in the shitter.

"What was that about?" my father asked. "I was eating my lunch and watching television and all of a sudden this bottle comes flying through the window."

I exchanged glances with my mother and Grandma. None of us wanted to tell my father about the contract on Grandma.

"Mistaken identity," I said.

"Prank," my mother said.

"Damn aliens," Grandma said.

My mother set the tray table back upright and picked the plate and napkin up off the floor. "Good thing you were done with lunch," she said to my father. "Would you like fruit or ice cream for dessert?"

"Ice cream," he said. "Chocolate. And then I'm going out with the cab."

My mother went to the kitchen to get the ice cream, and Grandma and I went out to the front porch to watch the car burn. Two cop cars were the first to arrive. A couple fire trucks and an EMT truck were close behind.

I got a call from Ranger. He decided a while ago that my safety was his responsibility, so he keeps tabs on me by installing tracking devices on my cars. Initially I was annoyed, but the truth is they come in handy every now and then. Obviously, he was just notified by his control room that his bug went dead.

"Babe," he said.

"I sort of firebombed my car," I said, "but no one was in it, so it's all okay."

"Good to know," he said. And he disconnected.

Morelli called next.

"I just heard from dispatch that there's a fire at your parents' house," Morelli said.

"Someone pitched a Molotov cocktail through the living room window. It didn't break because it landed on the rug, and I was able to toss it back out the window before it exploded.

Unfortunately, I accidentally pitched it at my car that was parked in front of the house."

"Anyone hurt?"

"No. We're all okay. The fire trucks are here."

"I assume this was meant as a message to Grandma."

"I assume you're right. Are you still looking for body parts?"

"Yeah. I think I just found a nose."

"Boy, you really know how to have fun."

"Gotta go," Morelli said. And he disconnected.

My phone rang again. It was Connie.

"There's black smoke coming from the vicinity of your parents' house," Connie said.

"It's my car."

"Again?"

"Someone tossed a firebomb into my parents' house, I tossed it back out, and it exploded my car."

"Bummer."

"You have any idea who might have done this?"

"It would be a long list," Connie said.

Another fire truck pulled up with lights flashing and sirens screaming, and I ended the conversation with Connie.

"This is going to put a crimp in my plans," Grandma yelled at me. "I was hoping you'd give me a ride to bingo. I usually go with Evelyn Malinowski, but she has hemorrhoids and doesn't want to go to bingo with her whoopee cushion."

"You should give up bingo tonight," I said. "Someone just tried to firebomb you."

"We don't know that for sure," Grandma said. "They could have been after you. You get firebombed all the time."

"Not *all* the time."

"Well, once in a while. Anyway, you get firebombed more than I do."

No one was doing much for my car. Mostly everyone was standing around waiting for it to burn itself out.

"I hate to miss this bingo," Grandma said. "It's not every day I get to be a celebrity. Once Jimmy's put in the ground my days of glory are going to be over."

My great-uncle Sandor had bequeathed his '53 powder blue and white Buick Roadmaster to Grandma. The car was kept in the garage and was available for anyone desperate enough to use it. And that would be me.

"I can borrow the Buick," I said. "What about Mom? She's not going to want you to go."

"She's inside nipping at the hooch," Grandma said. "She'll be nice and mellow by bingo time."

It was close to four o'clock when I finished with the police report and arranged to have my car towed away. I backed Big Blue out of the garage and drove the short distance to Morelli's house. I got Bob hooked up to his leash, and we followed his usual route. It was slow going since Bob did a lot of bush sniffing and leg lifting, but it was a pleasant walk, not counting the occasional whiff of cooked car carried on the wind.

"What would you think of magenta extensions?" I asked

Bob. "It could be the start of my makeover program. Who knows what would follow. Maybe a new job. Or a new boyfriend. I might join a gym."

Bob turned his head and looked at me.

"Yeah, you're right," I said. "I'm not going to join a gym. I mean, let's not get stupid about this makeover."

A black Cadillac sedan cruised by and pulled to the curb. The passenger door opened and a young guy with slicked-back black hair got out and walked over to me.

"Stephanie Plum?" he asked.

"Yes."

"Get in the car. Someone wants to talk to you."

"Who?"

"I'm not at liberty to say."

"Is he in the car?" I asked, looking into the car.

"No. We're going to take you to him."

"I don't think so. I'm walking Bob right now. Tell him to text me."

So this all sounds pretty tough on my part, but the truth is I was a little rattled. I'd seen this scene countless times in mob movies, and it never ended well.

"Look, lady," he said. "Just get in the car, okay?"

I pressed the speed dial to Ranger. He picked up, and I told him I might have a problem.

"Who are you calling?" the slick-haired guy asked.

"Ranger."

"Oh jeez," he said. "He's the Rangeman dude, right? He threw my cousin out of a window once."

"Was your cousin okay?"

"Eventually. Sort of. It was a third-floor window."

"What did your mystery boss want to talk to me about?"

"I don't know. I just ride around with Lou. We go for coffee, and we snatch people sometimes."

"Bob is getting impatient," I said. "I need to move on."

"Sure," he said. "Have a real nice day."

Bob and I walked to the corner, and a Rangeman SUV pulled up.

"Everything's okay," I told them.

"Ranger would like us to escort you home. Would you like to ride, or would you rather walk?"

"We'll take the ride," I said. "Bob has already pooped. We have nothing important left to do."

CHAPTER FOUR

RANGEMAN DROPPED ME at Morelli's house and waited until I was safely inside. I closed and locked the door and looked out the window. They were still at the curb.

"Whatever," I said to Bob.

I poured his dinner kibble into his bowl, gave him fresh water and a hug, and told him Morelli would be home soon. Maybe. I left the house, got into my borrowed Buick, and chugged away. The Rangeman SUV followed me. Okay by me. As far as I was concerned, they could follow me for the rest of my life. Or at least until my life improved.

I parked in my apartment building lot, gave the Rangeman SUV a friendly wave, and took the stairs to my apartment. Rex was asleep in his soup can when I walked into the kitchen. I tapped on his cage and some hamster bedding moved, but Rex stayed snug in his nest. I lifted the lid on my brown bear cookie jar, looked in at my gun, and thought maybe I should put bullets in it. Just in case. I searched my junk drawer. No bullets. I could go out to buy bullets, but I wasn't sure where one went to do this. Dick's Sporting Goods, maybe. Dick's had everything. I went to the window. The Rangeman SUV was still there. They'd follow me to Dick's. And then they might follow me inside and see me wandering around, trying to figure out where to buy bullets. It would be embarrassing. I'd look like a moron.

I put the lid back on the cookie jar. At this time of the day the traffic would be horrible getting to Dick's. And did I really want to shoot someone? No. So, what was the point in getting bullets? If I felt like I needed bullets tomorrow, I'd have Lula get some for me. They sold ammo at her hair salon.

Bingo doesn't start until seven o'clock, but Grandma likes to get there early so she can get her lucky seat. I rolled to a stop in front of my parents' house at six-thirty and Grandma was waiting on the porch. She had her big patent leather purse hung in the crook of her arm. This meant she was carrying. It was the only purse that could accommodate her .45 long-barrel.

"How'd you get out of the house with that purse?" I asked her when she climbed in.

"I waited until your mother went to the bathroom and then I sneaked out."

A glass repair truck was parked in the driveway, and two men were on the porch fixing the broken window.

"Fast service," I said.

"The guy with the ball cap is in the same lodge as your father. They stick together."

Five minutes later I pulled up to the fire station.

35

"Evelyn isn't going to be here tonight," Grandma said, "so there'll be an extra seat next to me if you want to play. It's going to be a good night. Marvina is calling, and they got a grand prize donated by Dittman's Meat Market."

I imagined my mother whispering in my ear. *Do not leave your grandmother's side. I'm holding you responsible. Do not let her break any more fingers or shoot anyone.*

"Sure," I said. "I'll play. Hold the seat for me while I park the car."

I dropped Grandma off and circled around to the lot behind the firehouse. Rangeman followed. I parked and walked up to their SUV.

"I'm going to be a couple hours," I told them. "I'm making sure Grandma doesn't shoot anyone at bingo."

There was a moment of silence while they digested this.

"Seriously?" the driver asked.

"Instructions from my mother," I said.

I went into the bingo hall and took my position next to Grandma. She was the center of attention, accepting condolences and sharing wake details. Marvina was at the front table, checking out the basket holding the bingo balls. Women were beginning to take their seats and lay out their cards. The door opened and Tootie and Rose walked in. A hush fell over the room, and everyone but me took a step back from Grandma.

Tootie reached into her purse, someone yelled, "She's got a gun!" and everyone hit the floor. Tootie pulled a bingo dauber out of her purse, and there was a collective sigh of relief.

"I got a good feeling about today," Grandma said, getting to her feet. "I feel lucky."

"You got firebombed!"

"Yeah, but it didn't burn the house down. And I'm wearing my lucky shoes. I was wearing these shoes when Jimmy hit the jackpot."

I assumed she was also wearing the shoes when he died, but no point mentioning it and ruining her lucky high.

Marvina gave her bingo basket a spin, and there was a scramble for seats. Tootie and Rose settled on the opposite side of the room from Grandma. They set out their equipment, straightened their cards, and glared at Grandma.

"They're trying to put the hex on me," Grandma said.

"There's no such thing as the hex."

"Maybe not, but I'm glad I'm wearing these shoes. I'm planning on getting that grand prize tonight. I heard Dittman put a rump roast in the basket."

After ten minutes of play, Ginny Barkalowski called out "*Bingo!*"

"Dang," Grandma said. "I'm not keeping up with my cards. I can't concentrate with Tootie hexing me. She's giving me the eye."

I glanced across the room at Tootie and saw that she was mumbling and had her finger pulling on her lower eyelid.

"Ignore her," I said to Grandma. "It's all baloney."

Grandma slid her middle finger alongside her nose and stuck her tongue out at Tootie.

"Are you giving her the finger?" I asked Grandma.

"It's just that my nose itched," Grandma said. "Was I using my middle finger?"

"Yes. And you were doing it on purpose."

"I got a bunch of slick moves like that," Grandma said.

"If you dial back the moves I'll take you to the diner for rice pudding after bingo."

"I'll do my best, but it's hard when you keep getting provoked."

Morelli called at eight o'clock.

"I can't talk long," I said, stepping outside the bingo hall. "I'm at bingo with Grandma. Tootie and Rose are here, and Grandma thinks they're trying to put a hex on her."

"She's probably right," Morelli said. "I hear emotions are running high over Dittman's rump roast."

"You know about the rump roast?"

"I'm a cop. I know everything."

"How did it go with the guy who exploded himself? Did you find all his parts?"

"Mostly," Morelli said. "A cat ran off with something, and we couldn't catch it. We think it might have been a finger. How's your day going, aside from bingo?"

"It's been routine. I was offered a ride while I was walking Bob, but I declined. Black Cadillac sedan. Two morons inside. Said someone wanted to talk to me. Wouldn't give me a name."

"Did you get a picture of their plate?"

"No. I was a little flustered."

"Do you need a big strong guy to come over to protect you?"

"Thanks, but I've already got two of those hanging out in the parking lot."

We exchanged a few more pleasantries and disconnected. I turned to go back inside and saw a black Cadillac sedan idling across the street. I gave it a little finger wave, and it drove away.

At nine o'clock an argument broke out over the Dittman's grand prize. Suzanne Blik was declared the winner, and Karen Barkley instantly accused her of cheating. The accusation had some merit because we all knew Suzanne cheated all the time. We also knew that almost *everyone* cheated all the time at bingo.

"I won this fair and square," Suzanne said.

"You never won anything fair and square," Karen said. "That Dittman's basket belongs to the runner-up. And that would be me."

They both had a grip on the big wicker basket. Karen wrenched it away from Suzanne, and the basket went airborne. Cans of gravy and green beans, a loaf of rye bread, and the massive rump roast flew out of the basket. The empty basket hit Tootie square in the face, and Tootie sat down hard on the floor. Blood gushed out of her nose.

Marvina panicked and hit the big red FIRE EMERGENCY button on the wall. Overhead sprinklers went off and gushed water, and everyone ran screaming for the door. A bunch of firefighters rushed in and carted Tootie out of the room.

Grandma and I exited the building, and Grandma immediately took off for the parking lot.

"Hurry up," she said to me. "Where's the car? I gotta get in the car."

The parking lot wasn't well lit, but it's easy to spot a powder blue and white '53 Buick Roadmaster. I slid behind the wheel, and Grandma climbed in next to me. I looked over and realized she had the rump roast.

"Omigod," I said. "I can't believe you took the rump roast."

"Someone had to take it," Grandma said. "It wouldn't be right to waste a good rump roast."

Ranger was waiting for me when I slogged into my apartment. He was dressed in the standard Rangeman uniform of full utility gun belt, black cargo pants, and long-sleeved shirt with the Rangeman emblem on the sleeve. He owned the company, but he still did the occasional shift when they were short on manpower.

I was soaked to the skin, and I had two layers of mascara streaking my face. Water dripped off the hem of my jeans.

"Babe," Ranger said, "your lips are blue. We need to get you out of those wet clothes."

"I think my lips might be blue from my mascara."

The hint of a smile twitched at the corners of Ranger's mouth. "Maybe, but I'd still like to get you out of your clothes."

I got rid of my shoes and peeled my socks off. "What are you doing here?"

"Mental health check. I was ending a patrol shift and heard you were heading home after a bingo disaster."

"Marvina panicked when Tootie got hit in the face with the Dittman's basket. She punched the button on the fire alarm and set the overhead sprinklers off. I imagine she thought she was hitting an emergency help button."

Ranger was lounging against my kitchen counter. Arms crossed over his chest. Watching me strip down to my sports bra and stretchy bikinis.

"It's been a while," Ranger said. "I've missed you."

Ranger and I have had our moments in the past. It's not like this was the first time he's seen me in my undies. Or for that matter without them. And it's not as if my sports bra and bikinis were all that revealing. Not any more revealing than my swimsuit. Maybe less. It was that Ranger emits a sexual pull that is hard to ignore. He enters my field of vision and I get a rush. If I'm at arm's length and close enough to get a hint of his shower gel or feel his body heat, I'm in serious danger of turning into a slut. I want him. Bad. And that's not good since Ranger is an opportunist, and I have an awesome boyfriend who doesn't look kindly on sharing me. Yet another indication that my life isn't on track.

"As you can see, I'm perfectly okay," I said to Ranger. "I just need to wash the bingo hall water out of my hair, and I'll be good as new."

"We need to talk," Ranger said. "We can talk while you shower."

Oh boy. Ranger watching me in the shower. Just the thought gave me heart arrhythmia and a massive dose of Catholic guilt. I'd pretty much lost my blind faith, but the guilt was still strong.

"That doesn't work for me," I said. "We can talk *after* I shower."

Ranger checked his watch. "As long as you don't take the hour shower. I have paperwork stacked up at Rangeman. I've been out all day."

Yay for me. The no-cheating stars must be in alignment. I took a fast shower, toweled off, and ran a comb through my hair. I wrapped a towel around myself and stepped out of the bathroom and into my bedroom. Ranger was sitting on the bed, checking his mail on his phone. He looked up and smiled at me.

"Babe," Ranger said.

This time it was easy to guess what *Babe* implied. His voice was soft. His gaze traveled the length of me and settled on the towel.

"No," I said. "Don't even think about it."

"Hard not to think about it when you're in front of me in a towel."

"I just took a shower! What did you expect?"

"I was hoping for naked."

"And I was hoping you'd wait in my living room."

"I tried that," Ranger said. "Your couch is covered in dog hair."

I ratcheted up my grip on the towel. "Bob is a shedder."

"Babe," Ranger said, "your knuckles are turning white, and I'm running out of time. Here's the short version. The two errand boys who tried to get you into the Cadillac work for Benny the Skootch. He's got his name on a La-Z-Boy at the Mole Hole, and I'm guessing he wants to talk to you about Grandma and the missing keys. You know about the keys, right?"

"Only that they're missing."

"I don't know much more than that, but I know if the keys don't turn up soon, things are going to get messy. These Mole Hole guys are old-school. They do things the old-fashioned way."

"Broken bones and blood everywhere?"

"Yes. I don't want it to be your blood, so try not to lose your Rangeman escort. And talk to Grandma about the keys. Make sure she doesn't have them."

His cellphone buzzed, and he looked at the screen. "I have to go." He pulled a packet out of a pocket on his cargo pants and tossed it onto my bed. "Be careful."

"What's in the package?"

"Ammo. Get your gun out of the cookie jar."

I watched him leave the room, and I heard the front door click closed. I was sort of disappointed that he hadn't ripped the towel off me. There are times when Ranger doesn't pay total attention to *no*. It might not have been so bad if this was one of those times, being that I was in a state.

I opened the towel and looked down at myself. I didn't have

big boobs like Lula, but mine were sort of perky. I had a flat stomach and a nice, neat landing strip below that. Legs were okay. I needed a pedicure. Not bad since lately I'd put in minimal effort. Good thing I wasn't actually fifty-six. I imagined I'd be a wreck by then.

CHAPTER FIVE

I STUMBLED INTO THE OFFICE a little after nine and went straight to the coffee machine.

"You look terrible," Lula said. "You got big bags under your eyes. I hope you're not coming down with something. It's Friday and I can't afford to catch the flu for the weekend. I got a killer date coming up."

"I'm fine," I said. "I just didn't get a lot of sleep last night. I'll be okay after coffee."

"You need more than coffee," Lula said. "You look like you need the rest of the donut box."

I brought my coffee to Connie's desk, poked around at the leftover donuts, and selected a maple glazed.

"Anything new come in?" I asked Connie.

"No, but I heard Charlie Shine is back in town. He was one of the La-Z-Boys until he jumped bail a year ago. It's going around that he came back to pay his respects, but my Uncle Emilio says it's about the keys."

"Does Uncle Emilio know what the keys look like? What they open? Why they're so important?"

"Only the La-Z-Boys know, and no one's saying," Connie said.

"Does anyone know where we can find Shine?"

"I bet he's with his honey," Lula said.

Connie and I went raised eyebrows.

"Shine has a honey?" I asked Lula.

"Hell, yeah. Darlene Long. She's been sitting pretty, living the good life the whole time he's been away."

I got a refill on my coffee. "Isn't Shine married?"

"I don't know about him being married," Lula said. "I just know about Darlene, being that we used to work together until she lucked out and got her sugar daddy. She retired to a nice apartment with an elevator, and I retired to this sucky job."

I ate a second donut. "You know where she lives, right?"

"I went to a lingerie party there once. Darlene and me aren't that friendly, but we get along okay. She worked on the second block of Stark, and I was further up Stark with the hardworking 'hos."

"Shine was a mega-bucks bond," Connie said. "There's no guarantee that we'll get it all back since it's a year later, but it's worth a shot."

I hiked my messenger bag higher on my shoulder. "Let's boogie."

Lula and I went out to the sidewalk and stared at my car.

"You got the Buick," Lula said. "I'm sorry, but that's a

hardship car. It got no sound system or anything. We're gonna have to take my car." She cut her eyes to the Rangeman SUV parked behind me. "*Hello!* Who's here?"

"Ranger thinks I need protection."

"There's two fine-looking men in that car. Maybe we should take *that* car."

"I don't think that's a good idea."

"I can see their muscles from here," Lula said. "They spend time in the gym. I wouldn't mind seeing more of what they got, if you know what I mean."

"We're supposed to be working. And *they* are *definitely* working."

"And?"

"And they might be gay. You never know these days."

"They aren't gay," Lula said. "I could tell a gay man. They got wonderful complexions. These two are blotchy. They don't know nothing about skin-care products. I'm guessing they don't exfoliate."

"Well, I don't want to ride with someone who doesn't exfoliate."

"Say what?"

"I'm not interested in Ranger's men. I'm interested in Charlie Shine. Could we please get going?"

"Hunh," Lula said, "you're Miss Cranky Pants today."

Darlene Long lived in a midrise condo building by the river. We parked in the condo lot and looked up at what we guessed were

Darlene's windows. Third floor, rear-facing unit. No balcony. Shine scrimped a little on his honey's digs. Not that I should throw stones. At least she had digs.

"Now what?" Lula asked.

"Now we snoop around."

We got out of the Firebird, and I told the Rangeman guys who were parked behind us to *stay*. I gave them the same firm voice and hand signal that I use with Bob.

"Does that work?" Lula asked.

"Sometimes."

The building's lobby was dated but clean and brightly lit. Tenant mailboxes were lined up in an alcove. Darlene's name was on one of them. We took the elevator to the third floor and walked the length of the hallway.

"This is her condo," Lula said. "It's a corner unit. 304."

We stood in front of the door for a couple beats and listened. We leaned in closer.

"I don't hear anything," Lula said. "Maybe we should kick the door in."

"Maybe we should try ringing the doorbell and knocking first."

"Sure. That would be another way to go."

I rang the bell and Darlene came to the door.

She looked past me to Lula. "Long time no see."

"I've been busy," Lula said. "I'm in the law enforcement business. We got a lot to do."

"We represent Charlie Shine's bail bondsman," I said.

48

"Charlie missed his court date, and we need to get him rescheduled. We thought he might be here."

Darlene managed a small smile. "Sorry I can't help you. I haven't seen Charlie in ages."

"You don't mind if we look around?" Lula asked her.

"Go right ahead, but don't move anything. My housekeeper is very picky about things being out of place."

"I have that problem too," Lula said.

Lula lives in a one-room apartment on the second floor of a lavender and pink house. It used to have a bedroom, but she converted it into a closet, so now she sleeps on her couch. Her kitchen consists of a half refrigerator and a hot plate.

We checked out Darlene's bedroom, bathroom, and kitchen. No Charlie Shine.

"It's not like we doubted you," Lula said to Darlene. "It's just no stone unturned."

"Of course," Darlene said.

We left Darlene and returned to Lula's car.

"Did you see how Darlene smiles at everything?" Lula asked. "Like she's gracious, right? Real pleasant, even when she wants to stick a stake in your heart. That takes a certain talent. That's how she got her honey. Always being nice."

"Hard to believe someone like that."

"You bet your ass. She was fibbing about not seeing Shine. That apartment reeked of old man."

I hadn't personally picked up any reeking, but it seemed logical that Shine was staying with or at least visiting Darlene.

I paged through Shine's bond agreement. "He lists a house on Willet Street as his home address. Let's take a look."

Willet Street is on the edge of the Burg. I grew up in the Burg and I know a lot of people there, but I don't know Charlie Shine or his wife.

Lula took State Street to Broad Street and left-turned into the Burg. "Do we know if there's a Mrs. Shine?"

"There was a Mrs. Loretta Shine a year ago when this bond was written. She put her house up as security for her husband's get-out-of-jail card."

"So why doesn't Vinnie take the house?" Lula asked.

"It's not healthy to confiscate property owned by a high-ranking member of the mob."

Lula followed her GPS instructions to Willet and parked in front of a small but neat two-story white clapboard house. The Rangeman SUV parked behind us.

"I'm starting to worry," Lula said. "Ranger has these yokels following you around twenty-four seven. He must think you're in a lot of danger. And since I'm sitting next to you, that could put me in danger. I wouldn't be happy if I got killed 'cause I was sitting next to you."

"And?"

"Just sayin'."

"No one's going to get killed. If anything bad goes down, I'll get kidnapped and tortured while they try to extract information out of me about the keys."

"Do you know anything about the keys?"

"No."

"That's not good. You'll have to make something up and hope you die before they come back and torture you some more for telling a fib."

"I'm glad you've thought this through for me."

"I always try to be helpful. It's one of my best qualities."

Lula and I got out of her car and went to Shine's front door. I rang the bell and an elderly woman answered. She was wearing tan walking shoes that looked orthopedic, tan slacks, and a pink floral-print shirt. Her hair was cut short and curled, and the color matched her shoes. She squinted at me over the top of her granny glasses.

"Yes?" she asked.

I introduced myself and gave her my business card. "I'm looking for Charles Shine. Are you his wife, Loretta?"

"Yes, and he's not here. He's probably with his honey."

"You know about her?" Lula asked.

"I send her a fruit basket once a month," Loretta said. "God knows, she deserves it."

"Have you seen him lately?" I asked.

"He was here yesterday, getting clothes. He looked in the refrigerator, didn't see anything he liked, and he left."

"I'd appreciate a call if he returns," I said.

"No problem."

We left Loretta, and Lula drove slowly down Willet.

"Now where are we going?" Lula asked.

"The Mole Hole."

"I knew you were going to say that. I think that's an excellent idea because it's coming up to lunchtime and I could get a burger there. Plus, we could check it out for Grandma's wake."

The Mole Hole is close to the train station. It's on a side street along with several other sketchy businesses. A pawnshop. A tattoo parlor. A Chinese restaurant that's regularly cited for health infractions. Mixed in with the businesses are narrow townhouses owned by slumlords.

Lula parked in the lot attached to the Mole Hole and marched over to the attendant.

"I expect my car to be in perfect condition when I get back," she said. "I don't want a fingerprint on it."

The attendant was a scraggly kid with a gold tooth up front. "You gonna pay for extra protection, Mama?"

"First off, I'm not your mama. And second, I'm not paying nothing, but you need to take out some insurance on your nuts, because they're gonna be in your throat if I'm not happy with my car when I come back."

I gave the *stay* signal to the Rangeman guys, and Lula and I went into the Mole Hole. It was aptly named because we went from bright sunshine to no sunshine at all. We stood at the entrance while our eyes adjusted. It was one large room with tables on the perimeter and a circular bar in the center of the room. A stage and three poles were in the middle of the bar. A lone woman slithered around on one of the poles to music I didn't recognize. She was wearing heels and a G-string and pasties that looked like daisies. Several of the barstools were occupied, and a man and woman sat at one of the tables.

"Not a lot going on here," I said to Lula.

"It's early for the lunch trade. It'll pick up. This is going to be a good venue for a wake. It's got a parking lot and lots of room in here to mingle and hand out condolences. You could even have entertainment up on the stage. Not the daisy nipple lady, but something classy . . . like a harp player or dueling banjos."

I moved to the bar and flagged down a bartender. Lula was next to me with a menu.

"I want one of these man-eater burgers with extra curly fries," she told the bartender. "And I'll have that with a glass of chardonnay."

He looked at me.

"I'd like to talk to Charlie Shine," I said.

He took a beat. "No food?"

"No. Just Charlie."

"Do you have a name?"

"Stephanie Plum."

He punched Lula's order into a computer, turned his back to us, and made a phone call. A couple minutes later a guy who looked like he ate way too much pasta came out of a door behind the bar and walked over to us. He was in his early sixties, wearing a golf shirt and pleated pants. He had thick lips, little eyes, and a comb-over.

"Stephanie Plum?" he asked.

I raised my hand.

He pointed to a table. "Let's sit."

Lula started to go to the table with us, and he stopped her.

"Private conversation," he said to Lula.

"Well, I'm staying right here by the bar, and I'm watching," Lula said.

I took a seat, and he sat across from me.

"I'm Stan," he said. "Who's your friend?"

"Lula."

"She looks mean. Is she muscle?"

"No. My muscle is waiting in the black SUV in the parking lot."

"Ha. Good one."

He thought I was kidding.

"I hear you're looking for Charlie Shine," Stan said.

I gave him my business card.

Stan pocketed the card. "I know who you are. You're the widow's granddaughter. The boys in the back room wanted to talk to you, but you declined our offer of a ride."

"I was walking my boyfriend's dog."

"Well, you're not walking the dog now, so I'm going to talk to you."

"Are you one of the backroom boys?"

"Yeah, I spend some time there."

"Do you have a La-Z-Boy chair?"

"No. I got a couch. There's only so many La-Z-Boys."

"About Charlie Shine," I said.

"About Jimmy's keys," Stan said. "What do you know?"

"I know that they're lost. That's it."

"We searched everywhere, and we can't find them. So our conclusion is that your granny has them. She was with Jimmy at his last moment. We think he handed them off to her." Stan made the sign of the cross. "He should rest in peace."

"My understanding is that the last moment was more like half a moment. I don't think he had time to hand anything off."

"You need to have a conversation with Granny. Out of respect for Jimmy we wouldn't do anything to ruin his funeral, but after the funeral I can't guarantee your family's safety if we don't get the keys. And you should know we aren't the only ones who want the keys. There are others involved who aren't as civilized as us."

"Others?"

Stan stood. "So be real careful."

"Wait! What about Charlie Shine?"

Stan lumbered away and disappeared through the door behind the bar.

Lula was sitting at the bar, sipping her chardonnay and waiting for her burger.

"Well?" she asked. "Is Shine coming out?"

"No. I'm going in."

"In where?"

"In whatever is behind the door behind the bar."

"Are you taking the Rangeman guys with you?"

"No. I don't want to make a big fuss. I just want Shine to go with me to get bonded out again."

"I'd go with you but I'm waiting on my burger," Lula said.

"No problem. I'll be right back."

I walked around the bar and tried the door. Locked. A little plaque on the door said PRIVATE. I knocked and waited a couple beats. I knocked a second time. Two very large goons appeared out of nowhere.

"There are gentlemen playing cards in the private salon, and they don't wish to be disturbed," one of the goons said. "You'll have to leave."

"I'm not leaving until I have Charlie Shine in custody."

"Unfortunately, you're creating a disturbance for our floor show," he said. "We're going to have to remove you."

In the next instant I was bookended by the two goons, who each had a hand under an armpit. My feet were four inches off the floor, and I was whisked out of the Mole Hole. *Slam!* The door closed behind me, and I stood blinking in the bright sun.

A minute later, the door opened, and Lula joined me. She had her burger and fries in a bag and her chardonnay in a cardboard to-go coffee cup.

"This worked out good," Lula said. "They didn't charge me for my burger. Where are we off to now?"

"Drop me at the office so I can pick up my car and go to my parents' house. I want to talk to Grandma. I'll have lunch there and meet up with you later."

CHAPTER SIX

WHEN I WALKED IN, my mother and grandmother were in the kitchen, staring at the casserole dishes on the kitchen counters. They looked relieved when they saw me.

"Thank heavens it's you," my mother said. "We heard the door open and were worried that it was someone with more food."

"We've run out of refrigerator space," Grandma said. "We got seven dishes of lasagna, twelve cakes, at least ten pounds of potato salad, and that's just the beginning."

"It's for the wake," my mother said. "I don't even know half the people who dropped this stuff off. We're going to have to rent a truck to get it to the Mole Hole."

I lifted the lid on one of the casseroles. "This looks good. Do you mind if I have some for lunch?"

"Take what you want," my mother said.

"I'm going to dig in too," Grandma said. "It's not just for the wake. It's to help us through our time of bereavement."

I loaded up with mac and cheese, fried chicken, kielbasa, and a bunch of mini hot dogs wrapped in mini rolls.

"The funeral is at nine o'clock tomorrow," my mother said, sitting across from me at the kitchen table. "The funeral home is sending a car for us at eight-thirty. Your sister isn't going. Everyone in her house has the flu. So, there will be room for you in the car."

If I'd known about Valerie and the flu I would have gone over a couple days ago and gotten infected. I'd take the flu over the funeral any day of the week.

"I might be going with Morelli," I said.

"He can ride in the car too," Grandma said. "It's a big car. It's a limo. Not every day you get to ride in a limo. And you'll get to sit up front at the church. They're reserving a front row pew for us. It's a shame Jimmy isn't here. He would have liked riding in the limo."

There was a long moment of silence.

"There's times when it's quiet at night, and I wonder about him. And I hope he's okay," Grandma said. "I guess he did some bad things, so it's a crapshoot if he got into heaven." She pushed some macaroni salad around on her plate. "Truth is I'll be relieved when all this is over, and I can move on to what's in front of me instead of what's behind me. It's not like I want to forget Jimmy. It's just that he's in a different spot in my life now. He's in the good memories spot. If I didn't put him there, I'd be sad all the time, and I don't like being sad. I figure happiness is a choice that you make. Even in terrible times." Grandma slumped a little. "Sometimes you really gotta work at it."

So, here's Grandma Mazur with hot pink lipstick and flame red hair, dressing up like the Queen of England, appropriating a ten-pound rump roast from the bingo hall . . . and it turns out she's brilliant. She has a life philosophy. She can articulate it. She consciously tries to live by it. *Happiness is a choice that you make.* Wow.

"That's great, Grandma," I said. "Good for you."

"I got a strong sense of self-preservation," Grandma said. "You got it too. It's from our Hungarian farm stock. 'Course there's also some Gypsy in us, and it's best not to talk about those tendencies. The Gypsies were a little loosey-goosey, if you know what I mean."

I knew exactly what she meant.

"I ran into one of the Mole Hole back room boys today," I said. "It seems Jimmy had some keys, and now they're missing."

"Yep. He was Keeper of the Keys," Grandma said. "It was a big honor."

"Did you ever see the keys?"

"No. He said they were in a safe place."

"Did he say where that safe place was?"

"No, but I know he always kept them close to him in case he needed one."

"Did he say what the keys opened?"

"No," Grandma said. "I didn't care about it at the time, but now that it's a big deal I wish I knew. Everybody is talking about it."

"The La-Z-Boys think you have them."

"Why would they think I have them?"

"You were with Jimmy when he . . . you know."

"Died?"

"Yes. They think he passed the keys on to you in his last moments."

"There were no last moments," Grandma said. "He didn't pass nothing on."

"Is it possible that you have them and don't know you have them?"

"I guess," Grandma said. "I'll keep my eyes open, but seems to me I'd have seen them by now."

This was a big bummer. Life would be so much better if Grandma had been able to give me the keys.

"I don't like this business with the keys," my mother said. "Who knows what those old men will do to get them back? They're all gangsters." She shook her finger at Grandma. "You should have known better than to get mixed up with one of them."

"It seemed like a good idea when he was alive. He had a lot of money and almost all of his teeth. He was a real good dancer. He never said anything about having a bad heart. And he told me he was retired."

I finished my mac and cheese and stood. "I have to get back to work."

"Who are you after today?" Grandma asked. "A killer or a rapist?"

"Charlie Shine. Rumor has it he came back for Jimmy's funeral."

"He's probably with his honey," Grandma said.

I turned to Grandma. "You know about that?"

"Everybody knows about that," Grandma said. "Loretta would have divorced him if it wasn't for the honey. This way Loretta gets to keep the house, but she doesn't have to put up with Charlie. He's a bit of a drinker."

"I have your laundry all done," my mother said. "I had to throw some of it away. What's left is in the basket by the front door."

I stowed my laundry basket in the trunk and drove to the office. Going with Grandma's words of wisdom that happiness is a choice, I thought I might choose to keep driving until I got to California. Or at least Colorado. I was deterred by the fact that I was driving a '53 Buick, and I'd run out of gas money before I got to Ohio.

I parked at the curb and joined Connie and Lula in the office. Connie was touching up a chipped nail, and Lula was napping on the couch. Vinnie was nowhere.

"I have a problem," I said. "The La-Z-Boys think Grandma has the keys, but she doesn't have them."

"Have you explained this to them?" Connie asked.

"Yes, but they didn't completely buy it. I'll try again

tomorrow. Out of respect for Jimmy they aren't going to rough Grandma up until after the funeral."

"Those keys must be real important for them to want to pull the fingernails off a nice old lady like Grandma," Lula said.

"You have connections," I said to Connie. "Can you find out what this is all about?"

"My only La-Z-Boy connection is dead," Connie said, "but I'll ask around."

"It's gonna be interesting to see who gets Jimmy's chair," Lula said. "Anybody would want a La-Z-Boy. I sat in one of them, and I never wanted to get up. You could put your feet up and everything."

"Are you going to the funeral?" I asked Connie.

Connie nodded. "I have to take my mother. It's like the event of the century."

"I can see that," Lula said. "Not every day you get to go to a wake in a titty bar."

"I was thinking about putting some bullets in my gun," I said. "Ranger gave me some."

"I have a salon appointment to get glamorized for my date tonight," Lula said. "You could come with me and get pink streaks in your hair or magenta eyelash extensions. It could be the first step on the road to the new you."

It was almost six o'clock when Lula and I left the salon. Lula had silver glitter on her eyelids and her hair was fluffed up into a huge pink puffball. I had a bunch of metallic midnight blue extensions in my hair.

"You made a good choice on those extensions," Lula said. "It's dark as a witch's bum in the Mole Hole, and your extensions are gonna catch whatever light they got there. You'll probably be the only one who can tell the potato salad from the mac and cheese. Everyone else is gonna have to use the flashlight app on their smartphone."

I rolled my eyes up as if I could see the top of my head. "They look pretty though, right?"

"Hell, yeah. And they'll be the shit tomorrow when you gotta wear black. Black isn't a happy color, if you get what I'm sayin'. You gotta sparkle black up. If you haven't got a lot of diamonds, then aluminum foil is the next best thing. Or if it's all black leather you could break it up with chains."

"My extensions are aluminum foil?"

"I can't say for sure, but they look like foil and that's what counts."

"Can I wash them?"

"Yeah," Lula said, "but you might not want to use real high heat with the hair dryer."

"Are you coming to the funeral tomorrow?"

"Wouldn't miss it."

I watched Lula drive away, I waved to the Rangeman guys, and I climbed into the Buick. It was Friday night. Lula had a date. I had the Rangeman guys. I wondered if they'd want to go to dinner. And later we could all watch a movie. I checked them out in my rearview mirror. Dinner and a movie might be awkward. They'd have to clear it first with Ranger. And then they'd be overly polite and afraid to talk to me. And when they went off their shift Ranger would grill them. Okay, dinner with the Rangeman guys was a bad idea. That left my parents and Grandma. An equally bad idea. My mother would take one look at my blue hair and go straight to the liquor cupboard. Better to spring it on her tomorrow when she's distracted by the funeral. Ordinarily I'd be seeing Morelli on a Friday night, but he was off to Atlantic City with his cousin Mooch. Annual poker tournament. They always lost, but they went every year anyway.

I drove home on autopilot, parked, and took the stairs to the second floor. I walked the hall and stopped at my door. It was partially open. My heart stuttered in my chest. I took a couple steps back and called Rangeman. Three minutes later, my Rangeman escorts were in my apartment, guns drawn, doing a security check while I waited in the hall.

One of the guys came out to get me. "It's clear," he said, "but it's a mess."

I stepped inside and looked around. Drawers had been dumped out, cushions thrown onto the floor and slashed, linens torn off the bed, cereal boxes emptied. The lid was off Rex's cage, and his soup can sleeping den had been emptied onto the kitchen counter. Rex wasn't in his soup can or his cage.

I had several moments of breathless panic until I saw Rex peeking out from behind my brown bear cookie jar.

I scooped Rex up, told him I loved him, and gently set him back into his cage. I replaced his soup can and gave him a corn chip from the food spread across the counter.

Ranger called. "Are you okay?" he asked.

"Someone tossed my apartment."

"Was there much damage?"

"Rex is safe. The rest is just stuff."

"Babe," Ranger said and disconnected.

I declined the offer of cleanup help from the Rangeman guys. They had good intentions, but I doubted their domestic skills. Not that mine were all that wonderful, but I wanted to do my own cleanup. I wanted to put my handprint on everything that had been disturbed. I wanted to put things back where they were before my apartment was violated. My household possessions weren't expensive and I didn't even like half of them, but they were *mine*. They shared my life . . . such as it was.

I called my mom and asked if everything was okay there.

"As okay as it could get," my mother said. "We ate one of the casseroles for dinner. Noodles and some kind of ground meat. I'll be glad to get all of this out of the house. It doesn't feel right."

"How's Grandma doing?"

"Better than I am."

"Is she going out tonight?"

"No. Old Mr. Jameson is laid out at Stiva's tonight, and she said hardly anyone is going to the viewing. I guess everyone is gearing up for Jimmy's funeral."

"Make sure you keep your doors locked," I said. "Grandma kind of has a target on her back right now."

Not that a locked door had done me any good.

I said good night to my mom and browsed through the kitchen debris for dinner, settling on a peanut butter and pickle sandwich.

I vacuumed up the cereal and washed the counters. I returned the cushions to the couch, placing them slashed side down so they couldn't be seen. I slid drawers back into the dresser in my bedroom, folded the clothes that had been thrown around the room, and returned them to their appropriate places. I made my bed with fresh linens and crawled in.

I shut the light off, but I couldn't sleep. My door was more secure now that the bolt was thrown, but I still didn't feel safe. And knowing that someone had pawed through my stuff was creepy. I turned the light back on and checked my phone messages and email. I got up and looked in on Rex to make sure he was okay. He was running on his wheel, and he stopped and blinked at me when I flipped the kitchen light on.

"Hey, little guy," I said. "I guess you had a pretty exciting day. Big adventure for you, getting dumped out of your can and everything." I filled his food cup with fresh hamster crunchies, shut the light off, and padded barefoot into the living room. I curled up on the couch, channel surfed, and finally settled on *House Hunters International*. A couple from Houston was looking for a place in Oslo, and the woman was obsessed with getting an apartment with a bathtub. I gave up on the woman and her bathtub search, and I did more channel surfing. I'm not sure when I fell asleep, but one of the morning shows was on and the sun was shining when I woke up on the couch.

CHAPTER SEVEN

SATURDAYS ARE ALMOST always workdays . . . depending on how bad I need money. If I'm having a good month and my rent is paid, I might go to the shore, but that doesn't happen often. This Saturday was different. This Saturday was going to be hideous. Besides the funeral thing, I was going to have to convince the people who ransacked my apartment that Grandma had no knowledge of the keys.

I staggered to the bathroom and stood in the shower until I was moderately awake. I made a halfway serious effort at drying my hair, being careful not to melt my electric blue extensions. In the end, I concluded that the styling effort wasn't entirely successful, and this would be another ponytail day.

I have a black suit that I use for funerals and the occasional job at Rangeman. Tailored jacket. Knee-length pencil skirt. I coupled it with a short-sleeved, scoop neck white sweater and plain black pumps. I looked in the mirror and thought about applying mascara but decided it would take too much energy. Ditto coffee and breakfast. I could get it at my parents' house.

Rex was still asleep in his cage when I entered the kitchen. No doubt exhausted from running on his wheel all night. I had a pang of anxiety about leaving him alone. It wasn't a big deal to have my cushions slashed. The threat of having Rex hurt or worse was a very big deal. I squelched the anxiety by reminding myself that my apartment had already been searched, and it wasn't likely that it would be searched again.

A new Rangeman crew was in my parking lot when I walked to my car. I waved at them and they waved back. I would rather they sat in my apartment and watched over Rex, but I didn't think the idea would fly with Ranger.

It was a couple minutes after eight o'clock when I pulled into my parents' driveway. The church service was at nine o'clock, and Stiva's big black limo was already at the curb. I took a deep breath and went inside. My father was in his chair in the living room, and the television was droning on in front of him. He was wearing his gray suit and a facial expression that could best be described as *just shoot me*.

I bypassed my father and went to the kitchen, where my mother and grandmother were fluttering around. The cakes and casseroles were gone, and the kitchen looked a little bare without them.

"Thank goodness you're here," Grandma said to me. "I need

help with my makeup. Your mother thinks I'm wearing too much mascara. And I can't decide on a lipstick. The queen has been wearing pink lately, but I'm not sure that's a good color with my red hair."

I helped myself to coffee and looked in the fridge for leftovers. "Pink is okay with red hair."

"Stiva's driver brought us fresh bagels this morning," my mother said. "They're in the bag on the counter."

I selected a bagel, sliced it in half, and gave it a layer of cream cheese.

"Anyone want half of this?" I asked.

"Not me," Grandma said. "I can't eat. My stomach is a mess, and I just brushed my teeth. I'll be glad when this is over. I wanted to do the right thing for Jimmy, but having a big to-do like this is nerve-racking. What do you think of this dress? I had a hard time finding a good black one."

My mother squinted at me. "What's in your hair?"

"Extensions," I said. "I had them put in yesterday."

Grandma came closer and looked at them. "They're sort of glittery under the light. I wish I knew about this. I would have got some put in *my* hair. You need something like that when you gotta wear black. It breaks up the frump factor."

I didn't think Grandma had to worry about the frump factor. She had flame red hair all punked out, and she was wearing a black cocktail dress that would have showed cleavage if she had any. As it was, Grandma's cleavage was somewhere in the vicinity of her belly button.

70

I heard the front door open and close, and Morelli sauntered into the kitchen. He was wearing jeans and a black blazer over a blue button-down shirt. When you put Morelli in a suit he looks like a casino pit boss. This isn't a good look for a cop, so he almost always dresses down. His eyes instantly focused on my hair. His eyebrows raised ever so slightly and he smiled. He moved closer and draped an arm across my shoulders.

"I'm guessing this is one step beyond two coats of mascara," Morelli said.

"It's experimental."

He nodded. "Not necessary, but fun."

"Do I look like an idiot?"

"No. You look hot. Do we really have to go to the funeral?"

"Unfortunately, yes. It's important to Grandma. And it's even more important that I talk to the La-Z-Boys. Someone tossed my apartment yesterday. I'm sure they were looking for the keys, but they were also leaving a message."

"Would you like me to talk to them?"

"No. I need to do it. I need to make them understand that Jimmy didn't pass the keys on to Grandma."

"Are you sure she doesn't have them?"

"Almost positive."

I looked over at Grandma. She was sitting at the kitchen table all by herself. She had a cup of tea in front of her but wasn't drinking it. She was staring into the mug, her mouth set in a tight line.

I gave Morelli the second half of my bagel and went to Grandma. "Is everything okay?"

"I'm worried about the church service. I can get through everything else okay, but there's things to think about when you're in the Lord's house. Especially when it's for the last time, like Jimmy. You gotta look at your life and wonder if you should have done better. Jimmy might have made some bad choices. His chosen profession might not have been the best."

"You mean, that he worked for the mob."

"Yeah," Grandma said. "I'm pretty sure he whacked people. Maybe a lot of people."

I went through a mental search, looking for a way to put a positive spin on Jimmy, but I came up empty.

"He had a long, successful career," Grandma finally said. "You gotta give him that."

"It's time to get in the car," my mother said. "Everyone take their things. We'll go directly from the church to the cemetery, so take a sweater. It might be chilly. I have cough drops and tissues if anybody needs them."

We all trooped out of the house, climbed into the big black Lincoln, and sat in silence for the short ride to the church. We took our seats in the pew reserved for us. The pew reserved for Jimmy's relatives was wisely located on the opposite side of the church. I looked at the flower-draped casket in front of the altar and got a chill. Grandma could be resting there next if I failed to protect her.

Grandma dabbed at her eyes. "He was always nice to me," she said.

We managed to get through the service and back to our limo without incident, mainly because we surrounded Grandma and shielded her from seeing Tootie give her "the eye" and Rose give her the finger.

"That wasn't so bad," Grandma said on the way to the cemetery. "There was no mention of Jimmy burning in hell, and the organist did a real good job."

Morelli was next to me, smiling. His family was even crazier and more dysfunctional than mine. This was a walk in the park for Morelli.

Jimmy's family had primo property at the cemetery. It was at the top of a medium-sized hill and overlooked acres of graves. It was a nice fall day. Seventy degrees and sunny. Blue sky. Puffy white clouds. Neatly trimmed green grass dotted with granite headstones. Yellow backhoe idling in the near distance.

We parked a short distance from the gravesite, and what seemed like a mile of white-flagged cars parked behind us. We all got out and took stock of the walk ahead of us.

"Okay," Morelli said. "Let's do it."

He took a firm grip on Grandma's arm, I took the other arm, and we helped her navigate the slope in her fashionable pumps.

Graveside seating was similar to church seating. The Rosollis and the Plums were separated by a section of chairs reserved for the La-Z-Boys and their top wiseguys. Lesser wiseguys stood at the rear along with ordinary mourners, plainclothes cops, and a couple photographers.

"This is a good location for the Rosollis," Morelli said. "Hard to get ambushed up here. You'd have to have a sharpshooter in those trees down by the road."

"You mean the trees that are being guarded by all those cops?"

"Yeah, those trees."

"So, all you have to worry about are the people who are sitting next to us and want to kill each other."

"Ordinarily that would be the case, but I can't see anyone risking getting taken into custody this morning. No one is going to want to miss the wake at the nudie bar."

Grandma was sitting between me and my mom. She had her hands clasped tight in her lap, and she was staring straight ahead. The casket was in her line of sight, but I didn't think she was seeing it. She looked like her thoughts were elsewhere.

"This is a strange place where we live," she said.

"You mean Trenton?"

"I mean Earth. One minute you think you know where you're going, and then in a second it could all change. You don't even have to make a bad decision. You could be doing everything right, and the bad thing happens. It's like we're one of them videogames. Someone pushes a button, and *BANG* you're dead. It's gotta make you wonder what's next."

"What do you think is next?" I asked Grandma.

"Alien invasion. I don't mean Mexicans, either. It's only a matter of time. I wouldn't be surprised to have them landing in the backyard tonight. Or maybe they wouldn't land at all. Maybe they'd just wipe us all out in a flash of light, and we'd be gone. Like the dinosaurs."

"Jeez."

"Yeah, it would be a real bummer to get wiped out in a flash of light. I prepaid my funeral. Picked out my casket and everything. I didn't scrimp, either. I hate to think I wouldn't be laid to rest in that casket. I was counting on a good send-off."

"Aliens aren't a sure thing," I said.

Grandma nodded. "That's a comforting thought."

The priest took his place at the side of the grave, welcomed all attending, and began the recitation of rites. Some of the older mourners nodded off. Tootie fiddled with her oxygen machine. A few people discreetly checked their Twitter accounts.

"I should have gone with the shortened interment version," Grandma said on the final commendation. "I'd forgotten how this could drag on. My behind is asleep."

The priest finished with his remarks and invited everyone to pay their last respects. Grandma was given a flower to place on the casket. She rose and took a couple steps forward. Jimmy's sisters rushed up behind her. Tootie rammed her walker into Grandma's back, and Grandma almost took a header onto the casket. Grandma regained her footing, whirled around, and clocked Tootie on the side of her head with her handbag. Tootie fell down to the ground, still tethered to her oxygen.

75

"Excuse me," Grandma said to Tootie. "That was an accidental reflex reaction caused by you being rude at my honey's funeral."

Angie muttered something in Italian and rushed at Grandma, waving her bandaged hands in the air. Morelli restrained her before she got in striking range.

The funeral director stepped in and suggested that in spite of the brilliant blue sky he thought it might rain and everyone should immediately go to their cars. The suggestion was taken, and there was a mad scramble to be first out of the cemetery.

Grandma put her flower on the casket and told Jimmy he was invited to the wake but she'd understand if he didn't show up, being that he might have other things to do. We made our way down to the waiting car. Grandma took one last look up the hill, perhaps checking for aliens, and we all piled into the limo.

"That's a good-size purse you're carrying," Morelli said to Grandma. "Really packs a wallop."

"I gotta fit my essentials into it," Grandma said.

We all knew one of her essentials was a .45 long-barrel.

CHAPTER EIGHT

BY THE TIME we arrived at the Mole Hole, the parking lot was full, and cars lined both sides of the street. The front door was open, and people were spilling out onto the sidewalk.

"I knew Jimmy would get a crowd, but this is even more than I expected," Grandma said.

"Don't kid yourself," my father said. "It's about the free potato salad and the girls with the big hooters. You can't work here unless you've got big hooters. Even the men have hooters."

"Jimmy didn't have hooters," Grandma said.

We pushed our way in with Morelli leading the way. I was behind Grandma, keeping watch over her. My parents trailed behind me. The donated food had been set out on the bar. Liquor was flowing, compliments of the La-Z-Boys. Emma Gorse and Mary Ann Wozinski found Grandma and offered their condolences. Three more women lined up behind them.

Lula bustled over. "Your extensions are smokin'," she said. "I could see them all the way across the room." She elbowed Grandma. "Condolences."

"Thank you," Grandma said. "Have some kielbasa."

Connie pushed her way through the crowd. "This is insane," Connie said. "I've never seen this many people at a wake. They're going through the buffet like they haven't eaten in a week, and some of them want to know when the pole girls arrive and the show starts."

My father was at the bar shoveling food onto his plate. My mother looked like she wanted to iron a shirt.

"You're in charge of my family," I told Morelli. "I'm looking for Charlie Shine or Stan or Benny the Skootch."

"Benny was at the church and the cemetery. I haven't seen Charlie Shine, and I don't know Stan," Morelli said. "Lou Salgusta and Julius Roman are also club members. They were with Benny earlier. I don't see any of them now, so I'm guessing they're in the back room."

I glanced over at the door to the back room. Crap. Been there. Done that. Not a good experience.

"Is there a problem?" Morelli asked.

"Nope," I said. "Easy-peasy."

I marched over and knocked on the back room door. The door opened, and Stan looked out at me.

"My sincere condolences on your loss," he said.

I nodded politely. "Thank you. I need to talk to the La-Z-Boys."

Stan was blocking my view of the room, but I heard a voice some distance behind him.

"Who's there?" a man asked.

"Stephanie Plum," Stan said.

"Bring her over here. Has she got the keys?"

I stepped around Stan and took stock of the room. There was a huge safe against one wall, with a long folding table in front of it. I assumed this was for the convenience of the bagmen. There was a card table and four folding chairs in a corner, a big brown leather couch against the far wall, and six La-Z-Boy recliners lined up in front of a big flat-screen television. That was pretty much it. Disappointing. At the very least, I'd expected wood paneling and a private bar.

Four of the La-Z-Boy chairs were occupied. Charlie, Benny, Lou, and Julius. I knew the four of them by sight. Jimmy's chair had a framed picture of him resting in it. The sixth chair was empty. I didn't know who sat there.

"About the keys," I said.

"Are you sure you want to talk about this today, what with your recent loss and all?" Benny asked.

"Grandma doesn't have the keys," I told him. "Jimmy didn't pass them on to her. His death was sudden. He was playing at a poker machine, apparently had a massive heart attack, and died on the spot. He didn't say anything to Grandma. He didn't pass anything over to her. And he didn't give her anything that would resemble a key previous to that."

Benny exchanged glances with the other boys. "That's her version."

"It's the only version," I said.

"We got a witness who says it didn't go down like that,"

Benny said. "We talked to an attendant who said Jimmy, should he rest in peace, grabbed hold of your granny and said something to her before he fell out of his chair. We're thinking there was time for Granny to get the keys from Jimmy. We're thinking that Granny very unwisely has decided to keep the keys for herself."

"She would have told me."

"We got no reason to trust you, either," Benny said. "So, here's the deal. Because we're civilized good Catholic men, we're giving you a grace period due to your loss. You've got twenty-four hours, more or less, to get the keys to us. After that we have no choice but to exert some persuasive force on your granny."

"Why are these keys so important?"

"That's not for you to know. It's important to us and that's enough."

I narrowed my eyes at Benny. "If you do anything to cause my grandmother discomfort, you'll answer to me."

"Haw! We're real scared about that."

"I have friends."

"We know all about your friends, and we might have to take care of them too."

I took a moment to steady myself. I looked him in the eye and allowed a small smile to surface. "Good luck with that one," I said. "You would be smart to let this go and start looking for a good locksmith."

Benny leaned forward and squinted at me. "What's with

your hair? It's got blue streaks in it. Is that something new? Like a funeral thing?"

"It looks like metal," Julius said. "It could be a wire."

"Do you want me to look at it more closely?" Stan asked. "Do you want me to see if she's got a transmitter hidden somewhere?"

"They're extensions," I said. "I got them at the hair salon."

"What happens if you set them on fire?" Lou asked. "Do they burn or just melt?" He smiled. "I like burning things. It's my specialty."

"He's right about that," Julius said. "He's done some real good burn work."

"There's an art to it," Lou said. "I haven't lost my touch, either." Another smile aimed at me. "Maybe I could show you what I can do someday? I could do you and your granny."

"Lou likes to burn the ladies," Julius said. "He always starts by putting his initials on their lady parts."

I turned and calmly walked out of the room, closing the door behind me. By the time I reached the bar my heart was pounding in my ears. I picked a small sandwich up from a tray and realized my hand was shaking. Okay, so I was terrified, horrified, enraged, and had gone scramble brained. Perfectly normal for a person who is basically a wimp at heart and completely lacking in tough-guy skills. The important thing is that I was strong in front of Benny and the Boys. I was pretty sure I'd pulled it off. Whether it meant anything to them was a whole other issue.

I did slow breathing and thought about daisies in a field. Hummingbirds and butterflies. The sound of the surf at the Jersey shore. I forced myself to eat the sandwich. It was going to be okay, I told myself. I had to stay on my toes and keep my eyes open. And it wasn't as if I had no skills at all. I'd become good at finding people. I had to transfer that skill to finding *things*. Like some keys.

I looked around the room. The novelty of the Mole Hole was wearing off. The possibility of pole girls performing was slim to none. The food had been savagely picked over. The crowd had thinned out, and Grandma was accepting good wishes from a handful of stragglers. Morelli was back on his heels. My parents were sitting at a table. They both looked shell-shocked.

I sidled up to Morelli, and he slid an arm around me.

"How'd it go?" he asked.

"About as expected. We have twenty-four hours, more or less, to give them the keys."

"And then?"

"Those old guys are *sickos*. I don't even want to repeat what they said."

"I can lean on them."

"They'd probably like that. Make them feel like they were back in the game. There were six chairs in the club room. One was Jimmy's. The other chairs were occupied by Benny the Skootch, Charlie Shine, Lou Salgusta, and Julius Roman. Who sits in the sixth chair?"

"I don't know," Morelli said. "It used to belong to Big Artie.

He died last year, and I don't know if the chair was ever filled. I can ask around. Did you try to apprehend Charlie Shine?"

"It never even occurred to me. I just wanted to say my piece and get out of the room."

Grandma joined Morelli and me. "Stick a fork in me," she said. "I'm pooped. Do you think it's okay to go home now? There's still a couple people left, but I can't take any more condolences."

I signaled to my parents that we were ready to leave, and they heaved themselves up and shuffled over to us.

"It was like an invasion of meatball-eating zombies," my father said, glassy eyed. "It was like one of those videogames you see advertised on television where a screaming horde storms the castle."

My mother stared at the bar. "They ate everything. It didn't last a half hour. Gone. All of it gone."

"Yeah," Grandma said. "It was a pip of a wake."

Morelli herded everyone outside, Grandma took a selfie of herself leaving the Mole Hole, and we climbed into the limo.

"I didn't see the Rosolli sisters at the Mole Hole," Grandma said. "I guess they got worn out at the cemetery."

"You almost killed Tootie," my mother said. "I'm sure she's home with an ice pack."

"It wasn't that bad," Grandma said. "I caught her on the side of the head. I probably didn't even break her nose. And besides I could feel that I got a bruise where she ran into me."

I was relieved that no one got pitched into the hole in the

ground along with Jimmy. Between the mob and the gangs, Trenton funerals aren't always a model of decorum.

"I had a talk with Benny La-Z-Boy," I said to Grandma. "He claims to have a source who saw Jimmy have the heart attack. He said Jimmy grabbed hold of you and said something to you before he fell to the ground."

"Yep," Grandma said. "That's the way it happened."

"What did he say?"

"He said, *'Oh crap apples.'* And then he was dead."

CHAPTER NINE

THE CAR DROPPED US at my parents' house, and Morelli and I went our own way. He went home to walk Bob. I headed for my apartment because I had nothing better to do. I drove two blocks, and I got a call from Grandma.

"Someone broke into our house," she said. "There's stuff thrown everywhere. Your mother is in a state. I was hoping you could come back and calm her down."

"I'm turning around," I said. "I'll be there in two minutes."

Five minutes later, Morelli and I were walking through the house cataloging the damage and setting things straight.

"My apartment looked exactly like this when it got tossed," I said. "I'm guessing the same idiots did both jobs."

"I'll file a report," Morelli said. "Depending on the deductible, your parents might be able to put in an insurance claim."

"From what I'm seeing, the damage is more emotional than physical. A couple couch cushions were slashed. A candy dish was broken in the living room. It wasn't expensive." I replaced a dresser drawer in my parents' bedroom, scooped the contents

85

up off the floor, and refolded everything. "This is the second time my parents' house was targeted in less than a week's time. This shouldn't be happening. This is their home. This is their safe place."

Morelli checked his watch. "Agreed. You seem to have everything under control here, so I'm going to take Bob for a short walk, and then I'll go back to the Mole Hole and have a talk with the Boys. I'll let you know how it goes."

I moved into Grandma's room. She had everything put back together and was making her bed.

"I guess this is my fault," she said. "I got mixed up with the wrong man."

I picked her pillow up off the floor and placed it on her bed. "Jimmy might have been the wrong man, but this isn't your fault."

"I wish I had the keys so I could give them up and have it be over and done."

"Yeah, that would be good, but you don't have the keys, so we'll have to be careful until the keys are found."

"I don't know how we could be more careful," Grandma said. "The doors were locked and the windows were closed, and someone broke in anyway. I don't know what more we could do."

For starters, I was going to have Ranger install a home security system. It wouldn't stop someone from throwing a firebomb through the window, but it would give warning that someone had broken in.

"What's Mom doing?" I asked Grandma.

"She was working in the kitchen, putting stuff away and cleaning. They emptied a sack of flour and some cereal boxes. That must be where people hide keys if they've got them."

I went downstairs and found my father in his chair in front of the television. He was staring at the television, but the television wasn't on.

"Are you okay?" I asked him.

"No," he said. "I'm not okay. I'm mad. I'd like to punch someone. I'd like to find the guy who broke into my home and did this. It's not right that this happened."

"I'm going to have Ranger install a security system."

"I don't want a security system. This is a nice neighborhood. I shouldn't need a security system."

I left my dad and went into the kitchen. My mom was sitting at the kitchen table with a cup of tea.

"I thought you'd be ironing by now," I said, sitting across from her.

"Ironing is like meditation for me," she said. "It's calming. It's soothing. I like the way a warm shirt smells. It's clean. It's like spring grass growing. It helps me clear my head. And I guess it lets me feel like I have some control over things when I can iron away a wrinkle." She looked around the kitchen. "I had no control over this, and I don't like it. This started with your grandmother, and now we're all involved. Ironing isn't going to make this go away."

"I'd like Ranger to install a home security system here, but Dad is against it."

"Have it installed," my mother said. "We need help."

It was almost four o'clock when I left my parents' house. The Rangeman car that had been absent all day was back on my rear bumper. I circled the block, returned to my parents' house, and parked in their driveway. I went in through the front door and out the back door. I cut through the alley behind the house and old Mr. Sanderson's backyard. I looked around. No Rangeman. They were sticking with my car. Good deal. Now they were guarding Grandma. I walked the short distance to Morelli's house and got a call from Ranger just as I reached Morelli's front door.

"Babe," he said. "Your car is at your parents' house but your phone is approaching Morelli's."

"You pinged my phone?"

"Is there a problem with that?"

I did a mental head slap. "Some people would think that was an invasion of privacy. Not me, but *some* people."

"As long as it's not you," Ranger said.

"Are you laughing at me?"

"I don't laugh."

"Once in a while you laugh. And I'm pretty sure you just smiled."

"Why did you leave your escort at your parents' house?"

"Someone broke into their house when we were at the

funeral. It was searched and trashed just like mine. I decided my family needed the Rangeman protection more than I did."

"Some people might consider that to be sneaky. Not me, but *some* people."

"Would you have agreed to have your men watch Grandma?"

"No."

"There you have it," I said. "I have a favor to ask. I'd like to have a home security system installed in their house."

"Done."

And he disconnected.

Morelli's car wasn't parked at the curb, and he didn't answer when I knocked, so I retrieved the key from under the doormat and let myself in. Bob came galloping at me from the kitchen. I braced for impact, and he threw himself against me, delirious with happiness.

I gave Bob some hugs, told him he was a good boy, and called Morelli.

"I'm on my way home," he said. "I had an interesting talk with Benny, and then I stopped at my mom's house to pick up a tray of lasagna."

Morelli's batshit crazy Grandma Bella lived with his mom. Bella was a small, sharp-eyed woman who dressed in old-country black, put the hex on people, and scuttled around like a spider on the hunt. His mom was the movie version of an Italian mother. She'd endured her drunken, philandering, abusive husband and prayed for him when he passed. Her windows were clean. Her house was spotless. She kept her only unmarried son's refrigerator filled with lasagna, red sauce, good hard cheese, ricotta cake, meatballs, and prosciutto. She knew his girlfriend wasn't up to the task. And sad to say, she was right.

A couple years ago, Morelli inherited the house from his Aunt Rose, and little by little he was making it his own. He'd done a partial renovation on the kitchen, and he'd added a downstairs powder room. Rose's curtains still hung in two of the upstairs bedrooms, but the master had a new bed and sleek motorized shades. Downstairs, there were some leftover end tables and lamps. He'd kept Rose's toaster and pots and pans, but he'd traded her dainty couch for a big comfy leather job and added a flat-screen television.

The best lasagna on the planet was on its way to Morelli's house, so Bob and I moseyed into the kitchen. I gave Bob a doggy treat, and I set the small kitchen table for dinner. Morelli always ate in the kitchen or in front of the television in the living room. He didn't eat in the dining room because he'd swapped out Rose's dining room table for a pool table. Just because a man owns a toaster doesn't mean he's entirely domesticated.

The front door opened and closed, and Bob took off at top speed. Seconds later he was dancing around Morelli while Morelli attempted to get the lasagna onto the kitchen counter without Bob slobbering on it.

"It's still hot," Morelli said. "My mom just took it out of the oven. I know it's early, but I didn't get anything to eat at the wake and I'm starving."

"I figured. I have the table set. How did it go with Benny? Is he going to back off?"

Morelli got beer out of the fridge. He gave one to me and chugged half of his.

"Benny swears on his mother's grave that they weren't responsible for either of the break-ins," Morelli said.

I cut and plated the lasagna. "Do you believe him?"

Morelli took his seat at the table and shrugged. "I don't know. There've been whispers all along that someone else is interested in the keys."

I dumped a chunk of lasagna into Bob's food bowl, set it on the floor by his water bowl, and joined Morelli. "Do you have any idea who this other person could be?"

"The suspects would range from Jimmy's sisters to his ex-wives to the rest of the world. It was no secret that Jimmy was Keeper of the Keys, and that the keys were essential to unlocking the Boys' fortunes."

"The sisters and ex-wives were at the funeral when the break-in was going down."

"They weren't all at the wake. And they have nephews and old family friends who would do a job for them."

We polished off half of the lasagna, hooked Bob up to his leash, and took him to the dog park as a special treat. He sniffed out a bunch of dogs, ran around for about three minutes, and went to the gate, signaling that he was ready to go. We let him stick his head out of the window on the way home, and he was all about it.

"I'm not so sure he's a dog-park kind of dog," I said to Morelli.

"It's all about the journey," Morelli said. "He likes to go, and he likes to come home."

We parked in front of Morelli's house, and Ranger called.

"Babe, we're here, trying to install a security system for your parents, and we're meeting some resistance. Your father has a butcher knife and he's threatening to gut my installer."

"Where's my mother?"

"She's wandering around with a Big-Gulp-size glass of what she says is iced tea but smells strongly of whiskey."

"I'll be right there."

Morelli raised his eyebrows.

"Not worth talking about," I told him. "Could you drop me off at my parents' house?"

"Do you want me to stay?"

"Not necessary, but thanks for the offer."

My father was standing in the doorway. He had the knife in his hand, and he was trying hard to look fierce. Ranger and his men were keeping their distance.

"What's going on?" I said to my father.

"Nothing's going on," he said. "And nothing's *going* to go on. I don't want a security system. I don't need one."

"In less than a week's time you had a firebomb thrown through your window and you had someone break in and trash the place."

"It wasn't trashed. It was disrupted. I'll take care of it."

"How?"

"I'm going to get my guns back," he said.

"Not going to happen."

"I'll promise not to shoot your grandmother."

"That's a start," I said, "but you're not getting the guns back."

"Why not?"

"We sold your guns."

"*What?*"

"We bought your big-screen television with them."

My father's face turned red, and his eyes bulged out. "You had no right to sell my guns! Those were *my* guns." He pressed his lips tight together. "Okay, fine. No big deal. I can get new guns. I don't need them anyway. I have a baseball bat."

"And the security system?" I asked.

"No! No security system. It's like those TSA people at the airport. They don't make me feel safe. They're a big fat reminder that some nutjob wants to blow up my plane. You put a security system in because you're afraid. It's a sign of fear. Like those body scanners that show your privates."

"You're carrying a knife and a baseball bat around with you. Isn't that a sign of fear?"

"No. It's a sign that I'm pissed off."

I waved at Ranger. "No security system."

Ranger smiled and told his men to pack up and head out.

"I saw that smile," I yelled at him. "You have a sick sense of humor."

I went inside and took a position on the couch. Stephanie Plum, bodyguard, on the job. My mother sat on one side of me and Grandma sat on the other. My father settled into his chair, took possession of the remote, and clicked the television on. After that instant, it was all a blur of game shows and talent shows and commercials about drugs to cure psoriasis, drugs to give you a stiffy, and Marie Osmond helping you to lose fifty pounds.

My father fell asleep in his chair at nine o'clock. My mother finished her Big Gulp and went to bed. Grandma took over the remote and tuned in to a rerun of *Naked and Afraid*.

"I got all these shows recorded," Grandma said. "I got enough to take us to midnight."

One episode of *Naked and Afraid* might be fun. A marathon would be hell on earth. I love my family. Truly. But I'd have a hard time choosing between a *Naked and Afraid* marathon and letting someone firebomb the house.

"Gosh," I said to Grandma, "I'd love to stay, but I promised Morelli I'd spend the night with him."

"I can't compete with that," Grandma said. "He's hot. Jimmy was okay, but he wasn't no Morelli."

This was true. Not many men were Morelli. I packed up and told Grandma to call if there was a problem. I trudged out to the Buick, turned the key in the ignition, and the car sputtered and died. I looked at the gas gauge. Empty. I abandoned the Buick and bummed a ride to Morelli's house with the Rangeman guys.

I called Ranger and told him I'd be staying with Morelli

tonight, so his guys could leave. That was the deal when Ranger was in protection mode. If I was with Morelli, Ranger felt I was safe, and he could back off.

"Babe," Ranger said.

I wasn't sure what *Babe* meant in this instance. It sounded a little like he thought I was settling for second best.

Morelli was watching hockey with Bob when I walked in.

"So?" he said.

"Crisis averted."

I sat next to him, and he wrapped an arm around me. "I'm glad you came back," Morelli said.

"How glad?"

"Glad enough to shut the television off."

"Wow. That's really glad."

"Okay, I have to be honest with you," Morelli said. "It's only pre-season and the Rangers are losing. And it's not the same since they traded Zuccarello."

"So, are you hinting that you need pity sex because of Zuccarello?"

"Would that work?"

"Yeah, but what about me? Do I get Zuccarello pity sex too? Just before they traded him, I bought a Rangers jersey with his name on it."

"Cupcake, you're going to get pity sex that will be life changing. You're going to be a new woman when I'm done with you."

This had some appeal, since I was wanting to be a new woman anyway. Between the extensions and the pity sex, I'd be on my way to somewhere.

"Okay," I said. "Where do you want to do this? What's the first step?"

"I need the workbench to execute this properly."

The workbench was Morelli's nickname for his bed.

"Do we need candles?" I asked him.

"Candles would be a distraction. Plus, I don't have any."

"This isn't going to involve any kinky stuff, is it?"

"The only thing kinky is going to be you screaming for more."

Oh boy.

CHAPTER TEN

IT WAS DAYLIGHT when I woke up. Morelli was next to me, still asleep. I looked under the sheets and checked myself out. Naked. Not noticeably different. Not yet a completely new woman. Although the pity sex had been outstanding.

"Hey!" I said to Morelli. "Are you awake?"

Morelli half opened his eyes. "I am *now.*"

"I'm hungry."

"And?"

"I think we should go out for breakfast. Pancakes and eggs and bacon and stuff."

"Sure. But not now."

"Why can't we go now?"

"We can't go now because you poked the bear."

"I didn't poke the bear."

"You poked the bear awake. And you know how the bear always has this condition in the morning."

"Just once, couldn't the bear wake up and want waffles?"

"How could you possibly want waffles when you could have the bear?" Morelli asked. "I thought you had a good time with the bear last night."

"Best pity sex ever," I said.

"And I was right. You were screaming for more."

"I wasn't screaming."

"You were begging."

"Okay, maybe I was begging."

I felt Morelli's fingers walking a path from my navel to my hoo-ha.

"I don't think I've got a lot left down there," I said. "It needs to rest awhile longer."

His fingers reached their goal.

"Are you sure it wants to rest?" Morelli asked.

"I might not be completely sure."

Morelli and I had just laid waste to the endless all-you-can-eat Sunday buffet at Jerry's Diner.

"Jerry outdid himself on this buffet," I said.

Morelli signaled the waitress for our check. "I don't think there's a Jerry anymore. I think Jerry died and the diner got sold to Amazon."

"Well, whoever owns it put out a kick-ass buffet."

"Agreed."

Morelli's cellphone buzzed, and he checked for a text message.

"Not good?" I asked.

"Kelly has the flu, so I'm on call, and there's a dead juvenile on Stark with gang graffiti tattooed onto his forehead."

"That's ugly."

"Yeah, that's my world. I'll take you back to your parents' house so you can get your car, and then I'll go to work. This shouldn't take long. It's not like there are body parts spread all over."

Ten minutes later, we spotted Grandma a block from my parents' house.

"She's on the move," Morelli said. "She's got her big black patent leather purse, which means she's carrying. And I'm guessing she's headed for the bakery."

We pulled up alongside Grandma, and I lowered my window. "Get in," I said. "We'll give you a ride."

"No thanks," Grandma said. "I feel like getting some exercise. I gotta stay in shape now that I'm single again. I might want another boy toy after things calm down."

"I'll walk with Grandma," I said to Morelli. "Call if you wrap things up early."

"I'm going to the bakery," Grandma said. "We've got leftover rump roast, and I'm going to get rolls, so we can have sandwiches for lunch. I might get some Italian cookies too. There were some at the wake, but I didn't get a chance to eat any. I was too busy with my widow obligations."

"You must be relieved to have it behind you."

"In the beginning I wanted to do a real good job. And I have to admit, I was liking the attention. I didn't feel so bad about

Jimmy after I got over the shock. I figured he was going to do okay, making deals with Jesus or God or whoever is in charge of that stuff. Jimmy was good at making deals. But in the end, it was just sad and tiring. You know what was the best part of the funeral and the wake? Your hair. It has sparkly blue streaks, and it's filled with life, and I always knew where you were, except when I couldn't see you. Looking at it made me not so tired."

Jeez. Who would have thought?

"Thanks, Grandma," I said. "That's really nice to hear. I've been feeling boring lately. I thought the blue extensions might help."

"You aren't boring. The blue streaky things work because that's who you are. You're like the sky at midnight, when the moon is shining, and the wind is blowing."

I got totally choked up. It was such a beautiful thing for Grandma to say. And I wanted to be the moon and the wind, but I couldn't see it. At this point in time I felt more like a cloudy day with the promise of rain.

We reached the bakery and took a number.

"It's always crowded like this on Sunday," Grandma said. "Everyone comes here after church. It's like when you're praying, you ask the Lord for a babka and then you just gotta come pick it up."

We were next in line when I saw Jimmy's sister Rose enter the bakery. Angie was behind her. Both women narrowed their eyes when they saw Grandma and me.

"What's with these women?" Grandma said, catching sight of them. "They're everywhere. And they're giving us the stink face."

"Ignore them. We're next."

Patti Benn was working behind the counter. "Number sixty-four," she called out.

"That's me," Grandma said. "I want six sandwich rolls and a half pound of Italian cookies."

"That's my number," Rose said, pushing to the front. "We dropped it, and that slut gold digger picked it up before we could get to it."

"That's exactly right," Angie said. "I couldn't hold on to the ticket because the slut broke all my fingers."

"Liar, liar, pants on fire," Grandma said. "I got this ticket from the machine. You two old hags gotta go to the end of the line."

"Ladies," Patti said. "Let's all take a step back."

"I'm not taking a step anywhere until I get my rolls and cookies," Grandma said.

"Typical," Rose said. "Hungarian."

Grandma cut her eyes to Rose. "You got a problem with Hungarians?"

"They aren't Italian."

"You got that right," Grandma said. "And proud of it."

"Nobody likes Hungarians," Rose said. "They're all fornicators."

"You bet," Grandma said. "And I'm proud of that too. You're

just jealous because you're such a dried-up ugly prune you can't even get any fornicating."

Patti threw some rolls and about two pounds of cookies into a bag and handed it over to Grandma. "On the house," she said. "Next?"

Mrs. Ruiz stepped up. "I'm next," she said. "I have number sixty-five. And I'm from Guatemala. Everybody likes us."

I hustled Grandma out of the bakery, being careful to stay between her and Rose and Angie.

"Those women are so disagreeable," Grandma said when we were on the sidewalk. "Jimmy could never get along with them. They hardly ever talked, and now you'd think they were joined at the hip."

"It's about money," I said. "And who will inherit it."

"Jimmy had a will. He said he had it drawn up a while ago and it gave everything over to his wife . . . whoever she was at the time." Grandma shook her head. "It's a shame people get so worked up over money. It's not like Jimmy's sisters don't have any. They're all living okay."

There's never a lot of traffic in the Burg. On weekdays, people leave for work in the morning and come home in the evening. Saturday morning is for shopping and car washing. Sunday is church. We were a block from my parents' house when I heard a car come up behind us. I turned to look and saw that Rose was behind the wheel and Angie was next to her. They slowly drove past us and made a rude Italian gesture to Grandma and me.

"Va fangool!" Grandma yelled at them, and she gave them the finger.

Rose drove half a block, made a U-turn, and gunned it straight for us. She jumped the curb, and I yanked Grandma to safety with about three inches to spare. Rose cut across Gary Luckett's front lawn, spun around, and came back at us. Grandma dropped the bakery bag, pulled her gun out of her purse, and squeezed off three rounds. Rose swerved away from us and drove down the street.

"How'd I do?" Grandma asked.

"You took out a side mirror, but I think the other two shots went wide."

"I was rushed."

I picked the bakery bag up from the ground and looked inside.

"Well?" Grandma said.

"Everything's okay."

"Good thing, because your mother won't be happy if I don't bring rolls home."

Grandma and I decided not to mention the shooting incident to anyone, but there was always the chance that someone had witnessed it and called my mom. The subject didn't come up during lunch, and I felt I was home free when, after lunch, my mom didn't turn to ironing or chugging bourbon. Morelli hadn't phoned, and that was okay with me. Between the brunch buffet and the rump roast sandwiches for lunch, I was thinking

I needed a nap. Fortunately, my father had very nicely gassed up the Buick for me.

Grandma said she was taking the night off from socializing and was skipping Greta Nelson's viewing at Stiva's. I thought this was a good decision. She was probably safe if she stayed home. After all, my father had his baseball bat.

I took a baggie of Italian cookies from my mom, trudged out to my car, and drove to my apartment in a food stupor.

I let myself into my apartment and gave Rex half an almond cookie.

"Suppose you had a really important key," I said to Rex. "Where would you keep it?"

It was a rhetorical question because I already knew the answer. He'd keep the key in his soup can. That's where he kept everything. Jimmy Rosolli had other options.

I took my MacBook Air and a steno pad to the dining room table and asked myself the same question I'd asked Rex. Where would I keep an important key? My keys were all on a key ring that I kept in the messenger bag that doubled as my purse. Okay, but suppose I had some keys that were too valuable for the key ring? Safe-deposit box? Gym locker? Safe? None of the above for me. I didn't go to a gym. I didn't have a safe. And a safe-deposit box would require a trip to the bank, and that was a pain in the ass. I'd hide the keys in my underwear drawer. This did me no good, since rumor had it that multiple people had already looked in Jimmy's underwear drawer.

This was made even more ridiculous by the fact that I didn't know how many keys were involved or what those keys looked like. Big? Little? Key cards? I didn't know what the keys opened. And I didn't know what sort of treasure they kept locked away.

There were six La-Z-Boys. One was dead. One was unknown. One was going to avoid me at all costs because he was a fugitive. That left Lou Salgusta, Benny the Skootch, and Julius Roman. It would help if I could get one of them to talk to me. First thing tomorrow I'd have Connie run background checks. Next thing I'd start knocking on doors. Trying to talk to them at the Mole Hole wasn't going to work. I was going to have to get them alone. I suspected my funeral grace period was over, so I needed to be extra vigilant.

I checked on Grandma at six o'clock. It was all good. Maybe it would stay good. It could happen, right? The keys could turn up. They could be in the pocket of a jacket that was taken to the cleaners, or they could be in the freezer behind the cookie dough ice cream. Jimmy was old. He probably misplaced things all the time.

Morelli called at seven o'clock. "I got stuck doing paperwork and then I got talked into football with some guys from work. Is everything okay with you?"

"Jimmy's sister Rose tried to run over Grandma and me when we were walking home from the bakery, but we jumped out of the way. Grandma shot off a side mirror, and Rose took off down the road."

"I don't know who's crazier . . . Rose or Grandma."

"Yeah, that's a tough one. Where are you? It sounds like you're in a sports bar."

"I'm home. Some of the guys came with me to watch the game. There's still pizza left if you want to come over."

"Thanks, but I'll pass. I've got stuff to think about."

I called Grandma at eight o'clock and at ten o'clock. Nothing new going on. No firebombs. No break-ins. No attempted kidnappings. Yay!

CHAPTER ELEVEN

I DROVE PAST my parents' house on my way to work. There were no strange cars parked on the street, and the house felt benign, so I continued on to the bail bonds office. Connie had just arrived and unlocked the front door. Lula wasn't there yet.

"This doesn't happen often," Connie said, setting the box of donuts on her desk. "You get first pick."

"I woke up at four-thirty and couldn't get back to sleep. I'm worried about Grandma. Everyone's out to get her. Jimmy's sisters. The La-Z-Boys. Who knows who else."

"I thought the keys would have turned up by now," Connie said. "Hard to believe no one knows where Jimmy kept them."

"Maybe someone did know. Maybe someone got to the keys and is sitting on them."

"One of the other La-Z-Boys?"

I shrugged. "Could be anyone. There were six chairs in the back room at the Mole Hole. They belonged to Jimmy, Benny, Charlie Shine, Lou Salgusta, and Julius Roman. Do you know who owns the sixth chair?"

"I don't think it was ever occupied after Big Artie."

"So, when someone dies the chair stays empty?"

"That's my understanding, but I'm not sure," Connie said. "I'll ask my mom. She might know."

I took the lone Boston Kreme. "Rose tried to run Grandma and me over yesterday. She jumped the curb and almost took out Gary Luckett's maple tree."

"The sisters were counting on getting some money," Connie said. "Jimmy's ex-wife Barbara isn't happy, either. Word on the street is that Grandma's going to get everything. Being that they were only married for forty-five minutes, it's not sitting well."

The front door crashed open and Lula stomped in. She was in full-on biker chick mode with chunky black motorcycle boots, a black leather miniskirt, and a black leather vest with an eagle stitched onto the back.

"I can't believe you got here before me," she said. "And I see you got the Boston Kreme. I was counting on that donut. I needed it. I had a bad night. Just look at my hair."

Connie and I moved our eyes off the black leather up to Lula's hair. The first two inches off her scalp were still pink, but beyond that it was significantly reduced in volume and singed black.

"I was on a date with Mr. Amazing Saturday night and some yodel set my hair on fire," Lula said. "Me and my date were getting it on at a bar, and the idiot next to me had his electronic cigarette explode. Took out half his face and fried my hair.

Do you believe it? You know how long it takes me to grow quality hair? It's not like overnight. And I couldn't get an appointment with Lateesha until this afternoon."

"Jeez," I said, "was the guy okay?"

Lula poked around in the donut box and settled on a chocolate glazed. "I don't know. It didn't look like he was gonna die, but his nose is never gonna be the same. My opinion is it was better when people smoked and died of lung cancer. At least they didn't set innocent bystanders' hair on fire."

"What happened to Mr. Amazing?" Connie asked.

"He turned out to be not so amazing," Lula said. "He was all freaked out by the guy on the floor. And he said my hair smelled like I'd been incinerated. I don't know how he knew about incinerated hair, but anyway, he left, and I had to take an Uber home."

There was a lot of silence after that since Connie and I didn't know where to go with it. Finally, Connie's computer dinged, and she pulled off three new FTAs.

"Bad Friday," she said. "There were three no-shows in court. Vinnie's not going to be happy."

She printed them out and handed them over to me.

"Where is the little turd?" Lula asked.

"Vegas," Connie said. "Some kind of conference."

I looked at the three FTAs.

"What have we got?" Lula asked.

"A shoplifter. A hijacker. Attempted murder."

"That's a group with good variety to it," Lula said. "It could almost make up for me having to start my day off with a lame-ass chocolate glazed donut."

"And we need to find the keys," I said.

Lula finished her donut and picked out a second. "You got a plan?"

"I thought Connie could run the remaining Boys through the system for me. Then I can try to find a weak link to talk to me. It would help if I at least knew what the keys looked like and the number of keys involved."

"I'll get right on it," Connie said. "Give me an hour or two."

I thumbed through the three new files. "The shoplifter should be easy," I said. "Let's round her up while Connie does my search."

"You didn't read carefully," Connie said. "It's a guy. Carol Joyce. And he's a pro. Goes into a store with a shopping bag and walks out with stacks of T-shirts, lingerie, whatever is out of sight and easy to pick up. Knows how to avoid security cameras. He's been at it for years. Started shoplifting when he was seventeen, but this is the first time he's been busted. I know about him because my Uncle Sal fences for him sometimes."

I read his bio background. "He lives with his mother. Cherry Street. That's North Trenton. He's twenty-one years old. Looks younger."

Lula looked over my shoulder at the file photo. "Boyish. Clean cut. White. Someone you could trust to go into a store with a shopping bag. Boom."

I shoved the files into my outside pocket. "We'll be back," I said to Connie. "Call me if anything key worthy pops up."

Cherry Street is in a pleasant middle-income neighborhood. Houses and yards are small but neatly maintained. Interiors are filled with overstuffed furniture, flat-screen televisions, and technology only a fourteen-year-old could master. The Joyce house was no exception. It was a two-story white house with a red front door and a small front porch.

The woman who answered the door was perfect for the house. Medium height. Medium weight. Medium short brown hair. Dressed in tan slacks and a pink striped shirt. She smiled a hello to me and took a step back when she saw Lula in her biker dominatrix outfit.

"I'm looking for Carol," I said.

"I'm afraid he isn't home right now," the woman said. "I'm his mother. Is there anything I can relay to Carol?"

"I represent his bail bonds agent," I said. "Carol missed his court date, and I wanted to help him reschedule."

"That's very nice of you. I'm sure he would welcome the help."

"Do you expect him home soon?"

"He's at work right now. He's a personal shopper. He doesn't really have a set schedule."

"Do you know where he's shopping today?"

"Goodness, no. He shops everywhere. He's always on the lookout for a bargain. Although he is partial to Quaker Bridge

Mall, and there's another mall on the highway. I forget the name of it. He shops there first thing sometimes because it opens early."

We returned to my car, and Lula looked around. "You haven't got Rangeman guys with you today," she said. "What's with that?"

"Maybe Ranger thinks the danger level has dropped off to yellow. Or maybe last night when I was asleep, he installed cameras and listening bugs besides the usual GPS tracker."

"He's hot, but he's a little whackadoodle," Lula said.

"He's had a troubled past."

"He's someone else who would benefit from a cat."

Omigod, Ranger with a cat. That was a mental image that would haunt me for days.

"Where are we going now to find this personal shopper?" Lula asked.

I checked the time. It was a couple minutes after nine. "Quaker Bridge doesn't open until ten, so he isn't there," I said. "The other mall she was referring to must be Greenwood. It's not far from here." I handed the file over to Lula. "I'll cruise the Greenwood parking lot. He drives a black Cadillac Escalade. You have the license plate number in the file."

"I'm on it. I'm looking at all the cars we're passing, too. It's easy to spot a Escalade on account of they're so big. It's actually a good choice of vehicle for a shoplifter of his magnitude. You could fit a lot of T-shirts in a Escalade."

I turned in to the Greenwood lot and drove up and down the

aisles. Greenwood isn't half the size of Quaker Bridge, and there were only a few cars parked. None of them was an Escalade.

"Quaker Bridge will be opening soon," Lula said. "I vote we go to Quaker Bridge next. And if we take a small detour onto Sutter Boulevard, we could fit in a stop at the Dunkin' Donuts there. It's got a drive-thru, and it's an excellent Dunkin' Donuts."

"You didn't have enough donuts at the office?"

"I didn't have a Boston Kreme."

I left Greenwood, drove ten minutes down the highway, and exited at Sutter Boulevard. Dunkin' Donuts was immediately on the right side of Sutter. The parking lot was packed, and there were eight cars in line at the drive-thru.

"I'll run in," Lula said. "It'll be faster, and I'll get a better choice of donut."

Fifteen minutes later, Lula hustled back to the car with a box of donuts and two large coffees.

"This is great," Lula said, handing me a coffee and opening the box. "Just you and me and a box of donuts. This is the way people bond over good memories and shit."

I looked at the donuts. "They're all Boston Kremes."

"Exactly. It's so we don't have to argue who gets what. And I got a dozen so there's lots to go around."

It was almost ten-thirty when we reached Quaker Bridge. I went directly to the Macy's parking lot, and we spotted Carol's Escalade immediately.

"We're on a hot streak," Lula said. "This is gonna be three in a row. And I'm looking forward to seeing this person. I'm always interested in a successful entrepreneur on account of I got entrepreneurial tendencies too. Not to mention he's a cutie. You could tell from his photo he's a nice guy."

"It was a mug shot. He's officially a felon."

"Okay, but that don't mean he isn't nice. His mama likes him, so that says a lot."

We prowled through ladies' shoes, men's sportswear, and cosmetics, and found Carol walking through women's sportswear. He was carrying two large shopping bags with the Macy's logo on them. The bags looked full.

I approached him from behind and called his name. "Carol?"

No response. He kept walking.

"Maybe we got the wrong dude," Lula said.

"It's him," I said.

Lula moved up, practically stepping on his heels. "Hey!" she said, using her outdoor voice. "Are you Carol Joyce? Hold up a minute. We need to talk to you. What do you have in those bags, anyway?"

Carol swung around and caught Lula on the side of the head with a shopping bag. Lula staggered back, and Carol took off running. He was headed for the mall entrance, but he was burdened by the heavy bags, and he had to dodge early shoppers. I caught up to him and grabbed the back of his shirt, and he stumbled into two women in front of him. Lula was behind me, huffing like a steam train, pounding down the aisles in her big, clunky chopper boots. She didn't pull up in time, plowed into the four of us, and we all went down to the floor. The two women were screaming and flailing around. Lula was on top of me, trying to right herself. By the time I got to my feet, Carol was gone, out of sight. The bags were on the floor, and women's jeans and a colorful collection of men's three-button knit shirts were scattered around us.

A small crowd had gathered and was standing at a distance. The women were babbling about being attacked and knocked down, and Lula was adjusting the girls and tugging her skirt down over her ass. Two mall security guards approached us.

I explained the situation and handed the guards my credentials, including the Carol Joyce file that gave me the right to pursue and apprehend.

"You're going to have to come with us," one guard said. "We'll need a statement and verification of these papers."

"Are you kidding me?" Lula said. "We haven't got time for that. We got important shit to do. And why aren't you thanking us for stopping a shoplifter? He would have walked out with all this merchandise if it wasn't for us. And I'll tell you what else, it's obvious you're doing profiling here. You looked at this woman with metallic blue extensions and you decided she needed investigating. That's blatant extension discrimination."

Lula snatched the papers from the guard and handed them over to me.

"Hunh," she said to the guard as her parting remark.

We turned and walked out of the store. We got to the parking lot and Lula cut her eyes to me. "Are they following us?"

I looked over my shoulder. "No."

"Idiots," Lula said.

"We lost Carol. His car is gone."

"I'm rearranging my opinion of him. That wasn't nice of him to hit me with the shopping bag. It was heavy, and it could have broke something. I need a donut after that disillusioning experience. Good thing we got some."

I unlocked the Buick, we got in, and we each had a donut.

"Sometimes I find human nature to be real disappointing," Lula said. "I guess that's why God made metallic extensions and pink hair dye. Sometimes you gotta compensate."

I turned the key in the ignition. "So true."

CHAPTER TWELVE

CONNIE LOOKED UP from her computer when we walked in. "I'm almost done," she said. "There's a lot of information on the Boys. Mostly it falls into three categories. Crimes, social clubs and civic events, and personal history. Too much to print out right now, so I sent you most of it in digital form. You can read it when you get the chance. I figured you were interested in recent personal information, so that's what I printed. Not sure what you'll gain from any of this. The Boys have become pretty sedentary. Charlie Shine is the youngest and most active." Connie handed me the folder. "I also included information on the younger guys who hang at the Mole Hole. Probably some of them know more than they're supposed to know, and it might be easier to get them to talk."

I took the folder to the couch and paged through it. Charlie Shine was seventy-eight years old. The other three Boys were in their early eighties.

"Do you think we're all overly concerned about these men?"

ed Connie. "They all have medical problems, and I don't
ѕє them engaged in a lot of activities."

"From my firsthand knowledge of Italian mobsters, I can tell
you their biggest fear is to get put out to pasture," Connie said.
"The men who are sitting in the La-Z-Boy chairs are still
accorded the utmost respect, because they've gotten more
ruthless with age as they try to maintain the illusion of power.
The La-Z-Boys were all assassins and enforcers. There's less
opportunity for wet work in today's mob, so the four remaining
Boys hang at the Mole Hole, watching the pole dancers and
talking about the good old days. For whatever reason, they're
now focused on the keys, and I wouldn't underestimate what
they'd do to get them back. For that matter, they could be using
the keys as an excuse to flex their atrophied mob muscles."

"Have you seen Benny the Skootch lately?" I said. "It takes
two people to get him out of his chair."

"Yes," Connie said, "but he *has* those two people. In fact, he
has a whole *posse* to help him get the job done, whatever it is. He
has people who would help him in the bathroom. He has people
to help hold his hand steady while he cuts your heart out."

"That all is revolting," Lula said. "I need a donut. Do we got
any more donuts left?"

"How could you think about eating another donut?" I said.
"You've been eating donuts all morning."

"Donuts settle my stomach," Lula said. "Some people take
that antacid medicine, but I eat donuts. Sometimes I eat chicken."

I finished reading the printed pages after an hour and a half, and I wasn't sure I'd found anything useful.

"These men are never alone," I said to Lula and Connie. "Benny the Skootch is married. It's his second wife and there's not much information on her."

"Carla," Connie said. "When Benny lost his wife, he married her sister, Carla. They must be married for at least ten years now. She doesn't get out a lot anymore. She has Parkinson's, and she's unsteady. My mom visits her once in a while. The information I gave you about Benny includes what I hear from my mom. It's tagged onto the end of his bio. He gets picked up every morning precisely at eight o'clock, is driven to the Mole Hole, and stays there until seven at night. He has a woman who tends to Carla during the day. Lights are out in his house at nine o'clock. If he goes out to the doctor's office, a luncheon, or gets a haircut, he's driven in the big black Lincoln. He's short and fat. I know 'fat' isn't a politically correct description these days, but that's what he is. He's fat. He smokes cigars, drinks beer with lunch and whiskey with dinner. He eats a lot of bacon cheeseburgers and chili hot dogs. It's one of life's great mysteries that he isn't dead."

"Sounds to me like he's leading the good life," Lula said.

"Lou Salgusta and Julius Roman live alone," I said. "I suppose I could try to catch them at home, but my blood runs cold at the thought. I'd rather corner them somewhere with people around, and where they aren't within arm's reach of their torture tools."

"We could just camp out in the Mole Hole lot and wait for one of them to leave," Lula said. "Do we know their habits like Benny the Skootch?"

"Sometimes I see Lou at Saturday night mass," Connie said. "I can't tell you more than that."

I glanced at my watch. "I'm going to check on Grandma and grab lunch."

"Sounds good," Lula said. "I'm going to see if the hair salon can squeeze me in early. I'll call you later, and I think we should try to find Carol Joyce again. He's ruining our capture record. We were on a roll until he screwed things up."

Grandma was at the kitchen table. She had her laptop open and was taking notes on yellow lined paper.

I put my bag down and sat across from her. "What's going on?"

"I'm planning out how I'm going to spend Jimmy's money. I got a bucket list about a mile long, so I'm trying to prioritize."

"Do you know how much you're going to get?"

"No clue, but I figure it must be a lot for everybody to want it so bad. I'm thinking I might buy a house of my own. Or maybe one of those new condos that look out over the river. And I'm going to sign up to visit Antarctica on an adventure explorer boat. And I want to go to Gatlinburg. I hear it's a hoot."

"When do you find out about the money?"

"The lawyer said he would schedule a meeting for sometime next week."

"I guess that's pretty exciting."

"You bet," Grandma said. "I've never been rich before."

My mother was ironing, taking all this in. Periodically she would sigh and roll her eyes.

"How long have you been ironing that same shirt?" I asked her.

"Not long enough," she said. "It's got a wrinkle."

"It didn't have any wrinkles when she started," Grandma said. "Maybe we should all break for lunch."

"Just give me a couple minutes," my mother said. "I need to finish this."

The back door banged open and two men barged in. They were wearing balaclavas and holding guns.

"Don't nobody move," the taller of the gunmen said.

The other grabbed Grandma and yanked her out of her chair. I jumped to my feet, reached for Grandma, and the tall guy squeezed off a shot that came as such a shock to all of us, including the gunman, that everyone froze for a beat. I felt searing heat rip through my arm and realized he'd tagged me.

My mother's face contorted, and she produced a sound that rocked the kitchen and was somewhere between enraged mother bear and crazed hyena. She charged the man who shot me and swung the iron wide, ripping the cord out of the wall socket and smacking him square in the face with the iron. He crashed to the floor and didn't move.

The man holding Grandma said "Holy Jesus," released Grandma, and ran out of the house. I ran after him, he fired a shot at me, and I ducked back into the kitchen. When I peeked out a second time he was gone. I ran to the front door and looked out, catching a glimpse of a silver car racing down the street.

I returned to the kitchen, where Grandma and my mother were standing at a distance, staring at the guy who was motionless, toes up, on the floor. My mother was still holding the iron.

"Do you think he's dead?" Grandma asked.

"I don't know," I said. "I'm not getting close enough to find out."

I pulled my cellphone out of my pocket and punched in Morelli's number.

"Someone tried to kidnap Grandma," I said, "but my mother clocked him with her iron and we're not sure if he's dead." I realized blood was dripping off my elbow onto the floor, so I added that I'd been shot.

I hung up and wrapped a kitchen towel around my arm. The wound was throbbing, and I was feeling wobble-legged, so I sat down at the little table. I was joined by my mother and Grandma.

"Are you okay?" Grandma asked me. "Maybe you should lay down until the medics get here."

"I don't think it's terrible," I said. "I wasn't shot in any vital organs."

My mother had ice in a plastic baggie. "Try this on it. I don't know what to do for a gunshot wound."

She handed me the ice and put the iron on the table. We all

watched the man on the floor. If he moved at all I was going to take the iron off the table and hit him again.

In minutes there were sirens and flashing lights and the house was filled with cops and paramedics.

"What must the neighbors think?" my mother said. "We have cars burning up and shootings. If this keeps up, we'll have to sell the house and move where people don't know about us."

"You worry too much," Grandma said. "It's not like we're the only ones with emergencies. Herbert Kuntz goes into cardiac arrest at least twice a month, and the whole street lights up with flashing lights."

A paramedic had my shirtsleeve cut off and was working at the wound site. Sweat was beading on my forehead from the pain, but I was focused on the team of people tending to the guy on the floor. From the amount of activity, I assumed he was alive.

Morelli walked into the kitchen and shook his head at me. Not happy.

"What the hell?" he said.

"You were worried and you love me?" I asked.

He kissed the top of my head. "Yeah. How bad is it?"

"It's not bad," the medic said. "Looks like the bullet passed through the upper arm without hitting the bone. My guess is there was minimum muscle involved. I've got the bleeding under control, but she needs to go to the ER and get stitched up."

Morelli looked down at the iron, still on the table. "Your mom really took him out with the iron?"

"Yep. She was awesome. Totally terrifying."

Morelli cracked a smile. "Nice."

"How's the guy on the floor doing?" I asked Morelli. "Do you recognize him?"

Morelli stepped over to where the gunman was still sprawled and spoke to one of the uniforms standing watch. A stretcher was rolled in, and the gunman was loaded onto it. Morelli came back to me.

"I don't recognize him," Morelli said, "but then it's hard to really see what he looks like with the big iron imprint on his face. He didn't have any ID on him. The only thing in his pocket was a packet of what appears to be cocaine."

Lula swung into the room. "What's going on? What did I miss? I couldn't get a hair appointment so I came for lunch." She spied the guy on the stretcher. "Holy crap! What happened to him?"

"He tried to kidnap Grandma, so my mother took him out with her iron," I said.

Lula turned to my mom. "Way to go, Mrs. P.!" She did a high five and a down low with her. "Is he dead?"

"Not yet," Grandma said.

"Good thing," Lula said. "If California found out a guy got killed with an iron, they'd ban them, and all those movie stars would be wrinkled all the time."

The medic attending me packed up. "We need to get Stephanie out to the truck," he said to Morelli.

I glanced over at Grandma and my mother. "Are you going to be okay?"

"As soon as they get this guy out of here, we're hitting the bottle," Grandma said.

My mother nodded. "Then we're going to pull on some gloves and scrub the floor."

"I'll stay and help," Lula said. "I need to hear all the details."

It was close to six o'clock by the time I was released from the hospital. I was numbed up, stitched up, and hydrated. Morelli had waited with me, going between my bed and the gunman's bed in the ER.

"I told your mom we were bringing pizza for dinner," he said. "I thought you would want to check up on her and Grandma."

"Yes, thanks."

We stopped at Pino's. Morelli ran in and came out with a bunch of pizza boxes.

"That's a lot of pizza," I said.

"Some of it is for the Rangeman guys parked in front of your parents' house. We decided you would come home with me, and Ranger would leave a patrol to watch over your family."

"Sounds like a plan. I'm starving, but I'm exhausted. I can barely think."

"It's the adrenaline letdown," Morelli said. "You just need pizza."

My mother, Grandma, and my dad were lined up on the couch, watching the news on TV. They were slack-faced and glassy-eyed. My dad had his baseball bat resting beside the couch.

We ate at the dining room table. Nobody said anything. Finally, Grandma broke the silence.

"There's bingo tonight," she said. "It's at the firehouse. Margie Pratt said she'd pick me up."

My father's mouth dropped open and a piece of pizza fell out. "Jeez Louise," he said. "Why don't you just stand in the middle of the street and let a car hit you. Get it over with so I can stop carrying this baseball bat around with me."

"What my father is saying, is that maybe going to bingo tonight isn't such a good idea," I said.

Grandma gnawed on a pizza crust. "There's nothing on television that I want to see, and Marvina is calling numbers at the firehouse. It's always good when Marvina calls."

"I can't go with you," I said. "The local is wearing off and my arm is starting to throb again."

"It's okay. I'll be with Margie. She's a crack shot. We go to the rifle range together sometimes."

This was a surprise to me. "You go to the rifle range?"

"Sure. Thursdays are for the ladies," Grandma said. "That's when we go."

"I thought you went to the hair salon on Thursdays," my mother said to Grandma.

"I get my hair done first, and then Margie and I go shoot a

hundred rounds," Grandma said. "I wouldn't be telling you this, but pretty soon I imagine I'll have my own house and lots of money for ammo, and I'll be able to shoot every day if I want."

My mother made the sign of the cross, drained her iced tea glass, and cut a fast look to the kitchen. Undoubtedly wondering if anyone would notice if she got more iced tea.

"I'm running low on energy," I said. "I'm going home with Morelli, and I'm sure I'll feel better tomorrow. In the meantime, Ranger has a car out front. It'll stay with you all night. If Grandma goes to bingo, the car will go with her. Lock your doors. If there's a problem, call me."

My mother gave me a thumbs-up and winked at me. It was the first time I'd ever seen her wink. I didn't know she *could* wink. I guess if you drink enough iced tea anything is possible.

I looked around the table. Morelli was pushed back in his chair and smiling. Grandma was on her phone checking her messages. My father helped himself to another piece of pizza. We were the All-American Family.

CHAPTER THIRTEEN

I SLEPT THROUGH THE NIGHT. No phone calls from Grandma, Ranger, my mom. No requests for sex at three A.M. from Morelli. My arm ached, but not horribly. Life was good. The sun was shining, and Morelli was standing at bedside, dressed in jeans and a checked button-down shirt.

"What's with this?" I said. "Why aren't you at work?"

"I wanted to make sure you were okay."

"Wow, this is serious."

"Yeah, it scares the hell out of me," Morelli said. "How are you feeling?"

"My arm is sore, but overall I feel good." I rolled out of bed and went in search of clothes. "It's hard to get my mind off Grandma. Yesterday was scary."

"We've identified the gunman as Marcus Velez. He's been picked up on a couple vagrancy charges. Tried to rob a convenience store a couple months ago and failed miserably. Was given two weeks in the workhouse. Just got out."

"Do we know who hired him?"

128

"No. He was too out of it to talk last night. Loopy from drugs and a concussion. He's still at St. Francis. I'll drop in on him when I leave here."

"Let me know how it goes."

"What's your plan for the day?"

"I'm going to read over Connie's La-Z-Boys files one more time, and then I'm going to try to find the weakest link. I'm thinking Velez isn't associated with the Boys. They have their own men, and those men wouldn't have a rap sheet like Velez."

"Yeah, he's cheap labor. Someone picked him off a street corner and gave him a gun."

Morelli left, and I settled in with coffee and a frozen waffle. After an hour and a half of reading I decided to target Julius Roman. He wasn't a weak link, but he had a predictable pattern of behavior. Every weekday at precisely 11:45 A.M. he would leave the Mole Hole and walk three blocks to New Town Deli. He did this rain or shine. A small table toward the back of the deli was reserved for him. On rare occasions someone would join him, but usually he ate alone. He had chicken soup and a sourdough roll. He left without paying. We knew all this because Connie's cousin owned the deli. It was a small world.

I rinsed out my coffee mug, told Bob to be a good boy, and walked to my parents' house. I waved to the Rangeman guys and let myself in through the front door. My father's chair was empty. My mom and Grandma were in the kitchen.

"The front door was unlocked," I said. "I told you to lock your doors."

"We don't have to lock the front door," Grandma said. "We got the Rangeman guys watching it."

I tried the back door. It was unlocked.

"Must have forgot that one," Grandma said.

I locked the door and hiked my bag higher on my shoulder. "I can't stay," I said. "I'm on my way to work, and I needed to pick up the car."

"I guess your arm's not too bad if you're going to work," Grandma said.

"It's manageable. What are your plans for today?"

"I haven't got much plans," Grandma said. "We got laundry going, and after that we're making meatballs for dinner. Crystal Buzick is at Stiva's tonight. There won't be much of a crowd, but I'm interested to see how they covered up the big mole she had on her chin. It was all lumpy and it stuck out something awful and it had hairs growing out of it. It's going to take some skill to make that look good."

I slid my mother a look that said don't even *think* about sending me with Grandma to see the lumpy mole.

Lula and Connie were outside the office, staring up at the roof. I parked and went to stand next to them.

"What are we looking at?" I asked.

"Richie Meister," Connie said. "We aren't sure how he got up there, but it looks like he doesn't know how to get down."

"Hey, Richie!" I yelled.

A head with shaggy brown hair popped over the side of the

building. "All the king's horses and all the king's men couldn't get Humpty-Dumpty down again," Richie said.

"Richie's been snarfing magic mushrooms," Lula said.

"We should get a ladder," I said.

"No need for that," Lula said. "Mrs. Capello walked by and saw him up there and called the fire department. She said they got her cat out of a tree once, so she figured they could get Richie off the roof."

We looked down the street toward the firehouse and saw that a hook and ladder was chugging our way. It was followed by a police car and an EMT.

"Seems like overkill, but I guess they gotta be prepared in case he turns out to be a jumper," Lula said. "I like that they brought the hook and ladder. Shows that they take their job seriously. This should be real entertaining."

The fire truck stopped in front of the office, and a bunch of guys in full gear got out and looked up at Richie. I knew one of the guys. Butch Kaharski.

"This is the third time this month we've taken him off a roof," Butch said.

"Yo, Richie," he yelled. "How'd you get up there?"

"My dragon dropped me off," Richie said.

"Can your dragon get you down?" Butch asked.

"He flew away. I don't know where he went. He's sort of a free-spirit dragon."

Butch turned to Connie. "Are there stairs to the roof?"

"No."

"This building backs up to an alley," Butch said. "We'll drive the truck around and pick him off from there."

Everyone got back into the truck, and the truck chugged around the corner. Connie, Lula, and I went into the bonds office and had a donut. After a couple minutes there was a knock on the back door. We all went to the door and looked out at Butch.

"There's a dead guy back here," he said.

My heart skipped a beat. "Richie?"

"No. An unknown. We found him behind the dumpster. He's got a hole in his head. Do you want to take a look and see if you can ID him?"

"No," I said.

"I'll pass on that too," Lula said. "I don't like dead stuff. Especially people."

Connie went with Butch, looked at the dead guy, and came back to us. "I don't know him," she said. "I took a picture with my phone, if you want to see."

I looked at the picture. "It's possible that this is one of the men who tried to kidnap Grandma. I remember his shoes. Red Air Jordans. And he's the right size. I didn't get to see his face."

I called Morelli and told him about the body behind the dumpster.

"I'm already on my way," he said. "I just got a call from the uniform who's on the scene with you. He was at your parents' house yesterday and remembered you talking about the red shoes."

We went out and watched the ladder go up and Richie get helped down.

"This is a lot better than last time," Butch said. "Last time he was naked, and no one wanted to bring him down. We had to draw straws."

"The boy's got a problem," Lula said. "He needs to get a different dragon."

We all nodded agreement.

"I suppose you're going to want to wait for Morelli," Lula said. "I hope he gets here soon because I'm in a mood to go after the shoplifter."

"He said he was already on his way."

"What do you think of my hair?" she asked.

Lula's hair was cut short, dyed blue-black, and was totally slicked down.

"I like it," I said.

"It's one of them retro-French looks."

"Yep. I can see that."

"It's why I'm wearing this little scarf around my neck. It's the recommended accessory."

Richie was on the ground, flitting around like a butterfly, flapping his arms. The first responders were standing back, waiting for him to get tired.

"I don't know what he's on," Butch said, "but I want some."

Connie went into the office and came back with the donut box. There were two donuts left. She waved the box in front of Richie and immediately got his attention.

"If you go in the truck with the medics, you can have these donuts," Connie said.

Richie stopped flitting and took the donut box. "Yum."

"We've got to remember to bring donuts next time we get called out to rescue a crazy," Butch said.

Morelli angle parked behind the fire truck and walked over to us.

"Did Velez tell you anything?" I asked him.

"He met a guy in a bar, they got to talking, and the guy offered him a job. One-time hit. Fifty dollars."

"That's all? Fifty dollars?"

"Velez thought it was good money."

Morelli looked over to the dumpster. Two legs were sticking out from behind it. Attached to the legs were two feet stuffed into red Air Jordans.

"If I was going to kidnap someone, I wouldn't be wearing red Air Jordans," Morelli said. "But that's just me."

"What else did you get from Velez?" I asked. "Did he know who wanted Grandma snatched?"

Morelli shook his head. "No. At least he didn't say. It was hard to communicate since your mother broke his jaw and it's wired shut."

"Yep, she buys a quality iron. Heavy duty. She likes the one with the burst of steam."

"I'm going to go do my cop thing," he said. "Are you coming back to my house tonight?"

"Do you think I should?"

"Absolutely. You might need your dressing changed."

"And you're good at that?"

"Cupcake, I've got skills you haven't even experienced yet."

"We're talking about my bandage, right?"

"Yeah, that too."

Oh boy.

I moved over to where Connie and Lula were standing, and we watched Morelli walk away.

"That man is fine," Lula said. "He's got a good butt. There's only one other butt in Trenton, maybe the world, better than Morelli's butt."

"Ranger's?" I asked.

"Mine," Lula said. "I have a magnificent butt."

Connie and I looked at Lula's butt.

"Impressive," Connie said.

"Exactly," Lula said. "I need it to balance out my generously proportioned bosoms."

Connie and I knew this was an understatement. Lula's bosoms were way beyond generous.

"Did you find anything helpful in the files I gave you?" Connie asked me.

"Yes. I'm going to start with Julius Roman. I'm joining him for lunch today."

"While you have lunch with the mobster, I'm going to hunt down the shoplifter," Lula said.

———

New Town Deli was squashed between an office building and a pawnshop in a part of Trenton that got a lot of foot traffic at lunchtime. I sat across the street from the deli and watched for Roman. At 11:55 I saw him walking toward me. He was the exact opposite of Benny the Skootch. Roman was thin and spry. If he had a posse with him, I couldn't spot them. He was neatly dressed in a button-down shirt, gray slacks with a razor-sharp crease, and a blue blazer. I'd be disappointed if he wasn't carrying under the blazer. I gave him time to get settled at his table before I left the Buick. I wanted to make sure no one else was dining with him. At 12:15, I crossed the street and entered the deli. The room was long and narrow. Generic booths ran along one wall. Wood tables that seated four filled the rest of the space. All of the booths and half of the tables were filled. At the very back, next to the swinging door to the kitchen, was a small table with a white tablecloth. This was Roman's table. He was sitting quietly with a glass of red wine in front of him. He was smiling, thinking his own thoughts. That ended when he saw me. He looked around and relaxed when he realized I was alone. Not that he had to worry. I'm sure the waiter was adept with a garrote, and at a moment's notice the chef would be at the table with his carving knife.

"Mr. Roman," I said, "would you mind if I join you?" Going with polite and respectful.

"Not at all," he said.

A waiter immediately appeared at my side.

"Miss Plum will be dining with me," Roman said.

I waved the waiter away and turned back to Roman. "Thank you, but I just want a moment of your time. We have a problem. Apparently, the La-Z-Boys aren't the only ones interested in finding the keys."

Roman nodded. He knew this.

"And I'm sure you know that I was shot during an attempt to kidnap Grandma yesterday."

Another nod.

"One of the men is in the hospital, and the second man was just found dead behind the bonds office."

Roman's face showed nothing.

"Did you know?" I asked. And what I was really asking was, did the La-Z-Boys commission the hit?

"I didn't know about the second man," Roman said. "I'm not surprised. The stakes are high."

"Do you know this other party?"

"I have suspicions."

"And?" I asked.

"And they're just suspicions."

"You must be worried that someone will get to Grandma before you."

Roman shrugged. "We'll get her one way or another. We would prefer that she gives the keys up without violence. At least I would prefer that. I can't speak for Lou."

"She doesn't have the keys."

Another shrug from Roman.

"I'm good at finding things," I told him.

"People."

"Yes. But I might be able to hunt down the keys if I had a little help."

"What kind of help?"

"I don't know what I'm looking for. I don't know how many keys we're talking about. I don't know what they look like. I don't know their purpose."

"You don't need to know any of those things. If you're lucky enough to run across them, you'll know they're the keys."

The waiter approached. "So sorry to disturb you, Mr. Roman. Would you like your soup now, or would you prefer to wait a little?"

"I'll have it now," Roman said. "My guest is leaving."

I stood and settled my bag on my shoulder. "Can you give me a starting point? You knew Jimmy. What would he do with the keys?"

"If I knew the answer to that question, I'd be in possession of the keys," Roman said.

I left the deli and returned to the Buick. I was about to drive out of the lot when I got a call from Lula.

"I got him!" Lula yelled into the phone. "I got the little weasel. He was coming out of Macy's with a bag, just like last time. I chased him down, and I yanked him out of his Escalade. I was awesome."

"Where are you now?"

"I'm still in the Macy's lot. I thought I'd drive him straight to the pokey."

"You can't do that. You aren't officially hired to do that job. You haven't got any of the necessary papers to make a capture. Stay in the Macy's parking area, and I'll be there in ten minutes."

CHAPTER FOURTEEN

LULA WAS PACING BESIDE her Firebird when I pulled in next to her.

"Where is he?" I asked. "I don't see him in your car."

"He's in the trunk. I couldn't get him to calm down. He was thrashing around and yelling, so I had to stun him and cuff him, and then I put him in the trunk. It's nice and quiet and dark in there. I figured he'd be comfy. I keep my trunk real clean. It's got one of those all-weather liners."

"We can't keep him in the trunk. Get him out and we can put him in my Buick."

Lula opened the trunk and I looked in.

"That's not him," I said.

"Of course it's him," Lula said. "It looks just like him."

"Help! Police! Help!" the guy yelled.

I closed the lid on him. He was still yelling, but it was muffled.

I pulled Lula aside. "Did you check for an ID? Did you look in the bags to see if he had receipts for his purchases?"

"Hell, no, I didn't do any of that. I was too busy wrestling him under arrest. He was totally uncooperative."

"Maybe because you've got the wrong man."

"Well, I didn't have the file with me. I had to go on memory. And what about the Escalade? He was getting into a Escalade."

"Lots of people have Escalades. This one doesn't have the right license plate."

"Oops," Lula said.

I opened the trunk again, apologized, and helped him out. His face was red, and he was sweating.

"She stun-gunned me," he said. "I thought I was going to die."

Lula attempted to unlock his cuffs, and he kicked out at her.

"Get her away from me," he said. "She's nuts. She's a psycho."

I took the key from Lula and got the cuffs off him. I apologized again and told him Lula was on medication and had escaped from her handler. I carried his bags to the Escalade and promised him I would take Lula back to the rehab center. He wanted my name and I told him I was Joyce Barnhardt.

We watched him drive away.

"That was embarrassing," Lula said.

"We should leave before he comes back with the police."

"Are you going to the office?"

"No. I'm going to my parents' house to talk to Grandma about the keys."

"I'll follow you so I can make sure you don't get shot again."

Twenty minutes later we parked behind the Rangeman SUV

and walked into my parents' house. Grandma was at the dining room table, working on her bucket list.

"Let's see what you've got here," Lula said, sitting next to her. "Whoa, a trip to Antarctica. That's a good one. Although I heard the penguins are real stinky."

I didn't see my mother in the kitchen.

"Where's Mom?" I asked.

"Grocery shopping. That's why I'm sitting in the dining room. If someone busts in the back door again, I have more time to run out the front door."

I poked around in the fridge and found a container of leftover chicken salad.

"Anyone want to share this?" I asked.

"I had lunch," Grandma said.

"I had a pizza at the mall before I ran into you-know-who," Lula said.

I got a fork and ate the chicken out of the container. "I want to talk about the keys, again," I said to Grandma. "You married Jimmy. You had to know all kinds of things about him."

"I guess so. It happened pretty fast. It was like love at first sight, except it happened after sixty-three years."

"How did he feel about the keys? Was he worried about losing them? Did he offer to show them to you? Did he have a special place for them when he was in his apartment?"

"He didn't talk about the keys," Grandma said. "Other people talked about the keys. Not actually talked about them. Just that Jimmy was the Keeper of the Keys. And everyone knew that it was a big deal. I guess I got the feeling that Jimmy usually had the keys with him. So, they must have been small. Like regular keys. And if they thought he passed the keys to me as he was dying, they would have to be small and on a key ring."

"But he didn't pass them to you. And the keys weren't on him when he died. He had a wallet with credit cards and cash. That was it," I said.

"How about the ambulance people?" Lula asked.

"I was with him when they took him away," Grandma said. "I didn't see anybody take any keys from him."

"Okay," I said, "let's go at it from a different angle. If you were Jimmy, what would you do with the keys when you were on vacation in the Bahamas?"

"If it was me, I'd hide them in my underwear drawer," Grandma said.

"Yes, but suppose you were Jimmy."

"Jimmy could be real crafty," Grandma said. "He was clever. He might even put them someplace that was booby-trapped."

"In his hotel room? In his condo?"

"His condo. I'm thinking he didn't take the keys with him. We were going for just a couple days, and it was one of those last-minute decisions. He might not even have thought about the keys, what with all the other stuff going on."

"What other stuff?"

"He had to get more male enhancement pills. And he wanted a haircut. And he had to get the plane tickets and the hotel room. Jimmy didn't have a bunch of young wiseguys like some of the other La-Z-Boys. He didn't have a personal assistant or anything. He did everything himself. Even when it came to work, I'm guessing he mostly just went out and killed people."

"Did that bother you?" Lula asked. "Most people don't like people who kill people."

"I didn't think about it until after he was dead," Grandma said. "It's not like he took me out on a date and talked about whacking people. I went out with a butcher once, and all he could talk about was sawing cows apart and chopping the heads off chickens. It was awful. Jimmy and me played gin rummy and went to the movies. It was nice. Besides, it wasn't like he killed random people. He was a respected professional. He had a real good reputation."

"Have you been to his condo since he died?" I asked Grandma.

"No. It's not like I moved in. There wasn't anything of mine at his place. And I knew his sisters went through it right away. I figured they took what they wanted. There wasn't really anything I wanted. I was going to wait until the lawyer made it official and the condo was mine before I took a look at it."

"Do you have a key?" I asked her.

"No, but Jimmy was always forgetting his keys and getting locked out, so he kept a key in the potted plant by the elevator."

"Let's take a look at his condo."

The condo building was an ugly yellow brick cube on the edge of the Burg. It had originally been divided into apartments, and it was almost as old as the La-Z-Boys. The interior was dark and utilitarian. The halls were narrow. Jimmy lived on the third floor.

"Jimmy moved here after the second divorce," Grandma said, taking the key from the potted plant. "He liked the location. He wanted to stay in the Burg." She opened the door to his unit and flipped the light switch.

The shades had all been drawn, and even with the lights on, the room was dark.

"Jimmy didn't care much about decorating," Grandma said. "He felt comfortable with this old stuff. He said it suited him."

"I guess you get used to something, and you don't want to change," Lula said. "Anybody know the age of this building? This wallpaper looks like it's been on here about fifty years."

I knew several people had thoroughly searched the condo, but nothing looked disturbed. The two rolled-arm chairs in the living room had a floral print that was faded and threadbare. The cushions in the green velvet rolled-arm couch were in need of plumping. Magazines and newspapers were stacked on a small coffee table. Table lamps had shades that were yellow with age.

"I don't like to be a critical person," Lula said, "but this is a big disillusioning experience. I can't see the mob's number-one hit man sitting in this sad chair covered in Martha Stewart fabric. It's not even new Martha Stewart fabric. Where's the liquor cabinet? Where's the gun safe?"

"Jimmy didn't drink," Grandma said. "And I never saw him with a gun."

"Maybe he wasn't really a killer," Lula said. "Maybe he was a

145

big fibber. Like, the old guys would get together and talk about things they never did."

I recognized the decorating style. There were a lot of houses in the Burg that were exactly like this. Houses that had aged with their owners. Houses that had passed from one generation to the next with few changes. A new refrigerator. A new hot water heater. The wallpaper was unchanged because someone's grandma had picked it out when she was a bride, and it provided a treasured connection. Sometimes a new owner like Jimmy would come in and have no real connection, but the space just felt right. It felt familiar. It was the *fits like an old shoe* syndrome. I suspected if Grandma moved into the space, she'd gut it and decorate it like the Jetsons' penthouse.

"Jimmy sometimes forgot his condo key, so let's assume that he absentmindedly left the La-Z-Boys keys somewhere," I said. "Everyone else was looking for places he might hide the keys. Let's go on the premise that the keys were lost, and he ran out of time to find them."

After an hour we still didn't have the keys. We found an old lottery ticket and some loose change in the couch. We found a TV remote in the freezer, and a lot of expired food in the small pantry.

"He's got a can of beans in here looks like it's as old as the wallpaper," Lula said.

"Jimmy didn't cook," Grandma said. "He ate out all the time. He didn't even make coffee. He got his coffee at the Starbucks down the street. All he ate at home was ice cream. He liked his ice cream."

"He has a stacked washer and dryer but no laundry detergent," I said.

"Yep. Sent it out. Linens, towels, clothes, everything. It all came back folded and ironed."

"Do you know what service he used?"

"Blue Ribbon. It's the best. We take our dry cleaning there sometimes," Grandma said. "They came and picked it all up for Jimmy and brought it back two days later."

"I'm starting to like this guy," Lula said. "He had a good lifestyle going. He didn't do nothing for himself."

I called Blue Ribbon Cleaners and asked for the manager. I explained that I was calling for Jimmy's wife and that she was inquiring about clothes that might have been left there.

"Well?" Lula said when I hung up. "How'd that go?"

"The manager said all clothes had been delivered to Jimmy the day before he left for the Bahamas."

We locked the condo, returned the key to the planter, and stepped into the elevator.

"We're missing something," I said. "What about Jimmy's car?"

"It's probably in the garage under the building," Grandma said. "He had a slot for it. He was number seven."

I punched G on the elevator button, and the doors opened to the garage.

"It's the black Honda Civic," Grandma said.

"Say what?" Lula said. "He drove a Honda Civic? Not that it isn't a good car, but it's not what I would expect. The people I know who kill people drive *big* cars. Hummers and monster trucks. Of course, they're all gangbangers and dealers. They gotta make a statement. It's like look how big my car is and that's nothing compared to my dick. I guess it's different with mob killers. They're more in the professional category, keeping a low profile. Or it could be that Jimmy didn't have any money. Maybe wet work doesn't pay anymore." She stood in front of the car. "It's not even new. This here's an old Civic."

"It ran good," Grandma said. "And he kept it clean inside."

I tried the door and found it unlocked. Probably because forty-five people had already looked through it for the keys.

We did our own search, using our cellphone flashlights, looking under the seats and in the trunk.

"This is depressing," Grandma said. "I don't like looking for the keys. It's not what it was about with Jimmy and me. I don't even know if I want his money anymore."

"I get what you're saying," I said to Grandma, "but we're looking for the keys to keep you alive. The money is a different deal. You have to figure that one out yourself."

"We should have a change of pace and go looking for the shoplifter," Lula said. "That would perk Grandma up."

Grandma joining us on an apprehension? Disaster! "No, no, no," I said. "I'm sure Grandma has things she needs to do at home."

"Nothing that can't wait," Grandma said, "but a shoplifter

doesn't sound exciting. Don't you have something better? Like a bank robber or a terrorist?"

"I haven't got any of those," I said. "I have a hijacker and attempted murder."

"Tell me about the attempted murder," Grandma said.

"Barry Strunk. He got screwed at the Cluck-in-a-Bucket drive-thru and pulled the minimum-wage worker through the drive-thru window. He had the kid on the ground, and he was shoving a Double Clucky Burger down his throat and yelling *This is all wrong. It's all wrong!*"

"That's questionable attempted murder," Lula said.

"Strunk was also yelling to the Clucky kid that he was going to kill him. They have it on Clucky tape. He said it a lot. And according to this report, the kid almost choked to death."

"The problem here is that this man had unrealistic expectations. It's a known fact that you get fucked at the drive-thru."

"Let's go after this one," Grandma said. "I want to see the man who got fucked at the drive-thru."

"He didn't *really* get fucked," Lula said to Grandma. "You know that, right? He just got figuratively fucked."

"Good enough for me," Grandma said.

I read the file out loud. "Barry Strunk. Forty-two years old. Divorced. Works at the button factory. No priors. Looks crazy in his mug shot."

Lula and Grandma leaned in and looked at the mug shot.

"I could tell right off that this boy needs anger management,"

Lula said. "He's got big frowny marks in his forehead and his mouth is all snarly."

"He should be getting off his shift at the button factory soon," I said.

"We could catch him in the parking lot," Lula said.

"The parking lot is a mess when there's a shift change," I said. "I'd rather wait for him at his house. He lives in one of the little row houses on E Street."

"I didn't bring my cuffs," Grandma said.

"That's okay," I told her. "I have cuffs. And I don't expect him to be difficult. He's not a career criminal. He just had a bad day."

I didn't entirely believe this, but I didn't want Grandma going all Dirty Harry on me.

We'd been driving around in Lula's car with the Rangeman guys on our bumper.

Grandma was in the back seat, and from time to time she'd turn and wave at the SUV.

"Ernie and Slick are with us today," Grandma said. "Slick's real name is Eugene, but he likes to be called Slick. He doesn't usually ride on patrol, but Ranger was short."

"How do you know all this?" Lula asked.

"I go out to talk to them sometimes. They gotta sit in the car all day doing nothing but stare at our house, so I bring them cookies and sodas. Slick is Ranger's electronics guy. He sets up the security systems. He was a safecracker before he got a job with Ranger."

Parking was tight on E Street. Lula squeezed into a space

two houses down from Strunk's, but the Rangeman SUV was out of luck. I got a text message that they would be circling the block until something opened up.

"It's been a long time since I've been on a stakeout," Grandma said. "How's this gonna go down?"

"When we see Strunk walk up to his door—"

"Hold on," Lula said. "Where's he going to park? We just took the last parking spot."

"These streets all have alleys in the back," Grandma said. "There's usually parking there."

I checked my watch. "The shift is getting out now. You two stay here, and I'll run around to the back. Call me if you see him. He's driving a white Taurus."

I jogged around the block and walked the alley until I came to Strunk's house. There were no garages back here, but there were small yards where people parked. I didn't see a white Taurus. I took a position behind a pickup truck next door to Strunk's place.

A woman stuck her head out of a second-floor window and yelled at me. "This is private property. What are you doing by my truck?"

I took a couple steps away from the truck. "I'm waiting for a friend."

"That's a load of bull crap. You think I'm stupid? The only friend you're waiting for is the one who's gonna help you steal my truck. I'm calling the police."

There wasn't a lot of cover in the alley. There were a couple cars way at the end, but that was too far from Strunk's back door. There was a weathered privacy fence that ran for about fifteen feet between Strunk's house and the crazy truck lady's house. An overgrown, undernourished azalea bush clung to life at the end of the fence. I moved to the azalea bush and watched for the white Taurus. If I saw the car, I'd duck down into the bush and hope for the best.

After five minutes there was no Taurus and no messages from Grandma or Lula. I heard a door close behind me in the crazy truck lady's yard. I turned to see what was going on and was hit with a blast of water from her garden hose.

"You think I couldn't see you sneaking around in the azalea bush?" she said. "I see everything. Nothing gets past me. I got a gun too. I'm counting to three, and then I'm going to start shooting."

This is when it all came back to me. The dissatisfaction with my life. The desire to be somewhere else doing something else. *Anything* else.

"I'm waiting for Barry Strunk," I said, turning my back against the water, trying to shield myself with the bush and the broken-down fence.

"Strunk is a loser. Barry the Loser, that's what I call him. I should have known you were with Strunk when I saw the blue hair. You're all nutcases and losers."

This is just great. The crazy lady thinks I'm a loser. My worst fear is confirmed by a woman wearing fluffy pink slippers, soaking me with her garden hose.

"I'm leaving," I said, hands in the air. "I give up. I'm done. Fuck it. Fuck it all."

I sloshed down the alley, back to Lula and Grandma.

"What the heck?" Lula said.

"Don't ask," I told her. "I don't want to talk about it. I want to go home. Take me home."

"Hold on, you can't get into my car like that," Lula said. "You're all wet. You'll ruin my upholstery. You're gonna have to take your clothes off or else ride in the trunk."

I gave Lula the finger and blew raspberries at her.

"That's not nice," Lula said.

The Rangeman SUV rolled down the street and stopped.

"I need a ride," I told them.

"What about Edna?" Slick asked. "We're supposed to stay with Edna."

"Edna is coming with me."

I narrowed my eyes at Grandma and jerked my thumb at the SUV. "Get in."

"What about the stakeout?" Grandma asked.

"The stakeout is done," I said. "Finished. Over. Kaput."

"What about me?" Lula asked. "You want me to stay here awhile?"

"I don't care what you do. Do whatever you want. I've had it. I'm fed up! F-E-D up! I'm wet and I'm cold and my arm is killing me, and you wouldn't even give me a ride."

"That's not true," Lula said. "I gave you two good options. You're just feeling picky."

"They weren't good options. You wouldn't have taken either of those options."

"I wouldn't have to," Lula said. "I don't go around getting myself soaked. And if I had to choose an option, I would have removed my clothes. I don't have a problem with nudity. Especially my own."

Grandma was already seated in the SUV. "Are you coming, or what?" she said to me. "You're going to catch your death, standing out there dripping wet. And there's some blood soaking through your bandage."

CHAPTER FIFTEEN

I MADE CERTAIN that Grandma was safe inside the house, and then I drove myself home.

Rex was asleep in his soup can when I walked into the kitchen, but I talked to him anyway.

"Honestly," I said to Rex, "this is ridiculous. Who has a job like this? Grocery checkers don't get wet. People working the line at the Personal Products plant don't get wet. The lady working the counter at the Häagen-Dazs store doesn't get wet. Even hamsters don't get wet. Crappy bounty hunters get wet. Good ones, no. Ranger never got wet. Just crappy ones . . . like me."

Rex popped his head out of his soup can, blinked at me, and retreated. I couldn't blame him for retreating. Even *I* didn't want to listen to me. I was ranting.

My mood improved after a hot shower. I put a new giant Band-Aid over my stitches, got dressed, and called Morelli.

"What's new?" I asked.

"Pino's has a new sandwich at lunch. It's got fried chicken and melted cheese and they pour gravy over it."

"I was thinking more in terms of my crap-ass life and the stupid keys."

"Nothing's new on that front."

I blew out a sigh, disconnected, and went back to the office. Connie was surfing her social media sites, and Lula was reading *Star* magazine.

"Let's go," I said to Lula. "Let's see if we can catch someone."

Lula got to her feet. "Who'd you have in mind?"

"Anyone."

"That's entirely doable," Lula said.

We got outside and looked at the cars parked at the curb. Lula's Firebird and my '53 Buick.

"Let's take the Buick," I said.

Lula nodded. "Good idea."

I drove to Carol Joyce's house first. The black Escalade was parked in the driveway.

"He's got a lot of nerve," Lula said. "He's got that big-ass car parked right out front, advertising that he's home."

"The Superman syndrome," I said. "Thinks he's invincible."

"Just because he made fools out of us the first time, he thinks he can always make fools out of us."

"Let's hope he's wrong."

I parked in the driveway, behind the Escalade, so he couldn't drive off. Lula and I went to the front door. I rang the bell. No one answered.

"Maybe he's out with his mama," Lula said. "They could be in her car."

I rang the bell again. "I don't think so. I think he's in the house."

I tried the doorknob. Locked.

"What are we thinking here?" Lula asked. "You want me to shoot the lock off?"

"Do you know how to do that?"

"Sure. You shoot at the lock and it falls off."

"Let's save that as a last resort. I'll go around back. Stay here. And don't shoot *anything*."

I jogged to the back of the house and tried the back door. Locked. I looked in the kitchen window. Everything was tidy. Lula walked into the kitchen and opened the door for me.

"How did you get in?" I asked.

"The window was open. The one next to the door."

"I don't remember seeing an open window."

"It wasn't actually open."

"It was unlocked?"

"More like it had a crack in it," Lula said.

"A crack? How big was the crack?"

"Big enough that I could get my hand in and open the window."

"You broke a window."

"It was an accident. I sort of turned around too fast and my purse swung out and *CRASH!* Anyways, now that we're in we might as well snoop around, although I didn't see any sign of him on my way through the house."

A mug of tea was sitting on the kitchen counter. The tea bag was still in it. I put my hand to it, and the mug was warm.

"He's here," I said. "He's hiding."

"I'm good at this. I can find people like you wouldn't believe. I used to play hide-and-seek all the time when I was a kid. I was the hide-and-seek champion."

We started in the kitchen, opening every door, looking in cupboards. We moved on to the dining room and the living room. Downstairs powder room. We went upstairs and looked under beds, in closets, bathroom cupboards. Nothing. No Carol Joyce.

"I gotta give him credit," Lula said. "He's a good hider."

I looked down at the street from an upstairs bedroom window. The Buick was blocking one lane. The Escalade was gone.

Lula came over and looked out with me.

"Damn," Lula said. "No wonder I couldn't find him."

"He pushed my car into the road."

"Yeah, you gotta love that Escalade. It's got power. Your Buick is no lightweight, but that big ol' Escalade is a beast."

We trooped downstairs and left the house. I made sure the doors were locked, but there wasn't anything I could do about the broken window. Mrs. Joyce was still out somewhere. Carol was most likely lurking in the neighborhood, watching, waiting for us to leave.

Lula and I walked around the Buick, checking it out.

"Not a scratch or a dent," Lula said. "This car is a tank. They don't make cars like this anymore."

Thank heaven, I thought. The thing drove like a refrigerator on wheels, and it got four miles to the gallon.

"I haven't had my fill of humiliation yet," I said to Lula. "Let's see if Barry Strunk is home."

I drove past the front of Strunk's house and thought I saw the flicker of a television screen through a living room window. I drove down the alley and found his Taurus angle-parked in his backyard.

"Here's the plan," I said to Lula. "I'm going to drop you off, and you're going to keep watch that he doesn't come out the back door and drive away. Just make sure you don't get near the neighbor's truck."

"What's wrong with the truck?"

"The crazy lady who lives there doesn't like anyone getting near her truck. Also, don't break anything or shoot anything. Just don't let Strunk get into his car and drive away."

"Yeah, but what if I have to shoot him to stop him? What if he shoots at me?"

"He tried to kill a kid with a double cheeseburger. There was no gun involved."

"I could handle a double cheeseburger," Lula said.

I dropped her off, drove around to the front, and found a parking place. I hung my cuffs from my back pocket, shoved a pepper spray canister into my sweatshirt pocket, and walked up to the house. I heard the bolt slide locked just as I was about to knock.

I rapped on the door and called out that I was looking for Barry Strunk.

The answer came back muffled.

"He's not home. No one's home."

"Open the door. I want to talk to you."

"What about?"

"I represent your bail bondsman. You missed a court date and I want to help you reschedule."

"Are you sure?"

"Yes."

"Crap," he said. "What do I have to do? Do I have to sign something?"

"You have to go downtown with me and get a new date from the clerk."

Silence.

"Barry? Hello?" I banged on the door and tried the handle. "Open the door, and I'll let you see my blue hair."

Okay, that was stupid, but I thought it was worth a shot. I had my ear to the door, and I couldn't hear any sounds inside the house. Strunk was either crouched down, playing possum, or on his way to the back door and his car. I was betting on the latter. I called Lula to tell her to watch for him.

"Don't worry," Lula said. "I'm on the job. Nobody gets past Lula when she's on the . . . what the hell?"

There was a lot of screaming and the phone went dead. I jumped into the Buick, raced around the corner, and turned into the alley. Lula was standing in the middle of the road. She was soaking wet, and the white Taurus was gone.

"I hate this job," she said. "This job sucks. Who else has to put up with this kind of abuse? Almost nobody."

"You're wet," I said.

"No shit! Some crazy lady turned her garden hose on me. I was getting ready to take down Strunk, and next thing I'm freaking soaking wet."

"I told you not to get near the truck."

"Yeah, but I needed a place to conceal myself."

"Looks like he got away."

"He almost ran me over. I could be dead now with truck tire tracks on me. What's with people these days? There's no consideration. They'd just as soon run over a person." She shook herself like a wet dog. "I'm done. I'm wet, and I'm cold, and this hand-bedazzled top I'm wearing is dry-clean only. That Strunk is going to be in big trouble if his neighbor ruined my top."

"No problem," I said. "I'll pop the trunk."

"Say what?"

"You're going to get in the trunk, right? I mean, you're all wet."

"I'm not riding in no trunk."

"Then you're going to have to take your wet clothes off. I have vintage upholstery in this car."

Lula stripped her bedazzled top off, and her massive breasts flopped out.

Eeeek!

"I was just yanking your chain," I said. "Put the top back on!"

Lula got into the Buick naked from the waist up, and buckled herself in. The retrofitted seatbelt disappeared into her cleavage, and her nipples stuck out like giant Keurig K-Cups.

"It's better this way," she said. "I can dry out my top, so it won't get wrecked."

"Jeez Louise. It's not better. It's . . . distracting. And it might be illegal to flash nipples that big when you're in a Buick."

"All the ladies in my family have big nipples," Lula said. "It's one of our best features. We got nipples a person could be proud of." She glanced over at me. "Not that there's anything wrong with little nipples. I know you got little nipples on account of when we had to chase that guy on the nudie beach, and I got to see your nipples."

I looked down at myself. I couldn't see my nipples, but I knew they were there. One more thing to add to the list. Not only did I have a depressing job. Now I had to worry about my little nipples.

"Your nipples are dainty," Lula said. "You got dainty pink nipples."

This sounded a lot better than plain old *little* nipples, but I still wouldn't mind getting off the whole nipple topic.

"I'm done for the day," I said. "What about you? Do you have plans for tonight?"

"I've gotta work on my blog."

"You have a blog?"

"Everybody's got a blog," Lula said. "Don't you have a blog?"

"No."

"Well, I have a blog and I'm thinking about being an influencer. I could influence the shit out of stuff."

"No doubt."

I turned onto State Street, drove two blocks, and spotted the white Taurus parked at a 7-Eleven. Strunk was walking out the door with a monster drink and a hot dog.

"It's him!" Lula yelled. "That's our guy."

I pulled into the lot and before I came to a complete stop, Lula was out of the car, charging Strunk.

"You almost ran me over, you sonnovabitch!" Lula yelled.

Strunk froze with his mouth open and his eyes bugged out at the sight of the giant nipples and bouncing breasts coming at him.

Lula got to arm's length, and he snapped out of his catatonic state and threw his soda at her and hit her in the face with the hot dog. He turned to run, and I tackled him, taking him down to the ground. Lula jumped in and snagged his shirt and wrenched him off me. We got him facedown, and Lula sat on him while I cuffed him.

We hoisted him to his feet and stuffed him into the Buick's back seat. Cars were driving by and honking at Lula, and Lula would give them a V-for-victory gesture and thumbs-up.

"You should put your shirt back on," I said to Lula. "You'll get arrested if you show up at the police station like that."

"No way can I put it on now," Lula said. "I've got sticky titties from him throwing soda on me. You have to take me home first so I can get another shirt."

"I'll drop you at the office," I said. "Your car is there. I can get Strunk to the police station on my own."

Strunk was sullen and silent in the back seat all the way to the office. Lula got out, and after I drove for two blocks, Strunk started growling and thrashing around.

"Hey," I said, "get a grip back there."

"I hate you," he said. "And you're ugly."

"I'm not ugly," I told him. "I have blue highlights in my hair, and I have dainty pink nipples."

"Let me see them."

"You can look at my highlights all you want."

"I don't want to see the highlights. Show me your nipples."

"Not a chance."

"I'll hold my breath and make myself throw up in your car."

"People don't throw up from holding their breath. You have to stick your finger down your throat to throw up, and your hands are cuffed."

"I could stick my tongue down my throat. It's already halfway there."

He made gagging sounds like he was trying to get his tongue down his throat.

"How's it going?" I asked.

"I hate you."

"You already said that," I told him.

"Yeah, but I mean it. If my hands weren't cuffed, I'd punch you. You're ruining my day."

"Like the Clucky kid."

"Yes! Do you know what I do all day? I work the line at the button factory. Little tiny buttons roll past me, and I sort out the ones that are cracked or discolored. All day. Five days a week. Can you imagine? That's my life. So all day long I'm thinking about a Double Clucky Burger. It's my reward for getting through my hideous, boring, mind-rotting day. I would prefer drugs over the Clucky Burger, but I can't afford drugs. I can only afford a shitty Clucky Burger. I get myself through the day, and I go to the drive-thru and order my food, and it comes out all wrong. How could anyone get a Double Clucky Burger wrong? It's probably made by robots like me."

"You tried to kill the kid working the window."

"He deserved to die."

"What was wrong with the burger?"

"No pickles. It's supposed to have a layer of thinly sliced pickles between the special sauce and the minced onion."

"That doesn't seem like a good reason to kill someone."

"It seems like a good reason to me. If you don't do your job right, you die. You know what happens to me if I miss a cracked button?"

"No. What?"

"They take me to a back room and strip me naked and whip me."

"Really?"

"No. But it feels like that."

"Maybe you should see a doctor."

"Maybe you should show me your nipples."

Ten minutes later, I parked in the courthouse parking lot. I tried to help Strunk get out of the back seat, and he kicked at me.

"I'm not going," Strunk said. "You can't make me."

I got back behind the wheel and drove to the cop shop back door. I requested assistance, and three cops dragged Strunk out of my car and into the building. I followed so I could get my body receipt.

I was waiting on the docket lieutenant, and Morelli joined me.

"Are you okay?" he asked. "You're white and sweating."

"My arm is throbbing, and I have a horrible headache."

"Did it occur to you that you should take a day off after getting shot?"

"Not until now."

Morelli took the receipt from the lieutenant, put an arm around me, and steered me out of the building.

"Since the Buick is parked at the back door, I'm guessing your FTA wasn't cooperative."

"He has anger issues."

Morelli opened the passenger's side door for me. "I'll drive," he said. "I was leaving for the day, and you look like you need help."

I closed my eyes and leaned back. He was right. I needed help.

Morelli had me tucked in on his couch. I had a new dressing on my arm, and I'd popped a couple Tylenol. I'd had leftover lasagna for dinner. Ice cream for dessert. Bob and Morelli were snuggled next to me. Life was good again.

"We got an ID on Red Air Jordans," Morelli said. "Sylvester Lucca. He was a trainer at the fancy gym on State Street."

"The one with the statues of naked Roman gods out front?"

"Yep. He has no priors. A couple traffic violations. Originally from Newark. Twenty-nine years old. I couldn't find any ties to the La-Z-Boys or Jimmy's relatives, but it's early. We're still digging."

"I expected the La-Z-Boys to make a move on Grandma by now."

"Hard to say what's going on with them. Maybe they're being careful, waiting for the right time. Ranger's men are watching the front of the house, and Ranger probably has some cameras operating in the back. Grandma hasn't been going out alone, and when she does the Rangeman guys follow her."

"The Boys are patient."

"They have lots of years of experience," Morelli said. "They know when to wait and when to move."

CHAPTER SIXTEEN

IT WAS A little after seven A.M. by the time I rolled out of Morelli's bed, showered, and got dressed. I'd assumed Morelli was already at work, but I got to the stairs and heard men's voices coming from the kitchen. The voices belonged to Morelli and Ranger.

I considered turning around and hiding in the bedroom, but the two men were standing between me and my breakfast waffle.

"Good morning," I said, edging my way into the kitchen. "What's going on?"

"Ranger brought you a car," Morelli said. "It'll be easier for you to drive with your arm."

"And I can track it," Ranger said. "There's so much heavy metal in the Buick it interferes with my electronics."

"Anything else?" I asked.

Ranger held out a necklace with a silver medallion engraved with a cross. "Panic button. Press it and we can find you above or belowground."

"I suspect you could find me even if I don't press it," I said.

Ranger almost smiled. "I have an identical necklace for Grandma Mazur."

"We decided that he should pull his men back and replace them with surveillance equipment," Morelli said. "After you and I talked last night it occurred to me that we were just prolonging the inevitable. Better to have them make their move so we can react."

I put the medallion on, got a waffle out of the freezer, and dropped it into the toaster. "I guess that sounds reasonable, but I'm terrified that something awful is going to happen to Grandma. I'm trying to fix things, but I'm failing. I talk to people and I look under beds and nothing comes of it. But at least she's relatively safe while I'm bumbling around. You want to change that. You essentially want to set Grandma up to get kidnapped. I know I'm not alone in this. I know you're going to be there. I know you're smarter and bigger and braver than I am. But this is my grandma."

I heard my voice crack when I said "grandma," and I tried to swallow back the emotion that sat hard and painful in my throat. Both men were watching me. Their eyes were dark and serious. They understood my problem. It was their problem too.

"Okay," I said. "Let's do it."

Ranger gave me the keys to a black Porsche Macan. "This car has front and rear cameras that send to my control room. It has a lockbox containing a loaded nine-millimeter under the driver's seat. The box isn't locked. If you want to lock it, the key is on your key ring."

"Thanks," I said. "It's been difficult driving the Buick with my sore arm. It steers like a tank."

"The medallion will go a long way toward keeping Grandma safe," Morelli said to me. "But it's only effective if she's wearing it. You have to make sure she never takes it off."

"It's waterproof," Ranger said. "She can wear it in the shower."

I poured myself a cup of coffee. "I'll take it over to her as soon as I'm done with my waffle."

"Babe," Ranger said.

Ranger doesn't pollute his body with sugar and additives. He has salmon from Scotland and half an organic multigrain bagel for breakfast.

"It's a whole-wheat waffle," I said. "And I didn't add syrup."

Ranger smiled. I amused him. "Keep in touch," he said. And he left.

Morelli watched me drink my coffee. "He calls you 'Babe'?"

"I think he calls everyone 'Babe.'"

"He doesn't call me 'Babe.'"

"Because you would punch him."

"I wouldn't mind punching him anyway."

Morelli and Ranger tolerate each other. Their professional paths frequently cross, and there are times when it's advantageous to share information and skills. Like now. In an odd way I was the link between the two men, and I was also the wedge that drove them apart. Morelli thought Ranger was a loose cannon and not to be entirely trusted. I have no idea what Ranger thought of Morelli.

Morelli gave me a kiss on the top of my head and told me to be careful. He said he'd call me later in the day, and he left.

"Just you and me," I said to Bob.

It was too early to go to the office, so I hooked Bob up to his leash and took him for a walk. It was almost eight o'clock when we got home. I gave him a doggie treat and told him he was a good boy. I pocketed Grandma's necklace, hung my messenger bag on my shoulder, and drove to my parents' house.

My father was in his chair, watching the news with the baseball bat at his feet.

"What's up?" I said.

"I'm not watching the news anymore. It's damn depressing. What's with these nutcases who go around shooting strangers? It used to be people shot each other one at a time. It was personal. You could figure out why they did it." He shook his head. "I don't get this other stuff."

Grandma was standing to one side. "They have cracked souls," she said. "You know how some people are born with physical defects? Like those sweet Down syndrome babies. I think some people are born with souls that aren't all there. Or maybe their souls got a crack somewhere along the line. Like a broken leg, only it's a soul." She looked over at me. "Did you have breakfast yet? We got oatmeal in the kitchen. I was just going to have some."

I followed Grandma into the kitchen. "I don't want oatmeal," I said, "but I'll have coffee."

I helped myself to coffee and brought it to the little kitchen table. I'd eaten baby food at that table, and I'd done my homework at it too. I couldn't imagine the table not being there. The refrigerator and the stove got changed out, but the table remained. It was the heart of the kitchen, and the kitchen was the heart of the house. Even after the attempted kidnapping, the kitchen still felt safe. Even with my mother nipping at the whiskey and my grandmother reading the obits for entertainment, the kitchen felt sane. Going with Grandma's theory, I was pretty confident that all our souls were intact, and that the kitchen was partly responsible for keeping them that way.

Grandma brought her bowl of oatmeal to the table. "That's a pretty necklace you're wearing," she said. "Is it new?"

"Yep," I said. "Ranger gave it to me." I pulled Grandma's necklace out of my pocket and handed it to her. "He gave me one for you, too."

My mother was at the sink, washing out the oatmeal pot. She stopped scrubbing and looked over at Grandma and me.

"It's to help keep us safe until we get the key issue sorted out," I said. "It's a panic button. If you squeeze it, Ranger will send someone to find you. He'll know where you are as long as you're wearing the necklace. You should put it on and not take it off. It's waterproof. You can wear it in the shower."

Grandma put the necklace on. "I feel safer already," she said.

My mother rinsed the pot and set it in the dish rack. "I noticed the Rangeman car was gone this morning."

"Ranger's replaced it with the necklace and some surveillance equipment," I said.

"It would be good if we've seen the end of it," she said. "Hopefully those two thugs won't return."

I could guarantee it.

"I have to go to work," I said. "Text me if anything changes here."

I rinsed my coffee cup and noticed the ironing board had been put away, but the iron remained on the kitchen counter.

I missed the Boston Kreme donut by five minutes. Lula was enjoying it when I walked into the office. Just as well, I thought. It wouldn't hurt to clean up my act with diet as well as everything else. All part of the new Stephanie. The new Stephanie is adventuresome, with metallic extensions in her hair. The new Stephanie doesn't pay attention to body shaming because she has dainty breasts. And now the new Stephanie is going to be a model of good health.

"There's a chocolate frosted in there if you want it," Lula said. "It's not a Boston Kreme but it's got sprinkles on it. You don't often see that on a chocolate frosted donut."

I took the donut and ate it. Slight setback for the new Stephanie.

"I have a guy I'd like you to run through the system for me," I said to Connie. "Sylvester Lucca. He belongs to the feet in the red Air Jordans."

"And you're looking to connect him to someone associated with Jimmy," Connie said. "You want to know who hired him."

"Yes."

173

"I got my day planned out," Lula said. "I'm going to find that snot-nosed Carol Joyce. Just because he made fools out of us two times, I bet he thinks he can always make fools out of us."

"Always is a long time," I said.

Lula took another donut. "You bet your ass."

I checked the time. "It's too early for shoplifting. We can make a run past his house to see if he's home. I'll drive. Ranger took pity on me and gave me a loaner."

"I'm all about it," Lula said.

We left the office and went to the Macan.

"This here's some good wheels," Lula said, sliding onto the passenger seat. "You have to do anything special to get this?"

"No. Everyone felt I needed a safer car that was easier for me to steer with my bad arm."

"Too bad. I wouldn't mind doing something special for Ranger. He wouldn't even have to give me a car."

I bypassed the center of town and took Liberty to Cherry Street. Mrs. Joyce was in front of her house with a fat Chihuahua that was all hunched over.

"That don't look good at all," Lula said. "They need to give that dog some prunes."

"The Escalade isn't in the driveway," I said, pulling to the curb.

Lula rolled her window down. "Hey, Mrs. J.," she said. "Where's your boy, Carol?"

"He's at his office," Mrs. Joyce said. "Are you still looking for him?"

"Yep," Lula said. "We just haven't had any luck catching him. Where's his office at?"

"I don't know exactly. I've never been there. I know it's by the outlet mall, because he's always saying how convenient it is when he wants to be thrifty."

"I bet," Lula said. "Is it in an office building?"

"No. Carol doesn't like those high-rises where he has to cart everything up in the elevator. His office is in one of those strips of offices. More like little garden apartments. I saw a picture of it once. All the units were painted a salmon color." She looked down at the dog. He was slowly turning in circles, still hunched over. "Go poopoo," she said. "Make a poopoo for Mommy."

"Okay, we gotta go now," Lula said. "Good luck with the dog. I had an uncle who looked like that once. He had to get an enema, and then he about exploded. You might want to stand back a little, just in case."

I drove to the end of the street and got a bird's-eye view of the outlet mall up on my cellphone. I moved around the area until I found something that looked like strips of offices.

"I know where that is," Lula said. "It's a mix of self-storage units and office units. I was at a studio there a couple times during my short but highly acclaimed adult film career."

"It looks like it's off Rosewood."

"Yep. There's a whole complex between Rosewood and the highway. Must be a hundred of these little units that people use for all kinds of things."

I took Route One to the Rosewood exit, drove a half mile on

Rosewood, and came to a sign for Rosewood Light Industries and Storage.

"This is it," Lula said. "It's like a maze after you get inside the complex. You'll have to ride up and down a bunch of dead-end streets to look for the Escalade."

I cruised three streets and found the Escalade on the fourth. It was parked in front of a middle unit on Avenue D. Five units on one side of it and six on the other. The entire stucco building was painted salmon. Each unit had a door. No windows. Each unit had a number, and most had plaques with names. The Escalade was in front of CJ Enterprises.

"Lots of these are used for storage," Lula said. "They all have roll-up garage doors in the back and there's service roads behind them."

I was about to park behind the Escalade, blocking its escape, and immediately thought better of it. Been there, done that. I parked two units down, and we went to the door of CJ Enterprises. I knocked and no one answered. I tried the door. Not locked. I opened it, and Lula and I stepped in. It was basically an empty room. There was an old wooden desk and chair in the middle of the room. Some empty cardboard boxes lay in a jumble in a corner. A long folding table was against one wall. No stolen merchandise. No Carol Joyce, but the lights were on. There was an open door and a closed door next to the folding table.

"That's the bathroom and the utility closet," Lula said. "It's a pretty basic setup."

We crossed the room and looked in the bathroom. Sink and

toilet and a double-door closet. I opened the closet and found stacks of men's jeans.

"They're real nice," Lula said. "Ralph Lauren. They're pricey jeans. I wouldn't be leaving them in a bathroom."

We heard a scuffling behind us, and the door slammed shut.

"What the heck?" Lula said.

I tried the doorknob. "We're locked in."

"No problem," Lula said. "I'll shoot the shit out of this door."

"Where's your gun?"

"It's in my purse."

"Where's your purse?"

"It's in the car."

"Plan B," I said, pulling my phone out of my pocket. "I'll call for help."

"Babe," Ranger said on the first ring.

"I'm locked in a bathroom."

"And?"

"I can't get out. The bathroom is in the CJ Enterprises unit, Avenue D."

"Anything else you want to tell me?"

"Nope. That's it."

The line went dead, and I knew help was on the way.

"This is annoying," Lula said. "I bet it was Carol Joyce who locked us in here. I'm disliking him more all the time."

I checked my email and text messages, and before I had a chance to look in at Facebook, I heard footsteps and a rap on the door.

"Anybody in there?" a male voice asked.

"Yep," I said. "Can you get me out?"

"You're padlocked in. Hang on and we'll get the bolt cutters."

Five minutes later, Lula and I were set free.

"There are some real nice men's jeans in there," Lula said to the two Rangeman guys. "You should check them out and see if any of them are your size. Our treat."

We reached my new Porsche, and "losers" was written in lipstick on the driver's side door window.

"Looks like the little prick hit the cosmetics counter," Lula said. "How do you suppose he knew this was our car?"

"It's the only one here."

"He has a lot of nerve calling us losers. We might be inept at this job, but we aren't losers. 'Losers' implies a whole other thing. He doesn't know us well enough to call us losers. He could have written a lot of other stuff on the window that would apply better. For instance, he could have written 'pussy,' and it would be insulting but accurate, you see what I'm saying?"

I got a tissue out of my bag and tried to wipe the lipstick away, but it turned into a big pink smear.

"I got a wipe," Lula said, ripping a packet open. "Best invention ever. It's like taking a little bit of clean with you wherever you go." She scrubbed the window and got most of the lipstick off. "Now what? I think we should try Macy's. He likes that store."

"You still want to chase after this guy?"

"You bet your ass. Just because he made fools out of us three times, don't mean one of these times we won't luck out. Notice he called us losers and not quitters. That's on account of we never quit. In my mind, that's the difference between being a loser and a winner. A winner is willing to look like a idiot for as long as it takes to get the job done. I figure you stick with it long enough and you win. Unless you die or come down with some disease like shingles or cancer of the rectum. If I ever got cancer of the rectum, I'd go to the best rectumologist out there. Like I'd get a celebrity rectumologist. I wouldn't mess around with some local yokel."

"All good to know," I said, "but I vote we take a break from Carol Joyce and go back to the office to see what Connie has for me on Sylvester Lucca."

"Works for me," Lula said. "There might be some donuts left."

CHAPTER SEVENTEEN

CONNIE HANDED ME a slim manila folder. "Not much on him," she said. "The interesting part is that he needed money. He was living way beyond what he could afford. He was in an expensive apartment, and he had a flashy, expensive car. He was behind on his payments for both. He had three maxed-out credit cards. Two in collection."

"He had just the one job?"

"Yeah. He was a trainer at Miracle Fitness."

"No connection to Jimmy?"

"None that I could find. He fits the profile of a wiseguy, but I didn't see anything that would indicate he was part of the club. I called a couple of my friends that use Miracle Fitness, and they said Lucca was a real ladies' man. Came on to everyone. Didn't much care about age or marital status. I guess it was generally believed he fooled around on the side with some of his clients."

"Do we have a list of his clients?"

"Not exactly. He taught classes that didn't require a sign-up.

When you join Miracle Fitness you get to use the equipment and attend the classes. Some of the trainers had their own private clients, but it wasn't done through Miracle Fitness. I gave you a copy of the Miracle membership list. I sort of hacked into their system to get it."

"Did you look through the list?"

"No. I didn't have time."

"We should go check this place out," Lula said. "I always wanted to see what it was like inside. I figured it had to be good, since they had those naked statues on the outside. I even thought about joining a couple times when I wanted to tone up. It's in a convenient location."

"Why didn't you join?" I asked.

"I figured it was expensive. Anything that's got naked gods by the front door has to be pricey. And it's not like I don't already have some tone. I mean, I got tone coming out of my ass."

"So, it seemed like a waste of money," I said.

"Not so much a waste as I had to prioritize. Instead of putting my money into the *gym*, I put my money into the gym *clothes*. I got a bunch of those leggings and sporty bra tops. I got a set that's leopard print."

"Do you ever wear them?"

"Hell, yeah," Lula said. "I put them on every Sunday after church and then I go to the supermarket to do my weekly shopping. There's a lot of bending and lifting involved. I'm all about multitasking. And they're comfy. Gym clothes got a lot of stretch to them." She took the last donut and turned to me. "We should go get you some. It would be a good part of your 'new Stephanie' program. We could get a set that goes with your extensions. They'd be a excellent accessory. Gym clothes aren't real expensive, either, if you know where to shop. I get mine at Target and when the seams split open, I just go get some more."

"Maybe they wouldn't split if you'd go easier on the donuts," Connie said.

"Nope," Lula said. "It's not the donuts. It's that I get a workout at the supermarket on account of the beer I like is always on the bottom shelf."

I stuffed the file into my messenger bag. "Let's take a look at Miracle Fitness."

I parked the Porsche in the lot attached to the gym, and Lula and I walked into the lobby. The floor was polished marble, and the reception desk was high-gloss wood. The young woman behind the desk was in black workout clothes that showed she was fitness perfection. A glass wall running across the back of the lobby gave us a view of the fitness equipment and the women using it.

"They must all be beginners," Lula whispered to me, "on account of none of them look like the bitch behind the desk."

"I'm interested in a membership," I said to the woman. "Do you have a list of classes? And I'd also like some information on your trainers."

"Of course," she said. "I can give you a packet that will answer all your questions. It will also include a breakdown of our fees and various membership choices. Would you like a tour of our facility?"

"A tour would be great," I said, taking a glossy pink folder from her.

Four minutes later we were following a guy named Thor.

"This is the Pilates room," he said. "We have two of them. As you can see there's a class going on. The second one is almost always free for unsupervised use. Any questions?"

"I got one," Lula said. "Is Thor your real name?"

"No," he said. "My real name is Bruce. They make you take a godlike name when you come to work here."

"I got another question," Lula said. "Are there any more naked statues besides the ones out front?"

"Nope. That's it."

We looked in on a Zumba class and a spinning class.

"I couldn't do that spinning class," Lula said. "My cooter falls asleep when I ride a bike."

I have the same problem, but I wasn't comfortable discussing my cooter with Thor.

"I have a friend who took some classes with one of the trainers here and really liked him," I said. "I don't know his name, but he wore red Air Jordans."

"That would be Zeus," Thor said. "He's dead." Thor moved to the next door. "We also have a room with a heavy bag and a couple speed bags if you're into that."

"Whoa, wait a minute," I said. "Zeus is dead? What happened?"

"Don't know. They found him behind a dumpster."

"Who would want to kill Zeus?"

"Probably lots of people," Thor said. "He was an okay guy, but he messed around. And I think he owed a bunch of people money."

"Miracle Fitness won't be the same without a Zeus," Lula said.

"It's only temporary," Thor said. "The new Zeus starts tomorrow."

"The new Zeus," Lula said. "That's like the old Stephanie and the new Stephanie, only instead of changing himself, the old Zeus got dead and replaced. Gives you something to think about when you see how that's another route to take."

If Thor was confused, he didn't show it. He just stood there and calmly waited to continue his tour. Probably he smoked a lot of pot.

"I guess that's the cycle of life," Lula said. "Still, seems like it was awful easy to replace Zeus."

"They keep a file of applicants in the office," Thor said.

Lula and I peeked into the ladies' locker room and followed Thor back to the lobby.

"This has been helpful," I said. "I'll go home and look through the packet of information."

We returned to the SUV and buckled ourselves in.

"It's wrong that someone could kill Zeus," Lula said.

"He wasn't really Zeus," I said. "You know that, right?"

"Yeah, but he was sort of Zeus. It just seems wrong."

For sure.

I dropped Lula off at the office and continued on to my parents' house. I wanted to make sure everything was okay, and I wanted to mooch lunch and read through the information I got from Connie and Miracle Fitness. If one of the La-Z-Boys snatched Grandma, it would be worrisome, but at least we would have a place to start looking. This other player was much more frightening.

My father was watching television and eating an egg salad sandwich off a tray table. My mom and my grandmother were at the kitchen table. They each had an egg salad sandwich. The first thing I noticed was that Grandma wasn't wearing her necklace.

"Where's your necklace?" I asked, hanging my messenger bag on the back of a kitchen chair. "You're supposed to never take it off."

"It got wet in the shower, so I set it on the counter to dry, and then I forgot about it," Grandma said. "There's more egg salad in the fridge."

I made myself a sandwich and brought it to the table. "You can't forget about the necklace. You need to always wear it."

"I'll put it on when I go upstairs, but I don't see the need for it," Grandma said. "This seems like a lot of to-do about nothing."

"The man who tried to kidnap you is dead," I said. "I'm sure

185

he was killed so he couldn't divulge the name of whoever hired him."

"You don't know that for sure," Grandma said. "People get killed in Trenton all the time."

"Humor me and wear the necklace," I said. "Besides, it's pretty and it's a gift from Ranger."

"I understand the man who was murdered worked at Miracle Fitness," my mother said. "That place has a real reputation. It's practically a swingers' club."

Grandma leaned forward over the table and lowered her voice. "Marg Bowman said the ladies diddle themselves in the sauna. She said they wear nothing but a towel and they diddle."

I felt my face scrunch up. "Eeuuww!"

"I'd like to know how that goes," Grandma said. "Do they all sit down and one of them asks, 'Should we diddle today?' Seems like it would be rude if one of them just started diddling without asking."

"I'm eating egg salad," I said. "Could we talk about something besides . . . you know? Like, is there anything new going on?"

"I got a letter from the lawyer setting the estate meeting for Monday," Grandma said. "I'm thinking about giving some of my money to the animal shelter."

"Good idea," I said.

"I'm going to get more money than I need, so you all can have what you want and then I'll give the rest away to the homeless dogs and cats."

"That's nice of you," my mother said, "but I don't need anything. The house is paid off and my car is only two years old."

"Yeah, but you're gonna need a new liver one of these days, and that costs money," Grandma said.

I pulled Connie's folder plus the pink folder out of my bag. First up was the list of trainers. This wasn't worth anything because they all had phony names. Poseidon, Hermes, Apollo, Atlas. I went to the membership list next. Eight pages of small print. Mental groan.

"Something wrong?" Grandma asked. "Your eyes just rolled so far back in your head I was afraid you'd fall out of your chair."

"It's this list. Connie got me the names of everyone who has a Miracle Fitness membership. I thought I might find someone who was connected to Jimmy in some way and would want the keys. Someone who would hire Red Air Jordans and then kill him to shut him up."

"That's easy," Grandma said. "Jimmy's first wife, Barbara. She's always talking about the hot trainers at Miracle. She's in her late seventies, and I wouldn't be surprised if she's one of the diddlers. She's on hormone replacement, and Rogaine. I think she gets Botox, too. Did you see her at the viewing? Her face doesn't move. She's all frozen up. She belongs on that show . . . *Housewives of Hell.*" Grandma reached for a cookie from the white bakery box on the table. "Barbara never married again, after the divorce. She tells everybody she has PTSD from being with Jimmy. She'd take out a hit on me in a heartbeat. His daughter, Jeanine, goes to Miracle Fitness too. She's married to Bernard Stupe."

"I went to school with one of their kids," I said. "Don. He was a year ahead of me."

"He's in Seattle now," Grandma said. "And the other one is in the military. I'm sure Jeanine would know about the keys, but I can't see her killing over them. She's always been a nice person. Quiet. Not like her mother. Bernard's quiet too. Polite."

"What about the second wife?" I asked.

"Bunny," Grandma said. "They were married for less than a year. Rumor has it that she got a bucketload of money from the divorce. She's living in Arizona now. She was at the viewing and then she flew back to Phoenix. I think she just wanted to make sure Jimmy was dead."

I looked at my mother. "Can you think of anyone?"

"Sidney DeSalle owns Miracle Fitness," she said. "There are a lot of rumors about him and his business practices. He's known for being a pretty rough guy. I don't know if he would be interested in the keys, but I imagine he'd know about them."

I called Connie and asked her to run Sidney DeSalle through the system.

"No problem," she said, "but you've got to come get Lula. She's driving me nuts. She's all into fitness, doing squats across the room and jumping jacks in her spike-heeled shoes. She says she's working to look like the woman behind the desk at Miracle Fitness."

"That's only going to happen if Miracle Fitness is handing out miracles."

I disconnected, ran upstairs and got Grandma's necklace, then went back to the kitchen and put it on her.

"I have to go to work," I said. "I'll check back later."

CHAPTER EIGHTEEN

LULA WAS TRYING to touch her toes when I rolled into the office. She was doing a lot of grunting, and her fingertips weren't anywhere near her toes.

"My problem is I'm not wearing the right clothes," Lula said. "I'm not in my workout clothes. These clothes are too restrictive."

Lula was wearing a black spandex miniskirt, and every time she bent over there was a flash of red thong, which was ultimately lost in the Grand Canyon of Lula.

Connie had her hands over her eyes. "Tell me when she stops."

"I'm on a self-improvement plan like Stephanie, only mine is physical. I need to lose three or four pounds," Lula said, standing straight, tugging her skirt down over her ass.

Lula needed to lose fifty or sixty if she wanted to look like the woman behind the Miracle desk. An alternative would be to grow six inches, but that wasn't likely to happen either.

I called Morelli and told him about Barbara Rosolli and Sidney DeSalle.

"I'll talk to them," he said. "We looked at the recording from the security camera that covers the parking lot next to the bail bonds office. A car drove past at one A.M. Tuesday. Couldn't make out the occupants or the license plate. We also talked to Lucca's neighbors, but that was a bust. He lives in a big apartment complex where no one knows anyone else."

"What about the three sisters?"

"Angie, Tootie, and Rose? It looks like they were responsible for the searches and the firebomb. They don't seem to be interested in kidnapping Grandma. They just want to harass her. And they wouldn't mind finding the keys in the process."

"You have a snitch?" I asked.

"Yeah. My mom."

Never underestimate the value of the Burg gossip network. More news gets passed during bingo at the firehouse and daily mass at the Catholic church than from CBS, NBC, and Fox News combined.

"What's going on tonight?" Morelli asked.

"I need a night at home. I've gone through all my emergency clothes at your house, and I have to clean Rex's cage."

"How's your arm?"

"It's good. Nothing oozing out of the incision. Stitches are intact. Only aches a little when I use it."

"I know big, strong cops who would be sidelined for two weeks with your gunshot wound."

"I don't have that luxury. And I was lucky. It was only a flesh wound." I hung up and hooked a thumb at Lula. "Let's go."

I got behind the wheel and pulled the hijacker file out of my bag.

"Looks like we're going after a new guy," Lula said.

"Emory Lindal. Wanted for hijacking a truck full of beer. Took it while the driver was eating dinner. Made the mistake of drinking a six-pack, and the police found him asleep behind the wheel. Didn't show up for court."

"Probably embarrassed to show his face because he's an alcoholic idiot," Lula said. "Any priors?"

"Traffic violations. Domestic violence. Seventy-two years old and lives in a mobile home south of town."

"He doesn't sound like much of a hijacker," Lula said. "It sounds to me like he committed a crime of convenience. He probably doesn't even have a warehouse."

I drove south toward White Horse and turned off onto Old Bridge Pike. After five miles we still hadn't come to an old bridge, and we'd passed only one other car.

"According to my phone map, this guy's road is a quarter mile on the right," Lula said.

I got to the road and stopped. It was narrow and it was dirt.

"I don't like this road," Lula said.

"There's a sign on it that says Applegate Road. So this is it."

"I know what's going to be at the end of this road. There's going to be some nasty old guy living in a broken-down, rusted-out trailer, and he's going to have a pet snake. A big one. That's always the way it is with dirt roads going through the woods."

I turned onto the road and took it slow over the rutted surface. "That only applies to one guy and one snake," I said. "Maybe there are others, but we only know one. Simon Diggery and Ethel. And I think Ethel likes you."

I drove past a shack made of random lumber and half of a VW van. It didn't look habitable, and I didn't see any sign of recent use.

"I'm telling you this isn't going to end good," Lula said. "I'm totally creeped out. I don't even like woods when they got flowers, and this woods only has woods."

We came to the end of the road and stared out at a small mobile home. It was pocked with rust, and the windows were painted black. It was surrounded by high grass. A crude dirt path led to the door. There were signs plastered all over it warning off intruders. KEEP OUT. SURVIVALIST HABITAT. DO NOT ENTER. SECOND AMENDMENT IN FORCE. Vultures hunkered down on the roof and circled overhead. Some of the roof vultures were working at trying to rip the roof open.

"That's a lot of vultures," Lula said.

I agreed. It was a lot of vultures.

"You know what vultures like?" Lula said. "Dead things."

"We should go check it out," I said.

Lula's eyes bugged out. "Are you nuts? This is a horror movie. You step out of this car, and some freak is going to rush out of the woods with an ax and chop you up into tiny pieces. He's going to be bleeding out of his eyes, and his skin is going to be green and falling off him in chunks."

"I'm thinking that the dead thing in the trailer is Emory Lindal, and that's why he went FTA."

"I guess that's possible," Lula said. "The guy with the ax could have got to him."

"You stay here," I said. "I'm going to take a fast look."

I opened the car door and stepped out and was almost knocked over by the smell. I jumped back into the car and jerked the door closed. "Wow!"

"You know what that smell is?" Lula said. "It's the death cooties. I told you not to go out there, but do you listen to Lula? Hell, no. You have to see for yourself. Now we got death cootie smell in our car."

I put the SUV in reverse, backed up about a quarter mile, stopped, and called the police. Twenty minutes later a patrol car pulled up behind us.

Lula checked the car out in the rearview mirror. "Twenty minutes and all that responds is this lame-ass patrol car. Did you tell them about the guy in the woods with the ax?"

"No. I told them about the vultures and the smell."

The cop got out of his car and walked up to us. I rolled my window down, showed him my credentials, and gave him the short version of the story, omitting the guy with the ax.

He got back into his car, pulled around us, and drove to the end of the road. I rolled my window up and followed him. He parked, got out of his car, took a couple steps toward the trailer, and returned to his car. Ten minutes later a fire truck and an EMT rolled in, followed by another patrol car.

"This is more like it," Lula said. "Only thing missing is the helicopter."

I was getting antsy. I hadn't intended to spend this much time here. I didn't like leaving Grandma unattended, and I wanted to work on the Sidney DeSalle angle. I called Morelli a couple times, but he didn't pick up.

Two firefighters went into the trailer. They had their respirators on, and Lula pointed out that they carried axes. They came out after a couple minutes and walked back to the cop cars. None of this activity seemed to affect the vultures. They kept pecking and clawing and ripping at the top of the trailer.

I put my hand over my nose and mouth and joined the group of men at the cop cars. They were sufficiently far enough away from the trailer that the smell was almost bearable.

"What's in there?" I asked.

The fire guy had his respirator off and was smiling. "Raccoons," he said. "A lot of them. It looks like they broke in, ate everything they could find, including rat poison, and couldn't get out. Then they died and exploded. I don't know who owns this rust bucket, but he's got wall-to-wall raccoon guts in there."

"No human guts?"

"None immediately visible."

I went back to Lula and inched the Porsche around the fire truck and EMT.

"Raccoons," I said, leaving the cop cars behind, bumping my way over the crude road.

"Say what?"

"Raccoons broke in, died there, and exploded. No humans. No snakes."

"That's damn disappointing," Lula said. "That's anticlimactic."

I called Morelli again and still no answer. I called Grandma, and she said she was on her way to the bakery. She was in the mood for a cannoli.

"Are you alone?" I asked her.

"Yep," she said, "but it's okay because I'm wearing my necklace. After I get my cannoli, I thought I'd stop in to see if Dolly has time to fluff up my hair. Stanley Bonino is at Stiva's tonight. He was a big deal in the K of C, and he was friendly with Jimmy. I hear he's laid out in Slumber Room Number One. They're expecting a crowd. Shirley Balog said she'd pick me up."

"Are you sure you want to go to Stiva's tonight? The sisters might be there."

"I don't care about the sisters. I already picked out my outfit. I'm going to wear my navy and red dress. It has a good neckline to show off my necklace."

"Tell Shirley she doesn't have to pick you up," I said. "I'll go to the viewing with you."

"You're a good granddaughter," Lula said when I hung up. "That viewing is going to be a nightmare."

I was in my apartment reading Connie's report on Sidney DeSalle when Morelli called.

"Sorry about the missed calls," he said. "My phone isn't holding a charge. I have to get a new one."

"Anything interesting to tell me?"

"DeSalle was out of town when Lucca was killed. That doesn't mean he didn't order the hit."

"I had Connie run a credit report on him. He's in the money with Miracle Fitness, so I'm struggling to find his motive for wanting the keys."

"We don't know what the keys unlock," Morelli said. "Everyone assumes it's money, but it could be incriminating evidence."

"The other player is Barbara Rosolli."

"She's a real nutcase," Morelli said. "I haven't had a chance to talk to her yet. Not looking forward to it. She hated Jimmy, and she thinks she deserves to get all his money. The entire Burg and beyond knows this. She's already got a lawyer ready to contest the settlement. If Grandma is out of the way, the money will go to Barbara's daughter, Jeanine. So there's a lot of motivation here."

"Is she capable of murder?"

"I'm not sure she could strangle someone, but murder once removed might not seem like a crime to her. She comes from a mob family, and she married into the mob."

"My quiet night of hamster cage cleaning has turned into a night spent at Stiva's."

"Stanley Bonino, right? Should be interesting. I'm sure the sisters will be there. Probably Barbara and some of the La-Z-Boys. Make sure you've got your medallion on."

CHAPTER NINETEEN

BY SIX-THIRTY I'd finished all my reading, cleaned Rex's cage, and chugged a bottle of beer and ate a peanut butter and olive sandwich. I was dressed in my go-to outfit of black pencil skirt and stretchy white scoop neck sweater. I debated flats or heels and went with flats. Just in case I had to chase down a bad guy. I added a short, fitted red jacket and hung my messenger bag on my shoulder.

Grandma was waiting for me on the porch when I pulled to the curb. Five minutes later, we were at Stiva's, and Grandma was pushing her way through the crowd to the front door.

"As soon as they let us in, we go straight for the casket," Grandma said. "That way I get to see the deceased, we get the condolences taken care of, and then we can hit the cookie table. That's where you get all the dirt."

Sounded like an okay plan. Maybe someone at the cookie table would know something useful.

The doors opened, and we all surged forward. I was directly behind Grandma and was scanning the area, watching to make sure no one came rushing at her. There was some initial jockeying for position, and then the line stabilized. We had about twenty people in front of us. The three sisters had elected to sit rather than get in the line. They were five rows back on the far side of the room. I didn't see Barbara Rosolli. Julius Roman took a seat behind the sisters. Our eyes met and he nodded at me. I nodded back.

My attention went back to Grandma. She was patiently waiting in line, and I couldn't imagine what she was thinking. My own thoughts were running in the direction of Snow White, who got saved when some hot guy kissed her, as opposed to more modern-day fairy-tale heroines who enjoyed kicking ass and saving the world. World saving was okay if you knew what you were doing. I wasn't in that category. I knew nothing. I had no martial arts skills. I wasn't comfortable with a gun. The thought of sticking a knife in someone made me gag. Of course, this was also true of my mom, but when it mattered, she came through with the iron. I'd like to think I have some of that same grit. I just wish I had a larger selection of tools in my toolbox.

We inched our way along and said our words to the bereaved. We headed out of the slumber room and into the packed foyer. The women had congregated around the cookie table, and the men were collected in small groups around the perimeter of the room, talking quietly, checking their watches, and wondering how much longer they would have to stay. The cocktails-before-dinner mourners were on the porch, smoking cigars and telling off-color, politically incorrect jokes. The wives and widows were enjoying the coffee and cookies and critiquing the viewing.

Grandma selected a couple cookies from the Nabisco collection and took a step back when Jeanine and Bernie Stupe approached us. Jeanine was the same age as my mom, and there were other similarities. Short brown hair, average height and weight, friendly but reserved. Bernie's sandy brown hair was showing male-pattern baldness. He was slightly paunchy and an inch shorter than his wife. He was standing behind her, looking like he needed a Red Bull.

"I didn't get a chance to talk to you at the wake," Jeanine said to Grandma. "There was such a crush of people, and I'm a little claustrophobic. Bernie and I left early."

"I'm sorry about you losing your dad," Grandma said.

"Thank you," Jeanine said. "And I'm sorry you weren't able to enjoy more time with him."

"If it's any consolation, he didn't suffer at all. It was so fast. One minute he was winning at the slots, and then he was gone."

"Not even a last word?" Jeanine asked.

"Well, he swore a little on the way down to the ground," Grandma said, "but that was it."

Jeanine nodded and pressed her lips together. "I should be going," she said. "I'm feeling a little sad . . . and panicky."

"Take care," Grandma said. "God bless."

We watched Jeanine and Bernie leave, and Grandma shook her head.

"Poor Jeanine," Grandma said. "It's hard when you lose

someone so sudden. Even at Jimmy's age, no one expected him to go like that."

I followed Grandma as she made her way around the cookie table, sampling the cookies and talking to the other women. The conversation ranged from comments on the deceased's complexion, to Melanie Glick's divorce, to the sudden disappearance of Bubbies pickles from Dittman's Meat Market. No one mentioned the missing keys.

We left shortly before closing and were ambushed on our way out by Barbara Rosolli.

"Edna!" she said, rushing up to Grandma. "I almost missed you. I didn't get to talk to you at Jimmy's wake, and I wanted to share sympathies on our loss. Just tragic."

"He was a good man," Grandma said.

"He was a vicious, cheating bastard," Barbara said, "but we loved him anyway, didn't we?"

"God don't like when you talk ill of the dead," Grandma said.

Barbara made the sign of the cross. "God knows what I went through with that man. I'm sure God understands when I speak candidly."

"You got something else you want to say?" Grandma asked.

"I didn't get a chance to drop something off for the wake, so I brought a box of cookies for you," Barbara said, handing Grandma a cookie tin decorated with a black bow. "Better late than never, right? I baked them myself."

"That's real nice of you," Grandma said. "Thank you."

"I need to be getting home now," Barbara said. "We should get together sometime. Have a coffee or a drink."

"Sure," Grandma said. "That would be okay."

Barbara walked away, and I looked at the cookie tin Grandma was holding.

"You aren't going to eat those, are you?" I asked.

"Heck, no," Grandma said. "I don't even like holding the tin. I can feel the evil burning my fingertips."

"Is she usually friendly like that to you?"

"I wouldn't say we were ever friendly. She moved out of the Burg after the divorce, and I didn't see much of her. Five years ago, she bought a house next to Jeanine on Chambers Street and she started going to bingo. All she could talk about was how Jimmy's second wife took all his money and she didn't get any of it even though she raised their daughter. I never sat by her, so I didn't have much to do with her. Then all of a sudden when word got out that Jimmy had died and we were married she went nuts. Emma Gorse said Barbara was going around telling everyone that I killed Jimmy for his money. She said that she had proof it wasn't a heart attack, and that three people at the casino saw him give me the keys. Can you imagine?"

I looked over Grandma's shoulder and saw the Rosolli sisters coming our way. Rose was leading the pack, shoulders hunched, mouth set.

"You!" she said to Grandma. "You have a lot of nerve showing your face with all these decent people."

"They aren't all decent," Grandma said.

"You should get out of this community. We don't want your kind here."

"I'm not so bad," Grandma said. "I'm going to take some of your brother's money and give it to the orphaned cats and dogs. I'm thinking there'll be a lot left over after my trip to the Galapagos Islands."

"I thought you were going to Antarctica," I said to Grandma.

"I'm stopping at the Galapagos on the way home," Grandma said.

"You should burn in hell," Rose said. "And your hair is a disgrace. You look ridiculous."

"I'm real sorry you feel that way," Grandma said. "I was hoping we could be civil. I even brought these cookies for you." Grandma handed Rose the tin with the black bow. "I baked them myself."

"Oh," Rose said, looking at the tin. "That was nice of you. Thank you."

"It's a pretty tin," Tootie said.

"We still don't like you," Rose said.

"We gotta go now," Grandma said. "You girls have a good night."

Grandma and I hurried to the car and locked the doors.

"I'm a terrible person," Grandma said. "She's probably right about me burning in hell."

"Those cookies could be perfectly okay. I'm sure Barbara wouldn't give you poison cookies."

"Would you have eaten them?" Grandma asked.

"No way."

I drove Grandma home and waited until she was in the house and waved to me that all was good. Fifteen minutes later I cruised into my apartment building parking lot and spotted Morelli's SUV. I parked next to it and went upstairs. Morelli was in the kitchen, watching Rex run on his wheel.

"Not watching television?" I asked.

"There's nothing on. I got bored at home, so I thought I'd stop in and see if you wanted to have some wild sex. I was going to make a sandwich while I waited, but you have no food."

"I have peanut butter and cereal. That covers every meal."

"Did you ever hear of a vegetable?"

"Pickles. I have two different kinds. Bread and butter and dill."

"I stand corrected."

"I might have hot dogs in the freezer."

Morelli opened the freezer, and his phone dinged with a text message. He checked the message and closed the freezer.

"I have to make a call," he said. "And I'm going to pass on the hot dogs."

He placed the call and rummaged through my junk drawer, coming up with a pen and a small sticky notepad. He took a bunch of notes from the person on the other line and hung up.

"That was Fitzgerald," he said. "He got called out to a shooting, and he thought I'd want to take a look. It's a couple blocks from here."

"Anyone I know?"

"Julius Roman. Shot execution style in front of his house. Close range. Single bullet to the head. He was found slumped over the steering wheel of his car."

My heart skipped a bunch of beats and I was breathless for a moment. "I just saw him. He was at the viewing."

"Obviously he didn't stay long. The ME hasn't gotten there yet, so time of death hasn't been determined, but it had to be around eight o'clock. Fitzgerald said a neighbor was out walking his dog and noticed Roman. I don't have a time on that, but the first responders rolled in at eight-thirty. Fitzgerald just got there and realized it was one of the La-Z-Boys."

"I feel sort of sick."

"Yeah, you're a little pale." Morelli got a cold bottle of beer from the fridge and put it to the back of my neck. "Breathe."

"This leaves Benny the Skootch, Charlie Shine, and Lou Salgusta," I said. "I don't like any of those men. I almost liked Julius Roman. He seemed more conservative than the rest. I thought he might be the voice of reason in the group. And he had an idea who hired Lucca to kidnap Grandma, but he wouldn't give me a name. He said it was just a suspicion."

Morelli stopped holding the beer against my neck. He cracked it open and handed it to me. "I have to go. I'll call when I know more."

I locked my door after him and chugged half the bottle.

"I hate this," I said to Rex. "I'm always nauseous. I keep

thinking about Lou Salgusta burning his initials into women. It's so disgusting. And people getting killed over stupid keys. What the heck is that about?"

I drank the rest of the beer and ate some Froot Loops out of the box. I ran a hand through my hair and felt the extensions. I'd forgotten about them. I went into the bathroom and checked them out in the mirror. I flipped my head around to make them move. They were pretty. Something was right in the world. It was a small something, but it was something all the same.

I found a Fred Astaire movie on the old movie channel and watched him dance with Ginger Rogers. Ginger was slim and Fred was slim and instead of talking all the time, sometimes they would sing. And then they would dance for no special reason and they'd be in perfect step without practicing. How cool is this? This is the planet I want to live on.

Morelli called at ten-thirty. He had nothing new to tell me, and he was going home to let Bob out and go to bed. He said all this to me in his flat cop voice. This meant that either he was exhausted, or he was putting a lid on unwanted emotion. I honestly don't know how he does it day after day, slogging through the horror. My job isn't nearly as demanding as his, and I'm burned out.

CHAPTER TWENTY

GRANDMA CALLED ME at seven o'clock in the morning. I was half asleep when the phone rang, and my first thought was that something horrible had happened. As it turned out I was partly right.

"Did you hear about Julius Roman?" she said.

"Yes. Morelli told me about the shooting last night."

"It's because of the keys, isn't it?"

"Probably, but I don't think anyone knows for sure. I'm sure Julius had enemies."

"When you live here in the Burg, you know you have neighbors who are in the mob, but you don't think about it a lot. I mean, people in the mob have to live somewhere. So why not in the Burg? And they look just like everyone else. Their kids go to school. The wives shop at Dittman's and Macy's. The men belong to the K of C. I guess that's why I could marry Jimmy. I saw the normal part of him. I wasn't thinking about the bad part. The crazy thinking that he had some sort of permission to do terrible things. People shouldn't think like that. You don't do bad things just because you want something . . . like the keys, or money, or to make someone think like you do. Nobody has the right."

"Are you wearing your necklace?"

"Yep. I got it on."

"There are a lot of people working to sort this out. In the meantime, you have to be careful."

"I'm staying home and making cookies all day. Fresh-baked cookies go a long way to filling a house with goodness and happiness. And I'm going to give some of the cookies to the sisters to make up for Barbara's. I hope they didn't get too sick from them."

"Maybe she wasn't trying to poison you," I said. "Maybe she was trying to butter you up, so you'd tell her about the keys."

"Well, she's in for a disappointment then, because I haven't got anything to tell anybody."

I dragged myself out of bed and stood in the shower until the water started running cold and my brain started functioning. I got out and towel dried and noticed one of my extensions was lying on the tile floor. Beauty doesn't last forever. Fortunately, in this case, I can buy replenishment. Just one of the many good things that can be said for extensions.

I made my way to the kitchen and surveyed my breakfast options. Coffee and cereal. I was out of milk. I had the fixings for a peanut butter sandwich, but probably I should save that for dinner. I looked in the freezer. Package of hot dogs covered in freezer frost.

I had my rent covered for the month. My credit card bill was minimal. I had a paycheck for the three FTAs I brought in. I could afford to make a quick trip to the supermarket.

Twenty minutes later I was in the cereal aisle trying to decide between one that was sugar and gluten free and one I actually wanted to eat. I looked up from reading the ingredients and saw Jeanine Stupe coming my way.

"I tried that healthy cereal," she said when she reached me. "I didn't think it was so bad, but no one else in my family would eat it. Now that it's just Bernie and me, we settle for toast and coffee."

"I haven't got a toaster," I said. "I've been thinking about buying one."

"Get a toaster oven," Jeanine said. "They're more versatile. I think they're better at heating breakfast pastries." She leaned in a little and lowered her voice. "Did you hear about Julius Roman?"

"Yes. I heard the news last night."

"He was such a sweet man. I know in his day he might have done some questionable things, but to me he's always been Uncle Julius."

"I just recently got to know him," I said.

Jeanine gave her head a small shake. "I'm sorry you and Edna had to get drawn into this over such a silly matter. I always thought the keys were ceremonial. Like they opened the liquor cabinet or something."

"Have you heard any talk about who killed Julius? I thought it might have been tied to the keys."

209

"Everyone has a theory. You know the Burg. We love a murder and a scandal."

"Who do you think did it?"

"I'm leaning toward someone on the outside. He had his share of enemies. I think it didn't have anything to do with the keys. I think the timing was coincidental."

I nodded. "That makes sense."

"I have to keep moving," Jeanine said. "I'm meeting my mom for coffee at nine o'clock, and she hates when I'm late. She's become so rigid with age."

"She gave Grandma a tin of homemade cookies last night. Please thank her again for us."

"Oh jeez," Jeanine said. "I hope you didn't eat any. She makes the world's worst cookies."

Besides getting staples like strawberry Pop-Tarts and coffee ice cream, I also got a bunch of frozen vegetables, frozen chicken nuggets, frozen enchiladas, and frozen turkey burgers. Next time Morelli looked in my freezer I'd have food in it. Whether I would actually get around to eating any of it, other than the ice cream, was something else.

Connie stood at her desk and waved a file at me when I came through the door.

"I have a priority job for you," she said. "This just came in. Steven Cross. Didn't show up for court yesterday. His judge set bail at six figures. High risk of flight. Vinnie should never have posted a bond for him."

"I remember when he was arrested. It made national news. Good-looking older guy. Worth tons of money. Hung out with movie stars and European royalty. Thought he was the Pink Panther. Robbed jewelry stores for kicks. Over a five-year period stole a couple hundred million dollars' worth of stuff. Got carried away at Stiffow Jewelers in Trenton and beat the seventy-year-old security guard senseless."

"Yep, that's him," Connie said. "He lives in a mansion-type house across the river. Also has houses in Monte Carlo, Palm Beach, Carmel, and Washington, D.C. If you're lucky he's still in Pennsylvania. He has a boyfriend here."

Lula was on the couch, taking it all in. "What's the boyfriend do?" Lula asked.

"He's a hairdresser," Connie said. "Has a salon in downtown Trenton. Sort of a local celebrity."

"I like it," Lula said. "This is right up my wheelhouse. I love those Pink Panther movies with David Niven and what's his name."

"Peter Sellers," I said.

"Yeah, Peter Sellers," Lula said. "And now you add a hairdresser into it. It couldn't hardly get any better."

I took the file from Connie and paged through it. Lula was looking over my shoulder.

"He even looks like David Niven," Lula said. "He's got the mustache."

"He might not have it anymore," Connie said. "I think it was a paste-on that he used when he was doing a heist."

211

I pulled his address up on Google Maps and went to bird's-eye view. "This is impressive. It looks out over the river, and it has its own tennis court."

"He's going to have a hard time adapting to prison life," Lula said. "Most prisons don't have tennis courts."

I shoved the file into my messenger bag. "Let's roll."

Thirty-five minutes later we pulled into the driveway and stopped.

"It's gated," I said.

"Maybe there's a button you push."

I looked at the keypad, pushed the red button, and smiled into the camera.

"Yes?" someone asked.

"I'm here to see Steven Cross."

"Steven isn't here."

"I spoke to him earlier this morning, and he said I should come over."

"One moment."

A couple minutes of silence passed, and the voice returned.

"Who's calling, please?"

"Stephanie Plum."

More silence.

"I'm sorry, Miss Plum. Steven isn't here."

"Do you know when he'll return?"

"I couldn't say."

I backed out of the driveway and pulled to the side of the road.

"He's there," I said to Lula.

"Probably out playing tennis."

I brought the area back up on Google Maps. Cross's house was squashed between two other large houses. A thick fifteen-foot-high ficus hedge ran between the houses. A wooded area bordered the back of the property. There was a generous front lawn, cut by a driveway that became a circular drive court when it reached the house. Garages were attached and to the side.

I was able to see part of the house when I was at the gate. White with black trim. Two stories. Big. I could bushwhack my way through the hedge and walk to the house, but I'd be visible, and he could send a pack of vicious dogs out to maul and eat me. I could sit on the side of the road and wait for him to leave for the airport. This could take a long time.

"We should launch a drone," Lula said. "We could use it to look in his windows and see what he's doing."

"I don't have a drone. Do you have a drone?"

"Not on me."

"Do you have one at home?"

"No. I don't have one there either."

There was big money involved in this capture. If I didn't bring him in, Vinnie would be out a small fortune. If I *did* bring him in, I'd make enough money to buy a car. It wouldn't be a new car. And it wouldn't be as good as the car I was currently driving. Still, it would be mine.

I looked at Google Maps again. If I went along the edge of the neighbor's yard and bludgeoned my way through the hedge by the garage I might not be seen. Probably there were security cameras everywhere, but they might not be manned. Especially if Cross was getting ready to leave the country for an extended period of time and was cutting his staff.

"I'm going to try to cut through his side yard," I said to Lula. "Are you in?"

"Hell, yeah. I'm not going to miss seeing David Niven."

The neighbor's property was heavily shrubbed but wasn't gated. I left the Macan on the side of the road, and Lula and I hugged the ficus hedge as best we could, scrambling around plantings. We broke through the hedge in the middle of the yard and looked around. Quiet. No dogs. Four garage bays with doors closed. A small porch with a single door to the side of the garage.

Lula and I sauntered across the yard, looking very casual and David Nivenish in case someone was watching. I went to the side door and tried the doorknob. Unlocked. I held my breath and cracked the door. No alarm. I let my breath out in a whoosh.

Lula and I stepped into a hallway that led to the kitchen on the ground floor and service stairs to the second floor. No one was in the kitchen. I could hear someone moving around above us. I motioned to Lula that I was taking the stairs, and she gave me a thumbs-up. I reached the second floor and stared down a long, wide hallway. A door was open toward the end of the hall. We tiptoed down and stopped just short of the open door.

As a designated representative of a licensed bondsman I can

legally enter a home if I believe my man is inside. It's considered polite to announce yourself.

"Knock, knock," I said, and I stuck my head around the doorjamb.

Steven Cross was in his gargantuan master bedroom suite. He was packing, throwing things into a large suitcase that was open on his bed. Another man slouched in a club chair nearby.

"Oh, dear God," the second man said. "Now what?"

"I bet you're the hairdresser," Lula said. "I could tell by your complexion that you have an excellent skin care regimen."

"Steven Cross?" I asked.

"Better known as David Niven," Lula said.

Cross stopped packing. "Yes?"

I held my fake badge out, so he could see I was official. "I represent your bail bondsman. You missed your court date and you need to reschedule."

"Sure. Reschedule me," he said. "Now go away. I'm busy."

"Looks like you're going on a trip," Lula said.

"Brilliant," Cross said. "What gave me away? The suitcase?"

"No need for sarcasm," Lula said. "I was just making conversation. Although the clever sarcasm is very David Niven."

"You need to reschedule in person," I said.

"Not gonna happen, cutie pie."

Lula was in Bohemian dress today with platform sandals, skintight poison-green tights, and a tie-dye tank top that was three sizes too small. The outfit was completed with a large faux-leather-fringed boho bag.

"We're official bond enforcement people," Lula said, rooting around in her bag. "We're almost like police, and I got a gun in here somewhere."

"I'm unarmed," Cross said. "And I have Georgio as a witness. You can't shoot me."

"How about if I knock you down and sit on you until you turn blue?" Lula said.

Georgio unslouched himself and stood.

"This is ridiculous," he said to Cross. "We're already behind schedule. Carmine is going to be here any minute, and I've been notified that the plane is in place. Forget the packing. You can buy new. Everything in that suitcase is horribly wrinkled anyway. I mean honestly, you can't just *throw* things in there."

Lula was still pawing through the junk in her bag. "I was almost sure I put it in here."

"As it turns out, I do have a gun," Cross said, taking a Glock out of his suitcase. "And I don't care if you're armed or not, I'd shoot you without remorse, because that's the kind of guy I am."

"David Niven didn't go around shooting people," Lula said.

"I'm not David Niven." He glanced at Georgio. "What should I do with them? Should I kill them? Cripple them? I could just shoot them in the knees."

"Only if they don't cooperate," Georgio said. "I hate to see this carpet ruined. It's hand-knotted from Nepal, and you know how difficult it is to remove bloodstains."

A car horn honked outside.

"That's Carmine," Georgio said. "We need to lock these two up somewhere."

Cross looked around. "Everything locks from the inside."

"The cellar door has a lock on it," Georgio said. "We can put them in the cellar."

"I'm not going in no cellar," Lula said. "There's always spiders in cellars."

Cross fired off a shot that missed Lula's little toe by an eighth of an inch.

"Okay," Lula said. "Maybe just this once."

Three minutes later we were standing in front of the cellar door.

"No good," Cross said. "The lock works both ways. Maybe I should just shoot them."

"How about the wine cellar?" Georgio said. "The new one you just put in the game room. It has a padlock."

We were marched into the game room. Cross unlocked the padlock and motioned us in.

"Wow, this is amazing," Lula said. "It's a real wine cellar. There must be a thousand bottles of wine here. And there's a little wine-tasting bistro table and everything."

There was also a glass door.

"You're looking at the glass door," Cross said. "Don't get your hopes up. It's impact glass. Bulletproof. No good to you even if your friend ever finds her gun. You can make a phone call, but by the time someone crowbars you out of there we'll be long gone."

Cross attached the padlock and waved goodbye.

"Good thing he looks like David Niven," I said, "because that's all he's got. He isn't very smart. And the hairdresser isn't a rocket scientist, either. The door might be impact glass, but it's not thick enough to be completely bulletproof," I said to Lula. "Empty a clip into it while I call Connie."

I went to the back of the wine cellar, dialed Connie, and told her to find Cross's plane. "It sounds like he's flying private," I said. "Does he have his own plane? Does his credit show any action with a charter company? We need to get to him before he takes off."

"The closest airport would be Trenton-Mercer," Connie said. "If he's flying private, he'd be flying out of an FBO. I think Signature is there. I'll see what I can do to stop him, and I'll get back to you."

"How's it going?" I asked Lula.

"I've run out of bullets, and the glass got all these spiderwebs going through it, but it didn't break."

I found a magnum of champagne and swung it at the door. The bottle broke, spraying champagne everywhere, and a small hole appeared in the door. I hit the door with another bottle and the door shattered. Lula and I cleared the door, bolted out of the house, and ran for the Porsche.

CHAPTER TWENTY-ONE

WE CROSSED THE DELAWARE and were back in New Jersey. Lula had the map app programmed for Signature Flight Support at Trenton-Mercer Airport. I hadn't heard from Connie, so I was going with my best guess.

"He has a good head start on us," Lula said.

"I'm counting on him wanting to use the restroom and visit the popcorn machine before he gets on the plane."

I was also *flying* in the Porsche, getting it into the nineties when I had open road. I knew it had a radar detector and a laser scrambler, and I was counting on them working.

I got a call from Connie just as I pulled into the Signature lot and screeched to a stop.

"Sorry this took so long," Connie said, "but I'm new at this airplane-tracking thing. I'm texting you his tail number. His plane is at Signature. Looks like he hasn't left yet. I'm trying to get a delay put on his plane, but so far, I haven't been able to get through to the right person. How close are you? I'm on hold with airport security."

"I'm on the ground and running," I said.

Lula was some distance behind me, trying to run in her stupid platform sandals. I pushed through the entrance door and stopped to look around. I didn't see Cross or Georgio.

"I'm looking for Steven Cross," I said to the woman at the reception desk. "I have papers for him."

She motioned at the side door. "He just walked through. You should be able to catch him."

I looked through the glass and saw Cross and Georgio and a uniformed pilot heading for a plane with the boarding steps down. The receptionist buzzed me out and I ran toward Cross. He was talking to the pilot and holding a big box of popcorn from the lobby machine. I was wearing my messenger bag across my body, and I had my cuffs tucked into the back of my jeans. Cross turned when I was about fifteen feet away. He one-handed the popcorn and reached inside his jacket with the other. I closed the distance and tackled him. There was an explosion of popcorn, his gun discharged, and was knocked out of his hand when we hit the pavement. I got one bracelet on his wrist before the pilot and Georgio wrestled me away. Lula burst out of the FBO followed by a security guy. She was running full steam ahead in her green spandex tights, waving her arms in the air, yelling, "Stop! Police!"

"She misspoke in her excitement," I said to the security guard. "We aren't police. We're apprehension agents. This man is in violation of his bond agreement and is attempting to flee."

"We're almost police," Lula said.

Georgio shook his head at Cross. "You just had to get popcorn. I told you there was food on the plane, but you insisted on using the restroom and getting popcorn. And then you had to pick out a magazine."

"I should have shot them when I had the chance," Cross said.

"You're no David Niven," Lula said. "You probably don't even play tennis."

I'd torn the knee out of my jeans and scraped my elbow when I tackled Cross. By the time we got things sorted out and security released him into my custody, I was already scabbing over.

"You're a fast healer," Lula said to me. "I don't know why you're so opposed to being a bounty hunter. You got all the qualifications for it. You don't want to underestimate good clotting time."

We dropped Cross off at the police station, made a stop at Cluck-in-a-Bucket for a large bucket of fried chicken and a quart of macaroni salad, and went to the office to eat lunch.

Connie was all smiles when we rolled in. "That was amazing," she said. "Ranger couldn't have done it better. If we'd lost that bond, we might have been looking at bankruptcy."

"You should have seen Stephanie doing a hundred miles an hour on the way to the airport," Lula said. "And then she tackled Cross when he had a gun in his hand and took him down. It was like she was Bruce Willis in one of those *Die Hard* movies."

Lula set the chicken and macaroni on Connie's desk and pulled a bottle of champagne out of her boho bag. "Compliments of Steven Cross, who, by the way, is a horrible human being."

I ate two pieces of chicken, had a mug of champagne, and called Grandma.

"We got cookies all over the place," Grandma said. "I'm all baked out. It'll be nice to get out of the house and go to bingo tonight."

Bingo. Groan.

"I'll pick you up at six forty-five," I said.

"Do you think I should give new cookies to the sisters?"

"No. I think you should avoid the sisters."

"We haven't heard anything about them dying, so that's a good sign," Grandma said.

I hung up and thought about having another mug of champagne, but I had to drive home, so I passed.

"Gotta go," I said. "Big night at bingo. I need to patch myself up." I looked down and saw a shiny blue extension lying on the floor. No problem. I still had lots left.

My elbow was scraped, and my knee was scraped. Fortunately, I had some big Band-Aids left over from my gunshot wound. The jeans were unsalvageable.

I went to my office, which was better known as the dining room table, and reread my information on the La-Z-Boys and Sylvester Lucca. I knew there had to be a connection. I knew I was missing something.

I fell asleep facedown on the table halfway through the Miracle membership list, and I woke up a little before six o'clock. Another extension had fallen out and was lying on the table. I used it as a gossamer-thin bookmark, went to the kitchen, and looked in my freezer. I had all sorts of food, but it all involved defrosting and heating. As it turns out, defrosting and heating aren't in my current skill set. My current skill set includes peanut butter spreading. I'm good at it. Practice, practice, practice. If I spent as much time on the rifle range as I spend with my knife in the peanut butter jar, I'd be a crack shot. So, I made a peanut butter sandwich and washed it down with chocolate milk . . . because I also know how to squeeze chocolate sauce into a glass of milk.

I got dressed in boyfriend jeans that were comfortably loose over my newly bloodied knee. And I coupled them with a long-sleeved jersey that eliminated the need to explain the Band-Aid on my elbow.

I drove to my parents' house to get Grandma, and I could smell the cookies when I got out of the Macan. Chocolate chip. By the time I reached the porch the chocolate chip aroma was mingled with gingerbread. My father was asleep in his chair, in front of the television. No doubt in a post-cookie stupor. Grandma was in the kitchen packing a grocery bag with cookie tins.

"These are for you," Grandma said. "There's some of each kind."

"Where's Mom?"

"Next door. She went over with cookies. I kind of got carried

223

away with the baking. Now we gotta get rid of some before your father eats them all and explodes."

I helped myself to a sugar cookie from the glass cookie jar, and I took my grocery bag. Grandma shrugged into a sweater and hung her big patent leather purse in the crook of her arm.

"I'm ready," she said. "And I have an extra bingo dauber for you."

"I'm surprised you have room for daubers in your purse."

"I hear you," Grandma said. "From time to time I think about getting something more compact. Maybe a semiautomatic. I like the idea of having more ammo available in case I'm in a shootout, but I'm used to this big boy." She patted her purse. "It's been with me for a long time."

I know I'm supposed to be protecting Grandma, but I'm not sure she needs me. I suspect she's better equipped to do the job than I am.

"I've been getting phone calls all day, between my cookie making, about Julius Roman," Grandma said. "There's a lot of finger-pointing going on. I guess things are pretty tense at the Mole Hole."

"I saw Jeanine in the supermarket, and she thinks it was an outside hit. Someone not related to the keys business."

"I guess Julius could have been involved in something we don't know about," Grandma said.

I parked in the firehouse lot, and Barbara pulled in next to us.

"Oh jeez," Grandma said. "What are the chances? Maybe we should skip bingo and go to dinner."

Barbara got out of her car and walked over to us.

"Edna! So good to see you again," she said.

Grandma unbuckled and got out. "It was only just yesterday."

"Did you like my cookies?" Barbara asked.

"Yeah," Grandma said. "They were delicious."

"I used real butter," Barbara said.

Grandma nodded. "Yup. I could tell."

"And they weren't too spicy?"

"I like a little spice," Grandma said.

"Well, I guess they agreed with you. You're looking good. Healthy and all."

"Did you expect something else?" Grandma asked.

"No, no," Barbara said. "It's just that you're always so hearty for your age."

"I'm not so old," Grandma said. "I think you've got a couple years on me, but you look like you're doing okay, too. Mostly. I hope I look as good as you when I get to be that old."

"Time will tell," Barbara said. "Here today and gone tomorrow."

"I gotta get in and get my seat," Grandma said. "I'll talk to you later."

We went into the firehouse and looked around. The sisters were across the room in their usual places.

Grandma waved and they stared back.

"They look okay," Grandma said. "I bet they didn't eat the cookies."

Miriam Flock was at the head table with the bingo balls. "I'll be calling today," she said. "Marvina is under the weather. She came down with something at lunch today. We all hope it isn't anything serious."

"Marvina lives next door to Tootie," Grandma said. "They haven't gotten along in years. Dollars to donuts they gave the cookies to Marvina."

Tootie smiled at Grandma.

"Pure evil." Grandma said.

"We're sort of involved," I told her.

"I guess that's true," Grandma said. "I'll go to Mass with your mother tomorrow."

Two hours later, we were leaving, and Barbara followed us to our car.

"I heard more about Marvina," she said. "A friend of mine works in the ER, and she said Marvina was admitted to St. Francis. Some kind of stomach thing."

"That's terrible," Grandma said.

"Well, you know, stuff happens. I was wondering if you wanted to have coffee tomorrow. We could meet at the coffee shop on Hamilton."

"I'm pretty busy," Grandma said. "I'll have to get back to you on that."

"Sure," Barbara said. "Give me a call."

Neither Grandma nor I said anything on the five-minute

drive home. I parked in front of my parents' house and gave up a sigh.

"Yeah," Grandma said. "Me too. I don't know if she wants to pump me for information or just kill me."

"I feel really bad about Marvina."

"I'll go in and make some phone calls and see if I can get more information. I don't want to make a big deal about Barbara's cookies if it turns out Marvina didn't eat any."

I watched to make sure Grandma got into the house, and then I drove off with my bag of cookies. I pulled into my building lot and saw that the lights were on in my apartment. I looked around and spotted Ranger's black Porsche 911 Turbo parked close to the rear lobby door.

He was checking his texts when I walked in. I set the grocery bag on the counter and hung my messenger bag on the back of a dining room chair.

"Have you been waiting long?" I asked.

"Just got here. I know the bingo schedule."

I took all of the tins out of the grocery bag, set them on the counter, and opened them. Hungarian filled cookies, butter cookies, chocolate chip, gingerbread, oatmeal raisin, chocolate chocolate chip, peanut butter, and sugar cookies.

Ranger put his phone down and grinned at the tins of cookies. "There's a story here," he said.

"Grandma wanted to make the house smell happy, so she spent the day baking cookies."

He nodded. "She's a smart woman."

I took a sugar cookie, and Ranger took a chocolate chip.

"Whoa," I said. "I thought you didn't eat cookies. I thought you only ate tree bark."

"You thought wrong."

"Chocolate chip, too. You went right for the money cookie."

"They're my favorite," he said.

I chose a Hungarian filled as my second cookie. "You even have a favorite. You've been leading a secret life."

"In many ways," Ranger said.

I knew this to be true. "Is there a special reason for this visit, beyond cookies?"

"I heard you were a hero today. I thought I'd come by and say congratulations. Usually when we see each other anymore it's for something bad. I thought this was an opportunity to stop by for something good."

"Thanks. I appreciate the thought, but I don't feel like a hero."

"Connie said you saved the bonds office from bankruptcy. I know that's not entirely true because Vinnie is insured, but you still made a good capture."

"I don't want to do this job anymore. I'm not good at it. I don't like it. I don't like being in the bad neighborhoods, looking for the bad people."

"What would you rather do?"

"I don't know," I said.

"Do you have a direction?"

"No."

"Babe."

"Yeah, I'm a mess."

"You aren't a mess," he said. "You're just a little burned out."

"It's more than that. I'm stagnant. There's no growth in my life."

"That's okay as long as you like what you're doing. Not everyone needs to keep moving up the ladder."

"You moved up the ladder."

"I discovered that I had certain talents, and I found a way to use them to my best advantage. There's very little gray in my life. I see things as black or white, and sometimes the dividing line isn't always the norm for other people. I can be ruthless and aggressive. I have qualities that allow me to take advantage of people and situations. You don't have any of those qualities. You have the talent and intelligence to go wherever you want to go, but you aren't driven. The truth is that you're much too sane. You'll probably never amount to anything."

I threw a cookie at him, and he caught it one-handed.

"You weren't serious, were you? Do you really think I'll never amount to anything?"

"You're already more successful than I am. You've accomplished more."

"What have I accomplished?"

"You're a nice person."

"So are you."

Ranger shook his head. "I'm many things. Nice isn't one of them."

"You're nice to me."

"You're an experiment. I'm trying to learn."

"You're full of crap," I said.

That got a smile out of him.

"What I know about success in business is that it helps to have a passion," Ranger said. "I feel passionate about tracking down bad people and protecting good people. It's not a job for me . . . it's a calling. And I'm willing to wade through some ugliness to do it."

"Don't you get tired of the ugliness?"

"Yes, but you deal with it. And you hope you're helping to make things better."

"I don't have a passion."

"Sometimes it takes a while to figure it out," Ranger said.

Rex came out of his can to see what was going on in the kitchen. I gave him a piece of butter cookie, and he scurried back into his soup can with it.

"Life is easy when you're a hamster," I said to Ranger.

"It looks boring. I'll take ugly over boring."

I was going to tuck that statement away in a corner of my brain for future consideration.

"This is the part of the night where you have to make a decision," Ranger said. "You can ask me to stay or you can tell me to leave."

"I can't ask you to stay."

Not because I didn't want him to stay, but because he was

part of the problem, and I wasn't ready to confront him with the issue.

"There's another part to success," Ranger said. "You have to be brave."

I dropped four chocolate chip cookies into a plastic baggie and handed them to Ranger. "I'm working on it."

CHAPTER TWENTY-TWO

I **WOKE UP** thinking about being brave. Sometimes I believe I was brave on the job. I didn't think of it as being brave when I was doing it. It was just something that had to get done. Like taking a look at Emory Lindal's trailer. And tackling Steven Cross when I saw him reach for his gun. Okay, so it's not like a firefighter running into a burning building or a cop putting his life on the line every day. It's brave in a small way.

Anyway, I don't think that's the kind of brave Ranger was talking about. He was talking about taking a chance on a dream. And taking a chance on a personal relationship. And I was sorely lacking in this kind of bravery.

I called Grandma to see if she knew any more about Marvina.

"Appendicitis," Grandma said. "She'll be home in a couple days, and we might want to make sure she hasn't got that cookie tin sitting in her kitchen."

Lula was already in the office when I arrived. She'd eaten the Boston Kreme and many more. Her short hair was in a state of

232

natural frizz, and she was dressed entirely in pink. Pink tank top. Pink leather skirt that was obscenely short. Pink thigh-high boots.

"What happened to the boho?" I asked.

"That was yesterday. Today I'm in homage to the Pink Panther. And I'm not referring to Steven Cross, who was a total imposter."

"Is there any news on Roman?" I asked Connie.

"Nothing, but I'd keep a close watch on Grandma. I'm hearing that the La-Z-Boys are nervous."

"There are only three of them now," I said. "Are they going to be able to pull off a kidnapping?"

Connie shrugged. "It would be good if you could take Shine off the streets. That would narrow it down to Lou Salgusta, who is batshit crazy, and Benny."

"Were you ever able to get a current address for Shine?" I asked Connie.

"No. He's not leaving any tracks. No new credit action to indicate a hotel or a rental car. My mother and my Aunt Stella haven't heard anything. My guess is that he's staying with someone. He has friends and relatives who would be willing to hide him. He also has Darlene."

"Darlene is too obvious," I said. "He might visit her, but I doubt he's staying there."

"If the remaining La-Z-Boys are getting ready to make a move on Grandma, they could be huddling at the Mole Hole," Connie said.

I checked the time. It was early for the Mole Hole.

"Let's talk to Darlene," I said to Lula. "If we don't learn anything from her, we can stake out the Mole Hole."

"Sounds like a plan to me," Lula said.

We crept through town in rush-hour traffic. Retail wasn't open for business yet, but office buildings were filling up. Darlene's parking lot was already half empty.

"A lot of government workers live in this building," Lula said. "They get to work early so they can leave early and play golf."

We took the elevator to the third floor and rang Darlene's doorbell. There was no answer, so I knocked.

I could hear movement on the other side, and Lula put her face up to the security peephole.

"Hey, Darlene," she said. "It's Lula."

The door cracked open with the chain attached, and Darlene looked out.

"I'm not up to visitors," she said.

"Good lord," Lula said, taking in Darlene's swollen face. "What happened to you?"

"I can't talk right now," Darlene said.

"You need help," Lula said. "Open the door. If you don't open the door, I'll break it down. I could do it too. I got a lot of skills since I went into law enforcement."

Darlene slipped the chain, and we hurried in. Her eye was swollen shut. Her cheek was bruised and swollen. Her lip was split open.

"What happened?" Lula asked.

I looked around. A round end table was overturned, and a vase was smashed on the floor. The floor by the smashed vase had a blood smear.

"Are you alone?" I asked Darlene.

"Yes," she said. "And I'm going to stay that way."

She slowly walked toward the bedroom, holding her side. "I need to keep moving," she said. "I need to be out of here before he returns."

"Charlie?" Lula asked.

"Yeah. He let himself in around two o'clock. Drunk." She put her hand to her mouth. "Sorry, I know I'm hard to understand. It's painful to talk."

"Honey, you need stitches," Lula said.

"I need to get out of here first," Darlene said.

"No problem," Lula said. "We're gonna help you. Do you have someplace to go?"

"I'm going to stay with my sister in Piscataway until I get a job and a place of my own."

"Are you going back to hooking?"

"No. My sister said she might be able to get me something where she works. And I've been putting money aside. I have some savings."

"We're still looking for Charlie," I said. "Do you have any idea where we might find him?"

"He's staying with someone. I don't know more than that. He goes to the Mole Hole. That's where they all collect." She took a stack of T-shirts from a dresser and put them into a half-filled suitcase that was on the bed. "You want to be careful," she said. "He's in a nasty mind. I'm lucky he didn't kill me. He was drunk and angry. Ranting about Jimmy being an idiot. How the keys were a stupid idea, and he couldn't leave Trenton until they were found. He said if he'd had his way, Edna would have talked by now. He blamed the delay on Julius Roman. Said he had no guts."

"Do you think he killed Roman?" I asked.

"I'd like to pin it on him. And he's capable of doing it. Unfortunately, he was with me when Roman was killed."

Lula was emptying closets and stuffing clothes and shoes into large black plastic garbage bags.

"What else do you want?" Lula asked Darlene. "You got jewelry? Personal stuff, like photographs? Do you have a car parked outside?"

"Charlie owns the car and this apartment," she said. "I don't want to make more trouble by taking it."

Fifteen minutes later we had the apartment cleaned out and the Porsche stuffed full of bags. Darlene didn't want to get medical care in Trenton, so we drove her to her sister's house.

"I hated to leave Darlene like that," Lula said when we were back on the road.

"Her sister seems nice. She'll take care of her."

"I guess. But it's terrible to see someone get beat up like that."

It was almost lunchtime when we pulled into the Mole Hole parking lot. Lula and I went inside and sat at a table that gave us a view of the inner sanctum door. No way to know who was inside.

We ordered lunch and watched the door. The two slick-haired kids who worked for Benny the Skootch went in and came out five minutes later. No sign of Stan. We got our mega-burgers and fries, and a waitress exited the kitchen and went to the door. She had three plates, plus sides, stacked on a large tray. She balanced the tray on her shoulder and knocked on the door. It opened and she went in. She came out minutes later without the food.

"He's in there," I said.

"You don't know for sure," Lula said.

"I have a feeling."

"Oh boy." She added extra salt and ketchup to her burger. "How are you going to get him out?"

"I guess I'm going to drag him out."

"You and who else?"

"You. And Ranger."

"Okay, now you're talking."

I called Ranger and asked for help. I told him to give me ten minutes so I could finish my lunch.

"Babe," he said. End of conversation.

After eight minutes I pushed back from the table.

"Are you carrying?" I asked Lula.

"Do bears poop in the woods?" Lula said.

"Pass me your gun under the table."

"Say what?"

"I need a gun, and mine is home in the cookie jar."

"I got a Glock nine with me," Lula said. "Do you know how to use a Glock nine?"

"You pull the trigger and it goes bang?"

"That would be your little Smith and Wesson."

"It doesn't matter. I don't intend to use it."

I slipped Lula's Glock into my sweatshirt pocket and went to the bar. I ordered a Coke and watched the front door. At precisely ten minutes after I hung up with Ranger, the front door opened, and Ranger and Tank walked in.

Tank is appropriately named. He's huge and has tough guy written all over him. He was in special ops with Ranger, and he's the number-two guy at Rangeman. He's the guy who watches Ranger's back. They were in Rangeman black fatigues, wearing full gun belts. Sidearms strapped to their legs. If I didn't know them and was seeing them for the first time, I'd flat-out have a panic attack.

Since I'd slept with one of them and knew what he was capable of doing, the adrenaline surge that would have fueled a panic attack instead produced a rush of sexual desire so strong I almost dropped Lula's gun.

The bartender spotted them and reached for the phone, just as I thought he would. Standard operating procedure. This was how I got to meet Stan. I pulled myself together and discreetly pointed the Glock at the bartender, suggesting that he take a step back away from the phone. I caught Ranger's eye and directed his attention to the door behind the bar. By the time Ranger and

Tank reached the door, the Mole Hole had emptied out. The floor-show music was still playing, but there was no pole girl.

I gave the gun back to Lula, told her to keep her eye on things, and joined Ranger and Tank. I felt small in comparison but totally empowered, flanked by the two men in black. I knocked, and Stan opened the door.

"Hello again," I said.

He attempted to close the door, and Ranger stiff-armed it open. Benny the Skootch was in his chair with a napkin tucked into his shirt like a bib. Lou Salgusta was eating his lunch at a card table. Charlie Shine had been at the table with Lou, but he jumped up when I walked in with Ranger and Tank.

"What the fuck?" Charlie said. "What the fuck?"

"You missed your court date," I said to Charlie. "You need to come with us to reschedule."

"This is bullshit," Charlie said. "Benny, get my lawyer on the phone. Tell him to get the fuck down to the courthouse."

Ranger attempted to cuff Charlie, and Charlie struck out at him. In a nanosecond Ranger face-planted Charlie onto the card table. Charlie was searched and his weapon removed, and his hands were cuffed behind his back. Ranger jerked him to his feet and force-marched him out of the Mole Hole.

"Very sorry to have disrupted your lunch," I said to Benny and Lou. "It all looks delicious."

I paid for lunch and met Ranger in the parking lot.

"Would you like us to drop him off, or would you like to have the pleasure?" Ranger asked.

"I'll take him in," I said. "Thank you. I really appreciate the help. I didn't know who was in the room. And I probably couldn't have cuffed Shine without Lula shooting him first."

Connie gave us a double thumbs-up when we walked into the office.

"Another job well done," Lula said. "We took Shine straight to the court and the judge set his bail at twice the original amount. No one will put up that kind of money."

"For sure not this office," Connie said. "And we have one less FTA to worry about. Emory Lindal was arrested last night. Drunk and disorderly."

"That leaves our favorite person," Lula said. "Carol Joyce, the little wiener."

As far as I was concerned, he could shoplift for the rest of his life. I had no desire to attempt another takedown of Carol Joyce.

"How many attempts at capture will this make?" I asked Lula.

"I stopped counting," Lula said. "It's humiliating. It's not like he's the Pink Panther or Jack the Ripper. This idiot lives with his mother and steals T-shirts for a living."

"We can drive past his house and his office and look for his SUV," I said. "I guess we could cruise the Quaker Bridge parking lot."

"That sounds like a lame attempt," Lula said. "What would Dog the Bounty Hunter do?"

"He'd go to the Joyce house at one in the morning, kick the door in, and drag Carol Joyce out of bed," I said.

"That would seem extreme in this case," Lula said, "on account of it would scare the bejeezus out of Mrs. Joyce. She thinks her son is a personal shopper. And there's the ugly little dog to think about. It already has intestinal issues. I would hate to cause it more anxiety."

My mother called.

"Your grandmother was caught breaking into Marvina's house," my mother said. "Luckily it was Eddie Gazarra who investigated. He's got her in his patrol car, and he doesn't know what to do with her."

"Where are they now?"

"He's in the All-Day Diner parking lot just past the hospital."

"I'm on my way." I grabbed my bag and headed for the door. "Family problem," I said. "Not life-threatening."

I pulled into the diner parking lot three minutes later and parked next to the patrol car. I grew up with Eddie Gazarra, and he was now married to my cousin Shirley the Whiner. I got out of the Porsche and looked in at Grandma. She was in the back seat, eating a cup of soft-serve ice cream. She smiled when she saw me and pointed to the cookie tin in her lap.

"What's up?" I said to Eddie.

Eddie got out of the patrol car, stepped away, and turned his body mic off. "She bumped the lock on Marvina's back door and let herself in. Tootie saw her do it and phoned it in. Luckily,

241

dispatch sent me out, or Grandma would be sitting in the holding tank right now."

"Did she explain any of this to you?"

"No. She won't talk. She said she had a righteous mission to perform, and she has no regrets."

"So, you bought her ice cream and called my mother?"

"Yes."

Gazarra was great. It was a shame he married Shirley. He could have done much better. I gave him the long version of the regifting of potentially poisonous cookies. The more he heard, the larger the smile got until he was full-on cracked up.

"Let me get this straight," he said. "Barbara gave the cookies to Grandma. Grandma gave the cookies to the sisters. The sisters gave the cookies to Marvina. And Grandma broke in so she could get the cookies out of the house before Marvina came home and maybe ate another one."

"Yep."

"I love it," Gazarra said. "I might have to confiscate that cookie tin. You never know when you want to give someone poison cookies. Good to have on hand."

"I'm going to bury it," I said.

"I'll transfer Grandma over to your custody and write this up as mistaken identity."

"Thanks. I owe you."

"Really? I could use a babysitter next Saturday."

"Last time I babysat for your kids they set the kitchen on

fire. I'd rather let you keep Grandma, and you could lock her up with the hookers."

"I don't want her," Gazarra said. "I'd be laughed out of the building. I'd be known as 'Granny Cop,' and my mother would be mad at me."

CHAPTER TWENTY-THREE

I TOOK GRANDMA back to my parents' house. We emptied the cookies into a plastic bag, smashed them with a rolling pin, and put them in the garbage. If a pack of rats ate them at the landfill that was their problem.

"We'll never know if they were poisoned," Grandma said.

I nodded. "Another one of life's mysteries."

It was early afternoon when I drove away. I reached the cross street and stopped because I had a dilemma. If I went back to the office, Lula would want to go after Carol Joyce. Not only did I see riding up and down lanes in a shopping center parking lot as a waste of time . . . I also didn't give a fig about capturing Carol Joyce. I honestly didn't care about any part of the bail bonds business. I know this is a terrible attitude, but there it was.

Although, I had to admit I enjoyed taking down Charlie Shine with Ranger and Tank. It was nice to be part of a professional team. Nice to get the job done without a screwup and a skinned knee. And I was able to get Charlie Shine behind bars, where he wasn't a threat to Grandma.

I was still wearing the baggy boyfriend jeans because there was nothing else in my closet. I had to do laundry, and I should go shopping. I was short on work clothes. Thanks to Steven Cross I had some money.

Thirty minutes later, I was in Macy's. Buying jeans is a no-brainer. I always wear the same thing. Nothing fancy. After jeans it's more of a struggle. I was looking at a red dress with a short swirly skirt when Carol Joyce walked up to me.

"You don't want that dress," he said. "It's all wrong for you, and it's not well made. Not worth the money."

I gave up a moment of stunned silence before my brain kicked in.

"Carol Joyce?"

"Yes. And I'm going to save you the trouble of trying this disaster on. Trust me. I'm good at this. It's one of the reasons I'm so successful. I only steal quality merchandise."

"You're serious? You risked getting cuffed to tell me this?"

"I don't feel it's much of a risk. I can easily outrun you. And to be honest, the game is getting boring. I'm thinking of turning myself in and getting the whole court thing over and done. It's my first offense, and there weren't any high-end items involved. I expect I'll get a slap on the wrist."

"Why do you shoplift?" I asked him. "Why don't you get a real job?"

"This *is* a real job. I average a yearly salary of mid-six figures."

"But why shoplifting?"

"I'm good at it. I started doing it in high school as a stunt and discovered I had a real talent for it."

"Wouldn't you like to do something else? Move up the ladder?"

"No."

"You have no dreams? No aspirations?"

"No. I like what I'm doing."

"It's illegal."

"Yes. That's unfortunate."

"What about if you get married and have kids? What will you tell them?"

"I don't know. I suppose that could be a game changer."

We had a couple beats of silence while we thought about that.

"So, why don't you like this red dress?" I asked him.

"It's too short. It's going to hit your leg in an odd spot and be unflattering. The color isn't wonderful for your complexion. You would look best in a blue red. This is an orange red. And finally, I don't like the cut of the neckline. I would like to see you in a scoop neck."

"Wow. That's amazing. I looked at it and all I saw was that it was cute. Your mother thinks you're a personal shopper. Maybe that's your true calling."

"I have a couple clients, but I do it more as a personal favor than a profession. It's just not as satisfying as shoplifting."

I put the red dress back on the rack. "What dress would you suggest?"

He pulled out a deep blue silk shirtwaist. "It doesn't have a scoop neck, but it's very classy and at the same time it's sexy because of the way the silk drapes and moves. It's a little expensive but I can put it in my bag for you."

"No! I wouldn't want you to do that." I took the dress from him. "It's nice, but I'm not sure about the style."

"Try it," he said. "I think you'll be surprised."

I tried the dress on, and it was perfect. It felt elegant and sexy, and it was comfortable. I put my baggy jeans back on, left the dressing room, and Carol was gone. Vanished. Crap. Truth is, I wasn't that surprised. And I didn't much care, although it would have been fun to do more shopping with him. I bought the dress and was pulling out of the shopping center parking lot when my mother called.

"Usually we see you and Joseph for dinner on Fridays," she said. "Last week was a wash because . . . you know. So, I'm just checking before we set the table."

"Sure, we'll be there for dinner," I said. "I'm almost positive."

"Six o'clock," she said. "We're having pot roast."

I hung up and called Morelli. "Dinner at six o'clock at my parents' house?"

"Sounds good. Gazarra told me about Grandma. He made me promise not to tell anyone."

"He's the best. I also brought Charlie Shine in. I was hoping for no bail, but the judge chose to set a super high amount instead."

"I heard. Shine's lawyer is looking for money. I'm told he's liquidating some of Shine's assets so Shine can post his own bond."

"That would be a real bummer. That would defeat my purpose for apprehending him."

I hauled my laundry basket into my parents' house just before six o'clock. I was wearing new jeans and a new long-sleeved, scoop neck, silky-feeling sweater that Carol had dropped into my jeans bag without me noticing. The price tag was still on the sweater. $175.00. I was now aiding and abetting a shoplifter. Screw it. I didn't care. It was a great sweater, and I had bigger fish to fry.

"Don't you look pretty," Grandma said when I walked into the kitchen. "Is that a new sweater?"

"Yes. And new jeans."

"You must be doing good at work."

I smiled at the irony of that. Just when I decide that I hate my job, I have the best week ever.

My mother was working at the stove, and the kitchen was heavy with the smell of meat and gravy. I looked in the fridge. Pineapple upside-down cake smothered in whipped cream. This meal was a mainstay of my life and almost as good as sex. Okay, who was I kidding? This was as good if not better than sex. And I could enjoy it without reciprocating.

Morelli walked in, and my mom and grandmother got all smiles. They liked Morelli. They would like me to marry him and make a bunch of little Morellis. Grandma also liked Ranger, but not to marry.

"This is my favorite meal," Morelli said to my mom. "I could smell the gravy when I parked my car."

"You're just in time," she said.

She poured the gravy into the gravy boat and handed it over to me. Grandma took the bowl of mashed potatoes. My father was already at the table. My mother set the pot roast platter in front of him. He had the carving knife and fork in hand. We were Catholic and my mother and grandmother went to Mass almost daily, but we didn't say grace. We assumed God knew our thoughts when it came to food. We were thankful, we wanted world peace, yadda yadda yadda.

Morelli always sat next to me. Grandma was across from me. My mom and dad were at either end of the table. This was a good arrangement because Grandma was a reach for my dad if she went off on aliens doing anal probes on humans and he decided he had to stab her with the meat fork.

"What are you working on now?" Grandma asked Morelli. "Did you ever find out about the guy who tried to kidnap me? The dead one with the red shoes."

"We're running down some leads," Morelli said.

"So, in other words," Grandma said. "You got nothing."

Morelli took a slab of pot roast and passed the platter to me. "Yep. That's about it."

"I hear his body got shipped back to Newark for burial. Not even having a viewing here. That's a shame," Grandma said. "A lot of people would like to take a look at him. He would have drawn a good crowd."

My father had his head down, concentrating on his meat. My mother had emptied her iced tea glass and was gnawing on her lip, wondering if anyone would notice if she got more. Grandma had the bottle of red wine in front of her and poured out a glass.

"Who wants wine?" she asked.

Morelli and I raised our hands.

By the time the pineapple upside-down cake came out, I'd had three glasses of wine and my lips were numb.

"Did you see I'm wearing a special medallion necklace?" Grandma said to Morelli. "If you press it, like this, people know where you are."

Morelli whipped his phone out and called Ranger's control room. "That was a test drive," he said. "No reason to respond."

He stayed on the line for a couple beats and then said, "Hunh, for real?" He looked over at Grandma. "Press it again." Another thirty seconds of silence. Morelli turned to me. "Press your medallion."

I pressed it and waited.

"So, nothing?" Morelli said to the guy in the control room.

Morelli hung up and slid a glance at me. "They aren't working."

"Probably made in China," Grandma said.

My mother cut the cake and passed pieces around.

"All that technology is a bunch of crap," my father said. "You can't beat a baseball bat."

"Or an iron," Grandma said.

Just because I'd had three glasses of wine didn't mean that I was stupid. I didn't like that the medallions weren't working.

"What did Ranger say about the medallions?" I asked Morelli.

"I didn't talk to Ranger."

I was on my second piece of cake when Ranger came in. He sat in the chair next to Grandma and unhooked her necklace. He pressed it and spoke to his control room through an earbud. He dropped the necklace into his shirt pocket.

"It's not working," he said.

"Would you like a piece of cake?" my mother asked. "Coffee? Wine?"

"No. I need to get back to work. I'm going to leave a Rangeman car with you for tonight." He stood and looked at me. "I'd like to talk to you for a moment, outside."

I followed him out to the porch and punched him in the arm. "You wanted that piece of cake, didn't you?"

He grinned at me. "How much wine have you had tonight?"

"Thwee."

I attempted to lean against the porch railing, misjudged the distance, and went over the railing into a hydrangea bush. Ranger picked me out of the bush and set me on my feet.

"We can talk tomorrow," he said.

I smiled at him. "Okeydokey. Do you want to kiss me?"

"Not here," he said. "I don't want to risk a shootout with Morelli."

CHAPTER TWENTY-FOUR

IT WAS MORNING. I was in Morelli's bed, and I was loving the luxury of sleeping late. Morelli came in with coffee and my laundry basket. He was dressed in sweats and a T-shirt.

"I told the guys I'd play ball with them this morning," he said. "Bob's been walked and fed. And your mom dropped your laundry basket off on her way to church." He handed me the coffee, kissed me on the top of my head, and left.

I sat up in bed and drank my coffee, thinking this was nice. This was the way life should be. Drinking coffee in bed on a Saturday morning. I finished my coffee, took a shower, and went downstairs. I allowed myself the extra treat of toasting my frozen waffle, had a second cup of coffee, and was ready to start my day. I also had an epiphany. Maybe the reason I didn't have a work-related passion was that I actually didn't want to work at all. I had a passion for doing nothing. Now that I realized this, I just had to find a way to get paid for it.

I drove past my parents' house on my way to the office.

The Rangeman SUV was parked at the curb, and I didn't see any crazy old Italian men skulking around. It was all good.

Lula and Connie were listening to police chatter when I walked in.

"Richie is on another roof," Connie said. "They're trying to get him in the bucket, but he says he's waiting for his dragon to return."

"I'll say it again," Lula said. "That boy needs a more reliable dragon."

Connie and I looked at Lula.

"You don't really think he has a flying dragon, do you?" Connie asked Lula.

Lula leaned forward and cocked her head, eyebrows up. "Have you got a better explanation?"

"No," Connie said.

Lula sat back. "There you have it. Boom."

"Anything new come in?" I asked Connie.

"No, but it's early. Oliver Turkel had his hearing yesterday, and he has a history of no-shows."

"I remember him," Lula said. "He's the guy who robs people and then moons them. It's his trademark move. Last time we brought him in, he mooned Stephanie and me. I even got it videoed on my phone."

"Something to look forward to seeing," Connie said.

"Yeah, but I doubt he'll moon us again," Lula said. "Stephanie tagged him on his bare ass with her stun gun, and he went down like a sack of cement. And then he wet himself." Lula shook her head. "It wasn't a real pretty sight."

I did an involuntary shiver at the memory.

"I'm still up for finding the shoplifter," Lula said. "I vote we ride around and look for him. And we could ride down Maple Street and see if Richie is still on the roof. It's not far from where Carol Joyce lives."

This sounded like a decent activity. It was a nice day to go cruising around. And I didn't think anything would come of it. We could look for Carol for a couple hours, have lunch, and then I'd quit for the day and go back to Morelli's house to get my laundry. Maybe Morelli would want to go to the shore.

We started by checking out Richie Meister. He was still on the roof, and traffic was snarled for blocks.

"I can see the hook and ladder," Lula said. "They got the big ladder up."

"Do you see any dragons?"

"Nope. Not a single one."

I circled around the Richie mess and drove past the Joyce house. No SUV in the driveway, thank goodness. I wasn't in a mood to arrest Carol Joyce.

"I've been thinking about our job," Lula said. "And how you don't like it anymore. And I think it's that we aren't badass like Ranger and Tank. You know what the difference is between them and us?"

"How much time do I have to answer?"

"The difference is we haven't got a badass uniform. We're just as good as them, but they got the uniform, you see what I'm saying? Even Dog got a badass uniform. Okay, so his hair needs some help, but he's got the black leather thing working for him."

"I can't see you wearing a uniform every day."

"I would have to personalize it. Like I could bedazzle it."

"I have a uniform," I said. "I'm wearing it."

"See that's your problem. You need some enthusiasm, and there's no enthusiasm to those clothes. Only thing on you that's got enthusiasm is your hair extensions, and they're starting to fall out. We got to get you new extensions. I'm thinking fire red next time. That's a power color."

"It's not the clothes or the lack of extensions," I said. "It's what we see. It's Oliver Turkel."

"Oliver Turkel was great," Lula said. "You got him square on his ass, and he peed himself like a big dog. Sometimes when I need a laugh, I replay that video."

"It isn't funny. It's disgusting and horrible."

"Yeah, but it's funny in a disgusting and horrible way. You got to put things into perspective."

I got to Quaker Bridge Mall and drove up and down the aisles. No Escalade with Carol's plate number. So far, my luck was holding. I left the lot and returned to Route One, and my mother called.

"She's gone," she said, and the shaky note of hysteria in her voice sent an instant chill through me.

"Where are you?"

"I'm home. We were at the bake sale at the church and she disappeared. She went to use the restroom and never came back. I tried calling her, but she wasn't answering. Then I thought maybe we got our signals crossed, and she thought she was supposed to walk home."

"How long has she been gone?"

"I don't know. I can't think. Thirty minutes, maybe. Ranger's got everyone looking for her. The young men in the car felt terrible, but it wasn't their fault. She must have gone out through the side door."

"Are you sure she's not in the church? There are lots of rooms."

"I don't know why she would be someplace other than the restroom, but I guess it's possible."

"I'm on Route One. I'll be home soon."

I hung up and called Morelli.

He answered on the first ring. "I just heard," he said. "Ranger called. I'm sending some guys over to help them sweep the church. I'm heading there now."

"Is anyone with my mom?"

"Ranger has two men with her."

I'd taken the call on speakerphone, and Lula had been listening in.

"What can I do?" she asked.

"I'm going to drop you at the office. Tell Connie to start making phone calls. And then you can ride around the streets."

Morelli and Ranger were huddled in the vestibule when I walked into the church.

"Anything?" I asked.

"We're questioning everyone who was here to see if they saw or heard anything," Morelli said. "We have a team going room to room. So far, the church is clean. We haven't been able to find any signs to indicate struggle."

I looked around. "Are there security cameras?"

"No," Morelli said. "They have an alarm system that they use at night, but there are no cameras."

One of Ranger's men came up to him.

"We found this behind a trash receptacle by the side door," he said.

It was Grandma's big black patent leather purse. I looked inside, and her gun was still there. Her cellphone was tucked into a side compartment.

I had to take a couple breaths to steady myself. This wasn't a time to disintegrate into an emotional basket case.

"Are you okay?" Morelli asked.

I nodded. "I needed a moment."

"Understood," Morelli said.

"Where do we go from here?" I asked.

"I'm going to talk to the La-Z-Boys and explain the realities of life to them," Morelli said. "You and Ranger can work the Lucca angle."

"I need to check in with my mom," I said to Ranger.

"I'll meet you at the house. I want to give some instructions to my men."

It was a short drive, and I took it slow, scanning yards, taking notice of car occupants. I parked in the driveway behind my mom's car. The Rangeman SUV was at the curb. My dad was pacing in the living room.

"All these years I wanted to kill her, and now someone might do the job for me and I don't like it," he said. "Go figure that."

My mom was in the kitchen, sitting at the table.

"You aren't ironing," I said.

"I can't find the energy to iron. I'm heartsick. My chest aches with it."

I made coffee for us, and I laced my mom's with whiskey. "She's strong," I said. "She'll come out okay. We'll find her."

My mom nodded and sipped her coffee. "This is good," she said. "Thank you. I feel like I should be doing something, but I don't know what it is."

"Stay here in the house in case she tries to contact you or manages to get home. I'm working with Ranger to find her, and Morelli is doing his cop thing."

I finished my coffee, rinsed my mug, and went outside to wait for Ranger. I had my messenger bag with me, stuffed full of all the information Connie had printed out for me on the Lucca case.

Ranger cruised down the street and idled behind the

Rangeman SUV. He was driving a new black Porsche Cayenne Turbo, the big brother to my Macan. I slid in next to him and saw that the instrument panel had been tricked out so he could communicate with his control room.

"I don't think your passion is fighting crime," I said. "I think you have a passion for expensive James Bond toys."

"Success has its rewards. Where would you like to begin?"

"Someone hired Lucca and Velez to kidnap Grandma. We need to find that person. I have two potentials, but I'm only lukewarm about them. Barbara Rosolli and Sidney DeSalle."

"I know DeSalle," Ranger said. "He's a bad guy."

"He owns Miracle Fitness, and Lucca was a trainer there."

"Motivation?"

"Greed? Or maybe they have something on him and he's afraid of a document dump. Barbara Rosolli was Jimmy's first wife. She lives on Chambers Street next to her daughter Jeanine. Her motivation is clear. She wants the money. She also has a lot of anger, and she knew Lucca from Miracle Fitness."

"What about the sisters?" Ranger asked.

"I couldn't find a connection to Lucca, and they have a different agenda. I think they're just enjoying the feud. It's like the Hatfields and McCoys for them."

"Let's do the ex-wife first," Ranger said.

Barbara Rosolli lived in small two-story house that had a postage stamp front yard and a narrow front porch that ran the width of the house. The house was painted white with black window trim, and some of the trim was beginning to peel. Jeanine's house, next door, was similar. The two were separated by a driveway that led to a single-car detached garage that sat at the back end of the lot.

Ranger parked on the opposite side of the street from Barbara's house, and we watched for activity. Shades were up on the front windows. A car was in the driveway. I saw no flicker from a television. No one peering out a window at us.

"Let's do it," Ranger said.

We crossed the street, I rang the bell, and Barbara answered.

"Stephanie," she said, "I just heard about Edna." Her attention turned to Ranger, and her eyes got wide. "Well, *hello*! Who do we have here?"

"This is Ranger," I said. "We're working together to find Grandma. May we come in?"

"Is it necessary?"

"Yes," I said.

Barbara rolled her eyes, stepped away from the door, and made a sweeping *enter* motion. I hadn't been in her house before, and I was surprised at the decorating. It was very neat and quietly pleasant. Comfortable, basic furniture in neutrals. Fresh flowers on the coffee table. It looked like a nice person lived there.

Jeanine came in from the kitchen. "Stephanie, I thought I heard my mom say your name. We were just having lunch and talking about what happened at the church. We were at the bake sale earlier. We must have just missed your grandmother and your mom. What happened? Did Edna just wander away? It's not like her."

"We think she might have gone off with someone," I said.

"A friend?"

"Maybe," I said. "Or maybe someone who was unhappy with her."

"Oh gosh," Jeanine said.

"Did you see anyone who might fall into either of those categories?" I asked her.

"There were a lot of people there. There was a late Mass and then the bake sale. There were certainly some people who could be considered friends. A bunch of the women from bingo. I don't know about the people who might want to harm her."

"Any La-Z-Boys?"

Jeanine looked over at her mom. "Did you see any?"

"No," Barbara said, "but one of Benny's wiseguy caregivers was there. He bought a coffee cake."

"I guess you know that one of the men who tried to kidnap Grandma was a trainer at Miracle Fitness," I said.

"Of course," Jeanine said. "What happens in the Burg is instantly known by *everyone* in the Burg."

"I know you both take classes there. Did you ever hear anything that would make you suspicious? Was Lucca ever especially friendly with anyone who might be interested in the keys?"

"Sidney DeSalle, the gym owner, is a little sketchy," Jeanine said. "I didn't take any of Lucca's classes. I couldn't keep up. He was hard-core. Bernie took some of Lucca's classes, but Bernie hasn't been there lately. Things got too busy at the concrete plant. He's there now. Some sort of a breakdown."

We left Barbara's house and sat in the Cayenne for a couple minutes.

"What do you think?" I asked Ranger.

"Barbara didn't say much."

"Does that mean something?"

"Just that she strikes me as the sort of person who would dominate a conversation. And Jeanine, not so much."

"Jeanine can be very chatty."

"Her husband works at a concrete plant?"

"I think that might be the name of it, the Concrete Plant. It's a family business. Bernie's father started it, and when he retired Bernie's brother took over. Bernie works there too, but I'm not sure what he does. Some sort of managerial thing. Word in the neighborhood is that he isn't real bright. I don't know if that's true. I've always found him to be a nice guy. He's not Italian, and I don't think he was ever accepted by Jimmy and the rest of the Rosollis."

"Do they have kids?"

"Adults. Living out of state."

"Next up, Sidney DeSalle," Ranger said.

"I have multiple choices for him. He has an office at Miracle Fitness, an office in a building downtown, and a house in Hamilton Township. He has three adult children. They all live out of state. He's divorced. Ten years ago."

"It's Saturday. Let's try his house."

"It's north of town, toward Pennington. And I hate to say this, but I'm starving. I need lunch. Go back to my parents' house, and I'll get some fast food."

I called my mom and asked her to pack us lunch. When we pulled to the curb five minutes later, she was at the door with a grocery bag. I ran up and got the bag from her. Her eyes were red as if she'd been crying, and she looked exhausted.

"You need to iron," I told her. "Everything is going to be fine."

Back in the car, Ranger glanced at the bag as we drove away. "I have a feeling this is going to be good."

I pulled out two pot roast sandwiches and handed one to Ranger. The sandwiches were made on perfectly sliced bakery rye bread. They had the perfect amount of mustard, a dab of horseradish, a crisp romaine lettuce leaf, a thin slice of onion and tomato, and a couple slices of my mom's amazing pot roast. They were each cut in half to form triangles. On my best day I couldn't make a sandwich that would come even close to these masterpieces of deliciousness. She'd also packed a couple bottles of water. A cookie tin was at the bottom of the bag. I choked up when I saw the cookie tin, because I knew Grandma had made the cookies to make the house smell happy. I took a breath and swallowed back the emotion. No negative thoughts, I told myself. Everyone has to believe that she's okay and this will end well, and that energy will make it happen. I mentally repeated the thought until I convinced myself it was true.

We ate while Ranger drove. DeSalle lived about a half hour from the gym if traffic cooperated. At midday Saturday there was almost no traffic at all. I was working on the cookies when Ranger cruised into an area of obvious wealth.

DeSalle's house was one of the largest on a street of very large houses. It sat on about an acre of land. A small metal sign was attached to the elaborate mailbox at the entrance to the driveway. PROTECTED BY RANGEMAN.

"It doesn't get any better than this," Ranger said.

He called his control room and asked them to check if the alarm system was on. The answer came back *yes*.

"Does he have video?" Ranger asked.

"Yes. Inside and out."

"Check the video to see if anyone is in the house."

After several minutes the control room came back on. "We can't pick up anyone in the house. Twenty minutes ago, a single male got into a car and drove away. This was the same time the alarm was set."

"Turn the alarm off and shut the cameras down," Ranger said. "And go back over video starting at eight o'clock this morning. I want to know who was in the house."

"Lucky us," Ranger said to me.

He parked in the garage area, where his SUV wouldn't be visible from the road. He unlocked the side door and announced himself as Rangeman Security. No one answered.

We went room by room through the house.

"This guy has nine bathrooms," I said. "And I counted

twelve televisions. So far as I could see he's the only one living here. What the heck does he do with all the bathrooms and televisions?"

The control room got back to Ranger. "The one male that we saw leave is also the only one we picked up on the interior monitors."

We returned to Ranger's car, and reinstated the alarm and cameras.

"I'd still like to talk to DeSalle," Ranger said. "Let's try Miracle Fitness."

CHAPTER TWENTY-FIVE

MIRACLE FITNESS WAS PACKED. There were classes going in every room, and a lot of people in varying degrees of fitness were walking around in spandex. They were clustered at the healthy juice bar, chugging bottles of healthy water, stretching tendons while they chatted about trendy diets.

All this healthiness had me regretting that I'd just eaten half a tin of cookies made with genuine butter and a ton of sugar. I looked down at my jeans and didn't see anything hanging over the waistband, but it was only a matter of time before the butter and sugar turned to fat. And God knows what my arteries looked like.

I glanced at Ranger. He'd eaten one cookie. *One.* How is it possible to eat only one cookie? What kind of a weirdo can do that? He wasn't in Rangeman tactical gear today. He was wearing black slacks, a black dress shirt with RANGEMAN embroidered in black on the pocket, and a black blazer. It all fit him perfectly, and he looked like money, and muscle, and not someone you would want to mess with.

Ranger approached the woman at the desk and asked to see DeSalle. She said Mr. DeSalle was in conference and not to be disturbed.

"He'll see me," Ranger said.

"He doesn't like to be disturbed when he's in conference," the woman said. Nervous. Probably making minimum wage and told never to think.

"No problem," Ranger said.

He called his control room and asked where DeSalle's office was located. He turned and walked left, down a corridor, found a door that said PRIVATE, and knocked.

DeSalle opened the door.

"Aphrodite called and said you were on your way," DeSalle said. "She thought you might be a hired assassin or CIA. She's very fit but not very smart. If this is about increasing my security, I feel like I'm sufficiently covered. If you're here to tell me my house burned down, I don't want to hear it."

"I'm working with Stephanie," Ranger said. "I'm sure you've heard that her grandmother was kidnapped this morning."

"No," DeSalle said. "I hadn't heard. I know an attempt was made a couple days ago. The police were here, asking about the old Zeus. I believe he was involved."

"How well did you know the old Zeus?" Ranger asked DeSalle.

"Not all that well," DeSalle said. "I employed him. He had a following. Hard-core workout junkies and hard-up women. He had a reputation for making needy women happy. Not any of my business as long as it didn't take place on the premises."

"Someone hired him to do the kidnapping," Ranger said. "Do you have any ideas?"

"I imagine it would be someone who wasn't connected and wasn't real bright. The old Zeus had muscle and that's where his talent ended. I've been told that Marion Beggert was one of the women he regularly made happy enough to pay off his credit card. Have you seen Marion Beggert?"

Ranger shook his head, no.

"If you'd schtupp Marion Beggert for a couple bucks, you'd do most anything," DeSalle said.

"Have you talked to any of the La-Z-Boys lately?" Ranger asked.

"I used to play poker once a week with the La-Z-Boys, but poker night was discontinued when Charlie took off and Benny got too fat to fit at the card table."

"If you hear anything, let me know," Ranger said.

DeSalle nodded. "You bet."

"Did we get anything out of that?" I asked when we were back in the car.

"Not a lot, but I agree that an amateur hired Lucca."

"Barbara?"

"Maybe, but there are a couple issues that make her a long shot. She would have to assemble another kidnap team on short notice, because I don't think she's capable of actually doing the kidnapping herself. And she would need a place to hold Grandma. Does she own any other properties?"

I called Connie. She was closing up shop for the day, but she ran a property check on Barbara for me.

"I've got two properties," Connie said. "A house and a storage locker. The house is rented. It was Barbara's house before she moved next door to Jeanine. The storage locker is on the road to White Horse."

"We'll take a look," Ranger said. "We'll do the house first."

I called Morelli on the way to Barbara's rental.

"I talked to Benny," Morelli said. "He's in the hospital with heart issues. Between gasping for breath, he told me to go fuck myself, and that was about the extent of our conversation. Charlie Shine made bail and was released an hour ago. I just missed him, and I haven't been able to find him. I also haven't been able to find Lou Salgusta."

"We're running down Lucca leads," I said. "Let me know if you want us to change direction."

The house in Hamilton was in a family-oriented neighborhood of nice middle-income homes. Lots of swing sets visible in backyards. An occasional basketball hoop attached to a garage.

Barbara's rental house had a red and yellow Big Wheel tricycle parked on the short sidewalk leading to the small front porch.

Ranger and I walked around the tricycle and stepped onto the porch. A young woman carrying a baby answered the doorbell. Two toddlers and a dog were running around behind

269

her. The kids were laughing and yelling, and the dog was barking.

"I'm looking for Barbara Rosolli," I said to the woman.

"We rent the house from her," the woman said, "but she's never here. I've only seen her once, a couple years ago."

One of the toddlers turned and ran past the woman and onto the porch. Ranger snagged him and redirected him back into the house.

"Thanks," I said to the woman. "Sorry to have disturbed you."

We returned to the Porsche, and I buckled myself in. "You're good with children," I said to Ranger.

"You've seen my family in Newark. Lots of kids. Even more in Miami when I lived with my grandmother. I can change a diaper, make an omelet, and dance the salsa without my Hispanic machismo being threatened."

"Do you miss Miami?"

"Less as time goes on."

Thirty-five minutes later we were riding through two acres of storage lockers, looking for number 3175. Ranger found it and parked in front of it so that the SUV would shield us from view if other cars drove by. We got out, he picked the lock and unholstered his gun. The locker itself was the size of a small single-car garage. We rolled the door up and looked inside. No Grandma.

"This would have been too easy," Ranger said. "Now what? Do you have any other suspects?"

"I have a long list of people who belonged to Miracle Fitness. Drop me off at my parents' house so I can check on my mom and dad, and I'll comb through the list one more time."

"Sounds good. I'll go back to Rangeman and see what I can find."

My dad was in front of the television. The baseball bat was beside him, leaning against his chair. My mom was in the kitchen, staring into the refrigerator. No ironing board in sight. No Big Gulp of iced tea on the counter.

"Hey," I said to my mom, "how's it going?"

"I was just going to pull out some leftovers for dinner. Will you be eating with us?"

"Yep. I thought I'd grab something here. Why don't I order pizza?"

"Pizza would be great. Your father would like that."

I called Morelli to see if he wanted to join us.

"No," he said. "I want to keep on this. Shine and Salgusta are holed up somewhere. I know something is going down with them. We're looking for their cars, and we're talking to relatives and neighbors."

"What about Benny?"

"He's in St. Francis. Looking at getting a stent tomorrow. I think he's already got a bunch of them."

There's my weak link, I thought. I hung up with Morelli and called Pino's. Twenty minutes later we got pizza delivery. One large pie with extra cheese, one large pie with the works, one small pie with the works.

"I'm taking the small pizza to a friend," I told my mom. "You and Dad go ahead and eat without me. I'll eat when I get back. I won't be long."

St. Francis Medical Center is on the edge of the Burg and a three-minute car ride from my parents' house. I parked, got Benny's room number from the attendant at the lobby desk, and went straight to his room.

There were two beds. One was empty. Benny was in the other. He was in a hospital gown, looking like he was about to give birth to twins. He had an oxygen thing hooked up to his nose and an IV drip hooked up to his arm. He was clearly shocked to see me.

"What the hell?" he said.

"I heard you were here," I said, "and I thought you might be hungry." I opened the pizza box and set it on his bedside table.

"Oh man," Benny said. "That's a Pino's with the works." He pushed a button on the side of his bed, and it raised him up into a sitting position. "Close the door a little so the nurses don't see. I'm supposed to be on a special diet."

"I didn't know," I said. "Maybe you shouldn't eat this."

"You try to take this away and I'll kill you. I could do it too. I know I look like a pussy in this hospital gown, but I'll do whatever it takes to keep this pizza. They fed me Cream of Wheat and Jell-O for lunch. It was disgusting."

I closed the door and walked back over to him. "So, what's the deal here? You looked healthy last time I saw you."

"I got a lot of plaque, whatever the hell that is. They put these stent things in me and then I'm okay. Gonna get another one on Monday. Personally, I think it was stress this time." He took a bite and closed his eyes. Some pizza grease ran down his chin. "Oh boy. Oh man. There's nothing like a Pino's pie."

"What were you stressed about?"

"Your granny, what else? She's got the keys, and now it's a real cluster fuck. Excuse my language, but that's what it is. We should never have listened to Julius. He kept saying to give her more time. 'She'll come around,' he said. 'She's grieving.'" He finished the first piece and took a second.

"Did Charlie or Lou come to visit you? Do they know you're here?"

"They got their hands full. They got to negotiate now."

"What are they negotiating?"

"Price. The asshole who has your granny is nuts. If we'd snatched her in the beginning it wouldn't have cost us anything. Now this guy wants to ruin us."

"Do you know who it is?"

"No. It's all done by Internet and throwaway phones. If you ask me, technology sucks. Nothing's personal anymore."

"But you know it's a guy?"

"No. I just assume." He started on another piece of pizza. "You should have brought beer with this."

"Next time," I said.

"You're okay," Benny said. "You come here to pump me for information, but you're nice enough to bring pizza. And I like that you listen. It's like we're just having a conversation."

"I think you're okay, too," I said to Benny. "Take care. I hope everything works out on Monday."

"Walk in the park," Benny said.

My mom and dad were still at the table when I got back. I got a soda from the fridge and helped myself to a slice of the extra cheese.

"Who got the pizza?" my mom asked.

"Benny the Skootch. He's in the hospital. Needs a stent."

"Him and everybody else," my dad said. "You get to be our age and things start to clog up."

"I didn't know you were friends with Benny," my mom said.

"I wanted to ask him if he knew who took Grandma."

"Did he know?"

I shook my head. "No."

I finished eating and went into the kitchen with my mom. She tidied up and I sat at the little table and read through the Miracle Fitness list. It was a long list, and I took my time. Morelli and his co-workers couldn't find a connection between Lucca and the La-Z-Boys. Ranger and Connie couldn't find anything in Lucca's history that would connect him to the La-Z-Boys. The connection had to be on the list in front of me. I got through all the names and came back to Barbara. She had real motivation. She never got over the divorce. She had anger. And she wanted money. Maybe not for herself, but for Jeanine and her grandchildren. If she couldn't access whatever treasure the keys had locked away, she could ransom Grandma to the La-Z-Boys. It was smart. Actually, it was brilliant.

I called Morelli and told him about my visit with Benny and my theory about Barbara.

"I'm impressed," Morelli said. "I took the wrong approach with Benny, and you did the right thing. And I think you're right about Barbara. She has a motive, and she has the connection. I just can't see her acting alone."

"If she was able to talk Lucca into kidnapping Grandma, she probably is capable of finding another fall guy."

"I'm tied up right now. I was pulled off the kidnapping temporarily. Had a gang bloodbath in the projects. I'll be here all night, but tomorrow morning we'll visit Barbara. In the meantime, you might want to have Ranger do something illegal, like put her under physical and technical surveillance."

I hung up and looked over at my mom. "You're still not ironing."

"It isn't the same without your grandmother making fun of me."

"I'm heading out," I told her. "If anything scary happens, call me right away."

CHAPTER TWENTY-SIX

I DROVE FROM my parents' house directly to Barbara Rosolli's. Waiting for Morelli or asking Ranger for help would be the smart thing to do, but sometimes you need to go with your gut and just charge ahead. Morelli and Ranger were intimidating. Me, not so much. Barbara would be more willing to talk to me if I was alone. I didn't think she was going to admit to kidnapping Grandma, but she might slip and say something useful. And if she didn't make a slip, I had a speech prepared to spur her into action.

I rang her bell, and she answered the door with a glass of wine in her hand. Yes! Off to a good start.

"Stephanie," she said, looking around me. "Where's Mr. Sexy?"

"I'm alone."

"Too bad. He was hot."

"Can I come in for a moment?"

"Sure, what the hell, join the party. Jeanine and I were having a glass of wine. Her husband is working late again."

They were drinking wine at the kitchen table. This is something I would do with *my* mom. There was comfort at the table that couldn't be found anyplace else in the house. I sat down and accepted a glass of wine. There was a chunk of Parmesan on a cutting board, and some slivers had been sliced off.

It was disarming that I was invited to be part of this. Just as it was disarming that Benny was happy to have me visit. I was on the hunt for kidnappers and killers, and it would have been easier if everyone was rude.

"Here's to us," Barbara said, and we clinked glasses.

"And here's to Edna," Jeanine said. "Let's hope she's okay and returns to us soon."

"Oh God," Barbara said. "Do I have to drink to that?"

"Mom!" Jeanine said.

"Okay, okay," Barbara said. "Here's to Edna."

I took a slice of the Parmesan. "This is really good," I said. "Did you get this at Giovichinni's?"

"Of course," Barbara said. "You don't find hard cheese like that at the supermarket."

"It's nice that you live next door to each other and you can get together like this," I said. "Does Bernie work late a lot?"

"No. It's that they got a big order for precast and some machine broke down. Bernie wanted to stay with the mechanic who was working on the machine. These guys get time and a half for overtime. The Cement Plant looks like a big business, but the profit margin is slim. I guess it gets eaten up fast with time-and-a-half paychecks."

"It's disgraceful that you and Bernard should have to worry about those things," Barbara said. "Your father should have put money aside for you. And now even in death the money will go to *other places*."

"Bernie and I don't need Daddy's money," Jeanine said. "We're doing okay."

Barbara chugged half a glass of wine. "The whole La-Z-Boy thing is bizarre anyway. A bunch of old men sitting around in recliners in a nudie club. Ick!"

Here was the opening for my speech! I'd seen it done in Sherlock Holmes movies, and it always worked. Let the guilty person think you knew all about them, so they'd make a hasty move and screw up.

"I talked to Benny today," I said. "He's in the hospital waiting to get stented."

Jeanine went wide-eyed. "You talked to Benny? Isn't he a kidnapping suspect? What did he say?"

"He was angry that the La-Z-Boys didn't kidnap Grandma sooner. They dragged their feet on it, and now someone else has her and is essentially ransoming her to them."

Barbara gave a bark of laughter. "I love it."

"So, do you know who has her?" Jeanine asked.

"Yeah, I think I do," I said. "Benny didn't tell me any names, but I'm pretty sure I have it figured out."

"*Who?*" Jeanine asked.

"I don't want to say until I'm sure. I'm waiting for Morelli to get off work. I want to run it by him before I officially go to the police with it."

I watched Barbara when I laid the trap. She didn't look panicked. Mostly she looked like she'd had a skosh too much wine and was having a hard time focusing.

"Well, I should be going," I said. "Thanks for the wine. This was nice. We should do this more often."

I got in my Macan, drove around the block, and parked a couple houses down from Barbara's house. I cut my lights and settled back to wait. In the Sherlock Holmes movies it took no time at all for the guilty person to leave their home and go to the scene of the crime to make sure everything was still okay.

After I'd waited for almost an hour, a car cruised down the street and turned into Jeanine's driveway. Bernie was home from work. Barbara's lights went off in her house, and I had high hopes that she'd get into her car and lead me to Grandma. After twenty minutes I decided that Barbara had gone to bed. So much for Sherlock Holmes.

I rode past my parents' house. It was dark except for a single light in an upstairs bedroom window. I rode past Morelli's house next. Dark. No green SUV parked in front. He was still at work.

I went home and studied the Miracle list one more time. I turned the television on to Turner Classics. A Charlie Chan movie was playing. Black and white. 1936. Maybe it wasn't Sherlock Holmes who used the bluff to smoke out the villain.

Maybe it was Charlie Chan. Maybe it was every movie detective between the years 1933 and 1945. When you watch movies late at night with a glass of wine, they tend to blur together.

Halfway through Charlie Chan I went to the kitchen for a snack and heard what sounded like a kitten mewing on the other side of my door. I looked out my security peephole. Nothing. Nobody there. The mewing continued. I opened my door and looked down at a small gray kitten.

Something went *ZINNNG* in my head, and when I came around I was confused and in a state of utter panic. I couldn't move, and I couldn't open my mouth. I couldn't see. My heart was pounding in my chest, and I was struggling to breathe. I think I was crying, but it was impossible to know for sure in the confusion and darkness. I could have been sweating. I could have been having a nightmare and nothing was real. For a moment I thought I was buried alive.

The confusion started to clear, and I inched into survival mode. One step at a time, I told myself. Breathe. Think. Hard to tell if I was blind or simply in total darkness. I saw a thin seam of light above me. I wasn't blind. I was in a container. I could feel the sides. It had a lid, but the lid wasn't completely sealed. I couldn't remember being placed in a container. What *did* I remember? A kitten. And then a big blank space. I wasn't in pain, so I hadn't been hit on the head and knocked out. I'd probably been stunned. And it had been a big charge. That would mean I'd been completely out for just a few minutes. It could have been longer if I'd gotten stunned a second time. The confusion would have lasted five or ten minutes. I'd stun-gunned a lot of people, and I knew the progression of symptoms. I was okay with this. Better to be stunned than to have a concussion.

I couldn't open my mouth. Duct tape, I thought. My hands were bound behind my back. Not with cuffs or plasti-cuffs. More duct tape. There was vibration under me. I was being taken somewhere in a truck or a van. I could sense when we stopped and when we took a corner.

Charlie Chan came through for me. My bluff had worked. I'd been abducted by the amateur. Barbara. She'd found a couple new goons to work for her, and here I was getting trucked away and hopefully they'd take me to Grandma. The troublesome part of all this was that she'd already killed a guy who'd become a liability. I didn't have my cellphone on me. Nothing that Ranger could track. We slowed and bumped over a stretch of uneven surface. I hoped we weren't at the landfill. That thought gave me another moment of panic.

We came to a stop, and I heard a vehicle door slam shut and another get wrenched open. My container was tipped back slightly, and I was rolled a couple feet and then dropped a couple feet, hitting hard on what I assumed was the ground. I sniffed the air. It didn't smell like the landfill. I was tipped back again and rolled along. I couldn't tell how many people were walking with me. There was no talking. The person dragging me was breathing heavily. Out of shape or maybe nervous and scared. There were scraping sounds, and I was jerked up a step. Just one. Door threshold, I thought. Door slammed shut.

I heard muffled speech from someone a short distance away. A latch was released, the lid to the container was opened, and the container was dumped on its side. I blinked in the sudden light and saw that I'd been stuffed into a blue recycling container with wheels. Someone grabbed the back of my shirt and pulled me out. It was Bernard Stupe.

I was in a windowless room about the size of a two-car garage. Grandma was at the far end, standing beside a cot. She looked disheveled but alert. There were some water bottles and fast food bags on the floor by the cot. She was handcuffed to a chain that stretched through an open door behind her. I could see part of a toilet through the door.

"Asshole," Grandma yelled at him.

"Shut up," Bernie yelled back. "One more word and no more cookies."

Grandma gave him the finger. "Cookie this, you dirtbag."

He ripped the tape off my mouth and rolled the recycling bin over to the door.

"I didn't see this coming," I said. "I'm surprised you would throw in with Barbara."

"Barbara has no part in this," Bernie said.

"Jeanine?"

"Are you kidding me? Ms. Turn the Other Cheek and Be a Good Person? Miss Sweetness and I'm So Sorry? I don't think so." He went out the door and returned with a length of chain and a padlock. "I wasn't counting on this, so I'm going to have to improvise. I thought it was all finally moving along to a happy ending, and then Jeanine came home and told me you had it figured out. She said you talked to Benny and you'd figured out who was masterminding everything. Okay, so she didn't say 'mastermind,' but that's what she meant."

He dragged me up to my feet and over to Grandma. He wrapped the chain around my ankle and secured it with the padlock. He walked the other end of the chain into the bathroom, and I could hear him fidgeting with it.

He came out, took a pocketknife from his jeans pocket, and sliced the duct tape off my wrists. I reached out to grab him, but he jumped away.

"I don't get it," I said to Bernie. "Why did you hire those two guys to kidnap Grandma?"

"Zeus and what's his name? It was a reasonable idea in the beginning. It was supposed to be that this big strong guy waits for the right moment, snatches the old lady, and brings her here to stay for a couple days. It's calm. It's simple. It's relatively nonviolent. Turns out Zeus is a moron. He picks up some loser idiot at a bar and they decide to go in like a SWAT team on a suicide mission. What the heck was he thinking? He broke down a kitchen door and disrupted your mother's ironing. They weren't supposed to be armed. Guns weren't part of the plan."

"You hired the god of Thunder," Grandma said. "What did you expect?"

"I know," Bernie said. "It was a bad choice."

"You should have hired a less macho god."

"He was the only one who needed money," Bernie said. "Zeus was a big spender."

"And then you killed him?" I asked.

"I had to. He was in a panic. He was going to turn himself in. He would have ruined everything."

"Bernie," I said. "How could you do that? You aren't a killer."

"I am now," Bernie said. "And it was surprisingly easy. *BANG*. Ironic, right? All those years when Jimmy would have nothing to do with me. I wasn't fit to be in the mob. I wasn't good enough for them. I know what everyone said about me. Bernard isn't too bright. Bernard isn't Italian. His relatives are from one of those inferior eastern European countries. Tea drinkers." Bernie closed the blade on his knife and put it back in his pocket. "And it turns out I can kill without remorse. Go figure."

"So, what is this about?" I asked. "Getting even?"

"It's about getting even and about the chance to start my life over. Someplace far, far away."

"Why do you want to start it over? You have a good life. A good job. A loving wife."

"I have a shit job. I hate my job. My father left the company to my brother. He's two years younger than I am. The company should have been mine. Not that I wanted it. The Concrete Plant. Do you know what we do? We pour concrete into molds and sell the blocks."

"What would you rather do?" I asked him.

"As it turns out, I'd rather kill people."

"That's not a step up from concrete," Grandma said.

"Anyway, as it happens, I'm brilliant," Bernie said. "While the La-Z-Boys are going nuts because they can't find the keys, I found a way to benefit from their stupidity. I don't know what the keys look like. Don't care. I don't know what they open. Don't care. For that matter, I don't know if Grandma here is going to be any help to them. Don't care. What I do know is that they *think* Grandma has the sacred keys. And they're willing to pay big bucks for Grandma. Grandma is my ticket out of the Concrete Plant. Even Julius Roman thought I was a genius. He approached me at the Bonino viewing. Said he met a business associate in the alley and was on his way home when he saw me dump Lucca. Said he figured I was going to extort money from the La-Z-Boys, and he wanted in on it."

"So you killed him?"

"I didn't need his help, and I wasn't in a mood to share."

"What about Jeanine?" I asked.

"Jeanine will be fine. She can cross the driveway and drink wine with her dim-witted mother every night. She can go to Mass and talk to God or Jesus or Mary. Jeanine has lots of friends. The house is paid for. All she has to do is keep up with the taxes and cut the grass once in a while."

"What happens if they won't pay your price for Grandma?"

"We've already agreed on a price. We just have to work out the swap. Granny for a big bag of money."

"And me?" I asked.

"I don't know," Bernie said. "If they don't want you, I guess I'll kill you. That might be better for you anyway since I'm told Lou Salgusta is ready to fire up his tools of persuasion."

"You're a little nutty," Grandma said.

"Yeah," Bernie said. "And I'm tired. It's been a long day. I'll see you girls in the morning."

We watched him leave, dragging the recycling container behind him. The door clicked closed and locked.

"This is a real bummer," Grandma said.

I looked at the chain around my ankle. "There has to be a way out of here."

I walked into the bathroom. Toilet and sink. The chains were padlocked around the sink plumbing. I went back to Grandma.

"I don't suppose you have a nail file."

"No. I don't have a stick of dynamite, either."

"How did he get you to go with him?"

"He had a kitten. He said he wanted to take it to the shelter, and he asked me if I could hold it for him. And then when I got in the car with the little cutie, he zapped me. How about you? Did you fall for the kitten thing?"

"Yep."

"It was a really cute kitten," Grandma said. "I keep wondering what happened to it."

"It never occurred to me that it might be Bernie," I said. "I thought it was Barbara."

I looked around. Sacks of sand were stacked against one wall. A jumble of equipment was against another wall. A band saw. A leaf blower. Coils of hoses. Machinery parts that were alien to me. A long folding table and a single folding chair. A shop vac.

"Where are we?" I asked Grandma.

"I don't know for sure. He had a sack over my head, and my hands were handcuffed when he brought me here. You can't hear any sounds from outside. From the way he would come in and out I thought this must be part of the Concrete Plant. Like he would work some and then come check on me, even though it was a Saturday. This room looks industrial."

I agreed with Grandma. The room looked industrial. It seemed to be some sort of storeroom.

"Are you scared?" I asked Grandma.

"Sure, I'm scared. Aren't you scared?"

"Yes, and I'd be even more scared if I wasn't so tired."

"I don't like being scared," Grandma said. "It makes my stomach feel squishy. I always thought your job sounded so great. Putting your life on the line for justice. And going into all kinds of dangerous situations. But now that I'm in a dangerous situation I'm thinking it isn't anything I want to do again. I can see why you don't always like your job."

It isn't the danger that I hate, I thought. It's the *ick*.

It was late, and the cot was big enough for only one person. I persuaded Grandma to lie down on the cot, and I stretched out on the floor. It wasn't comfortable, but I was exhausted, and for the next several hours I slipped in and out of sleep.

Bernie showed up again at eight o'clock. He had a couple bags of breakfast sandwiches and two containers of coffee. He slid the sandwiches over to us and placed the coffee within reach, making sure he didn't get too close to me.

"We're making the swap this morning," he said. "It's going to take place here."

"Where is here?" I asked him.

"We're at the plant. This is a storage facility that's never used. It's behind the truck garages. Sometimes I come here when I want to get away from everyone and take a nap or watch a ball game. I get good reception on my iPad in here. I'm the only one with a key, and no one would come here anyway."

I ate half a sandwich and sipped my coffee.

"The police will track you down, and you'll spend the rest of your life in jail," I said to Bernie.

"They'll never find me. The instant I get my money I'm gone."

A half hour later, Charlie Shine and Lou Salgusta arrived. They were each carrying two suitcases.

"This is stupid," Shine said to Bernie. "Nobody demands cash in a suitcase anymore. We wire money now. Do you know how hard it was to get this much cash? We had guys working all night."

"Leave the suitcases by the door," Bernie said. "I'll take them from here."

Shine looked down the room at Grandma and me. "What's with this? We were supposed to get Jimmy's old lady. I'm not paying for a second hostage."

"She's a freebie," Bernie said. "If you don't want her, I'll take her with me and get rid of her."

"I like it," Salgusta said. "Two is always better. We'll keep her."

Bernie took a suitcase in each hand and staggered a little under the weight. He walked out of the building, Shine followed him, and there were two gunshots.

Grandma and I gave a start at the sound of rounds being fired. Grandma pressed her lips together, and I put my arm around her.

Shine backed through the doorway, dragging Bernie to the side of the room, leaving a fresh blood smear on the concrete floor.

"Fucking amateur," Shine said, and he walked away from Bernie and over to Salgusta. "Now that we got two of them, do you want to change the plan?"

"No," Salgusta said. "It's still a good plan. I can work here. It's isolated. Nobody's going to come bother us. And it's got good acoustics. You torture someone in a room with rugs and curtains, and it mutes the sound of their moaning and screaming. Takes some of the fun out of it."

"Jesus, Lou," Shine said, "you're a sick bastard."

CHAPTER TWENTY-SEVEN

"THE COT IS TOO LOW for me to work on," Salgusta said, "but the table over by the sandbags will be good. Help me move it so it's under the light. My eyes aren't what they used to be."

"Maybe you've got cataracts," Grandma said. "I've got a good doctor for that."

"Yeah, I'll have to look into it," Salgusta said.

They moved the table and brought two of the suitcases over. Salgusta opened the cases and stepped back.

"These are all my knives and pliers and restraints," he said. "We can put the women on the table face up and tie them down with the buckle straps and ankle and wrist cuffs. It'll work good. We attach one bracelet to a table leg and the other bracelet to a wrist or ankle. I got some big ones for ankles." He checked Grandma out. "The old one is kind of scrawny. Maybe we use a wrist bracelet on her ankle."

"I got good ankles," Grandma said. "They're one of my best features. They haven't started to sag yet."

"My torches must be in one of the other two suitcases," Salgusta said. "I always like to start with the torches." He looked over at me. "In the meantime, you should get undressed. I'm going to start with you, and I need you to be naked." He looked to Grandma. "You too, Granny. You might as well get undressed now too. It'll save time."

Grandma gave him the finger.

"Nice," Salgusta said. "How is that for an old lady to act?"

Shine brought a third suitcase over to the table and opened it. "This looks like the right one," he said.

Salgusta took a slim silver tool out of the case. "This is the one I always start with. This is a beauty. I do real pretty work with this. It's my precision butane soldering torch. This is the one that I use for my trademark signature. After I'm done with that one, I go to my Bernzomatic."

He exchanged the small soldering torch for the Bernzomatic. He attached a yellow cylinder to the torch and held it up for us to see.

"It's got a quick start-and-stop trigger," he said.

He pressed the trigger, and a huge blue flame shot out of the torch.

"Yeah," he said. "This is what I'm talking about. You could do a good burn with this baby."

I still had my arm around Grandma, and I felt her shudder.

Salgusta set the Bernzomatic on the table and went back to the little silver torch. He inserted a slim silver canister into the tool and pressed a tiny switch. Nothing happened. He removed the canister and shook it next to his ear. He reinserted it and tried again. Nothing.

"Empty," he said.

"You got a spare, right?" Shine said.

Salgusta pawed through the suitcase. "Doesn't look like it. I haven't had any use for this lately. Nobody wants burn jobs anymore."

"So, bypass the signature and go for the money," Shine said.

"No. That would be all wrong. I have a system. That would ruin everything. I just have to get a cartridge. Where's the nearest Home Depot?"

"I'm not going to no Home Depot," Shine said. "Can't you burn your initials into them with a match or a Bic?"

"Maybe," Shine said. "Do you have any matches?"

"No. I had to give up smoking. I got emphysema. Once in a while I have a cigar." He felt his pockets. "I don't have any matches. Don't you have matches? You're the burn guy."

"I don't usually burn with matches. It's not like I'm a pyromaniac. I'm an intelligence-gathering specialist."

"Okay, so you got a Bic?"

"No. I don't have a Bic. I have a Bernzomatic, and I'm not using it until I've autographed my victims."

"Okay, fine. Go to Home Depot. Take my car. I'll stay here and get the women stripped down."

"That won't work," Salgusta said. "I need someone to drive. I lost my license from when I ran into the school bus. Anyway, these women aren't going anywhere. We can leave them alone for a half hour."

"This better not drag on," Shine said. "I got a one o'clock appointment for a blood draw."

"You got a cholesterol problem?"

"Yeah, but I'm on meds for that. This is prediabetes."

"They're gonna tell you to lay off the grape."

"I'm already off the grape. I switched to vodka. It's potatoes. Vegetables are good for you."

Bernie had left the key in the door. They took the key, closed the door, and locked it.

"I'm going to get us out of here," I whispered to Grandma. I heard their car engine turn over, and I strained to hear them drive away.

"How are you going to do this?" Grandma asked.

"Shine dragged Bernie to this side of the room. I think I might be able to reach him. He's got the padlock key in his pocket."

I walked the chain out, but I was short. I lay flat on the floor and grabbed Bernie's foot. I pulled him a couple feet closer, was able to get to my knees, and pulled him far enough to reach into his pocket. I found the key and scrambled away from the body. I ran to the bathroom and discovered the key didn't unlock that padlock. I tried it on my ankle padlock and had success.

"Hang on," I said to Grandma. "There's another key."

I went back to Bernie and searched his pockets again. Sure enough, a second key. I unlocked the bathroom padlock and

Grandma was set free, but she still had the chain attached to her handcuffs.

"I didn't feel another key in any of his pockets," I said. "And I don't want to take any more time to look. Just hang on to the chain for now."

I grabbed the Bernzomatic that was sitting on the table and ran to the door. It was locked on the outside but not on the inside. I opened the door, looked out, and didn't see a car or a truck. Shine and Salgusta were gone. Bernie must have parked someplace else. The recycling container was still there.

The storeroom faced the back of the garage that housed the concrete trucks. I led Grandma around the garage and was about to cross a parking area when I saw a car coming at us.

"It's them," Grandma said. "They must have forgot something."

I pulled Grandma into the garage through an open door and hoped we hadn't been spotted. There were seven massive concrete mixer trucks parked inside. They were all red and yellow with the Concrete Plant logo on the mixing drum. I climbed up on the cab of the third truck and looked in the window. Keys were in the ignition.

"This is it," I said to Grandma.

I ran around and opened the passenger's side door for her. She got her foot on the high step and couldn't get any further.

"Alley-oop!" I said, shoving her up with my hand on her butt, sending Grandma sprawling across the seat.

I slammed the door closed, ran around, jumped behind the

wheel, and turned the key. The truck rumbled to life just as Shine and Salgusta appeared in the open doorway. I was desperately trying to find a garage door opener when Shine reached the truck and wrenched the driver's side door open. I grabbed the Bernzomatic and pulled the trigger. A massive flame shot out. Shine screamed and fell back. I pulled the door closed, put the truck in gear, floored the gas pedal, and crashed through the bay door. I careened to a stop in the parking area and put my hand to my heart. It was beating at stroke level.

"Holy shit pickles," Grandma said.

I didn't take the time to look for Shine or Salgusta. I drove the truck out of the parking lot, through the Concrete Plant complex, and onto the service road. I wasn't sure where I was going, but after after what seemed like a lifetime of blind panic driving, I saw the turnoff to Route One. I headed for the ramp and took out a highway sign. I was so frazzled I didn't know if I was going to or away from Trenton. I just knew I was on the highway.

"D-d-do you know where we're going?" I asked Grandma.

"We're heading for Trenton," she said. "You're doing good, but you might want to slow down a tad."

I checked the speedometer and saw that I was doing eighty. Pretty good for a concrete truck, I thought. Cars were moving out of my way. Not wanting to compete with the huge yellow and red behemoth that was rocketing up their ass.

A cop car passed me, and then another. I had two in front of me and one on the side. I looked in my rearview mirror. Three more cop cars. All with their lights flashing. I took this as a good sign. Even if I got a speeding ticket, it was still good.

I stopped the truck in the middle of the road and a Rangeman SUV immediately slid up beside me. Ranger jumped out, ran up to the truck, and pulled me out. He wrapped his arms around me and held me close, and I realized I was crying.

"Babe," he said. "Who knew you could drive a concrete truck?"

"Omigod," I said, wiping tears away. "This was a nightmare. How did you find me?"

"Surveillance cameras, and then I followed the trail of metallic blue extensions."

"I've got Grandma with me."

"Tank is with her. Do we need to have an EMT check her out?"

"No. She's okay. We were able to escape before the bad things started to happen."

"Morelli is dealing with Stupe. I'm supposed to take you and Grandma home. You can give a statement when you're up to it."

"Do the police have Charlie Shine and Lou Salgusta in custody?"

"Not that I know. Stupe was on the floor, dead, when I got there with Morelli. The chopper spotted you in the concrete truck. Charlie Shine and Lou Salgusta weren't on the scene."

I leaned into Ranger. He was warm and comforting. I always felt safe when I was with him. "Has someone told my mom that Grandma is okay?"

"I'll get a phone to Grandma. She can make the call."

He whistled to Tank and told him to give his phone to Grandma.

"Where do you want to go?" Ranger asked. "Do you want to go home or to your parents' house?"

"Home. I miss Rex."

Ranger commandeered the Rangeman SUV and wove around the cop cars that were clustered around the concrete truck. At least three miles of congestion was behind the cop cars. I called Morelli and told him Shine and Salgusta were responsible for Stupe and for kidnapping Grandma and me. I was hoping they were stuck in the three miles of stopped traffic.

We didn't talk on the ride home. I was too numb for conversation. Ranger maneuvered me out of the SUV, into my building, and into my apartment. I looked in at Rex and felt better. Everyone in my family was okay.

"Are you hungry?" Ranger said. "I can make you an omelet."

I managed a smile at that. "I hate to pass it up, but I'm exhausted."

He looked in my fridge and my freezer. "Ice cream?"

"Yes. Ice cream would be amazing."

We sat side by side on the couch and ate ice cream.

"It's a shame you don't want to get married," I said to Ranger. "You're actually reasonably domesticated."

"Babe," Ranger said. "Are you going to propose?"

"Not at this moment, but I'm thinking about it."

"Would you like me to stay here tonight?"

"It would be a waste. I can barely keep my eyes open. I'm going to go to bed and sleep for days."

"I might not care."

I punched him in the arm, and he got up and walked to the door.

"Call if you need me," he said.

I fell asleep on the couch, and Morelli woke me up at six o'clock. He had Bob with him and a bag of food from Pino's. Meatball sandwiches, fries, coleslaw, and ricotta cake. He clicked the news on, and we ate in front of the television.

"Did you catch Shine and Salgusta?" I asked.

"No. They're in the wind, but it's only a matter of time."

"Ranger said he found me by following a trail of metallic blue extensions."

"I called when I finally got home from work last night, but you didn't answer. When I called this morning and you still didn't answer I got worried, so I came here and found your door unlocked and the television on. I got in touch with Ranger, and he was able to access the security camera at the back of this building. He ran the video back and saw Stupe dragging a recycling bin out and wrangling it into a panel truck that belonged to the Concrete Plant. We went to the Concrete Plant and wandered around, finally finding the blue bin with your extensions all over it. The door to the storage building was open and Stupe was inside. We saw the cot and the food bags and all of Salgusta's equipment. And I have to tell you my heart stopped for a full two minutes, and Ranger went pale. We were inside the building when one of Ranger's men came to tell us about the garage door and empty bay. We must have missed you by seconds. The chopper was already in the air doing a traffic report. He spotted the concrete truck, we scrambled every patrol car in the area, and Ranger took off. One of the patrol cars said they clocked him at 110 miles per hour on Route One."

"Stupe was trying to extort money from the La-Z-Boys. He killed Lucca and Julius Roman."

"And then Shine and Salgusta killed Stupe."

"Yep. And eventually they would have killed me, but they had to go to Home Depot, and I was able to get away."

"They had all their torture tools out, and they decided to go to Home Depot?"

"Ran out of gas for the torch."

"God's will," Morelli said.

"Yeah, better to be lucky than good."

CHAPTER TWENTY-EIGHT

EARLY MONDAY MORNING I woke up happy to be alive and without a man's initials burned into my hoo-ha. It was now three o'clock, and I was still feeling happy. I was wearing my new blue silk shirtwaist dress to the lawyer's office. Grandma was wearing a magenta tracksuit. Her lipstick matched her tracksuit and her red hair was spiked up with Sumoclay. She looked even happier than I did. And I suspected her outfit was a stiff middle finger to intimidation of any kind.

Jimmy's lawyer, Ziggy Weinberger, was in a midrise office building in center city. When Grandma and I arrived at one o'clock, the small conference room was already packed with people: Jimmy's sisters, Barbara, Benny the Skootch's two wiseguys in training, a man and woman I didn't know, and empty chairs for Charlie Shine and Lou Salgusta.

When Grandma and I took our seats, Ziggy leaned forward in his chair at the head of the table. "I don't think we need to wait for Charlie and Lou," he said. "They're probably in Argentina. So, let's get started. Jimmy had a will drawn up several years ago. It addressed the possibility of another marriage, and in the event of that marriage, all of Jimmy's assets would go to his wife."

"That will is invalid due to senility," Barbara said. "I fully intend to contest it."

Angie jumped out of her chair and waved her bandaged hand at Grandma. "Whore woman!"

"Ladies," Ziggy said. "A little decorum, please."

Angie sat down, and Ziggy continued.

"Everyone should have a file folder," he said. "There are documents in your folders that give an accounting of Jimmy's assets at the time of death."

I paged through my documents, got to the bottom-line figure, and raised my hand.

"I'm not seeing any assets," I said.

"That's correct," Ziggy said. "He had an insurance policy to cover burial, but aside from that, he was broke. He spent the last of his money on his vacation."

"He was a successful professional," Barbara said. "How could he be broke?"

"He didn't get much work in his later years," Ziggy said, "but he kept spending money."

"What about his condo?"

"It isn't a condo," Ziggy said. "It's an apartment. And the Mole Hole was jointly owned. Jimmy's share goes to the remaining partners."

"Good thing I waited to book Antarctica," Grandma said.

"I don't believe any of this," Barbara said. "What about the keys?"

"There are no keys," Ziggy said.

"Of course there are keys," Barbara said. "Edna has them. We all know he gave them to Edna. And those keys are worth a fortune."

Grandma rolled her eyes. "What a bean brain," she said.

"Is that it?" Angie asked Ziggy.

"Yes," Ziggy said.

"We came downtown for nothing?"

"Yes," Ziggy said.

Everyone quietly filed out of the conference room. No one said anything. We all stood in front of the elevator, the doors opened, and everyone shuffled in.

"We'll take the next one," I said, stepping back.

"Good thinking," Grandma said when the elevator doors closed in front of us.

My mother was ironing when I brought Grandma home.

"We're okay," I said. "You don't need to iron."

"This is just ordinary laundry-day ironing," she said. "I heard about Jimmy's will. I started getting phone calls ten minutes after you walked out of Ziggy's office. Who would have thought Jimmy didn't have money?"

"My Galapagos trip is canceled," Grandma said, "but I'm still going to Gatlinburg."

"Are you staying for dinner?" my mom asked me.

"No. I think I'll see what Morelli is doing. I'm all dressed up, and I feel like going out to a fancy restaurant."

There was a knock on the door, and Grandma went to answer it. I followed after her just in case it was Lou Salgusta with a blowtorch.

"It's Benny's young men," Grandma said, looking out.

"Mrs. Rosolli," one of the slick-haired kids said, "I hope we aren't disturbing you, but we have a delivery to make from Mr. Benny the Skootch. Mr. Benny the Skootch said this is because Ms. Plum was so nice to him and brought him a pizza with the works. And Mr. Benny the Skootch always pays back. Are we allowed to deliver the package to you?"

"Of course," Grandma said. "That's very nice of him. How is he?"

"He's well. He's all stented up. He might get out of the hospital tomorrow."

The two junior wiseguys hustled to a white van and pulled something huge out of the back door. It was wrapped in moving blankets and secured with bungee cords. They carried it into the house, Grandma and I stepped back, and they set it down in the living room.

"This really wasn't necessary," Grandma said. "What is it?"

"Mr. Benny the Skootch had a special close relationship with the late Jimmy," the kid said. "He thought highly of him, and he wanted you to have this memento."

They released the bungee cords and pulled the wraps off and stood back, overwhelmed with the occasion.

It was Jimmy's La-Z-Boy.

Grandma and I were speechless. It was a lovely gesture, but it was horrible. The brown leather was scared and stained. The chair smelled like cigars and whiskey, and it had the clear imprint of Jimmy's behind on the seat.

"Well," Grandma said. "This is a . . . treasure. Please tell Mr. the Skootch that I'm very grateful."

The two wiseguys were all smiles. "Yes ma'am," they said.

They left, and Grandma closed the door after them. My mom came into the living room and gasped.

"What is that?" she said.

"It's a present from Benny," Grandma said. "It was Jimmy's chair."

My mother made the sign of the cross, and I thought it was a good thing she already had the ironing board up.

My father walked into the house. "I just pulled in and there was a white van leaving," he said. "Did we get a delivery?"

I hooked my thumb at the chair.

"Whoa!" my father said. "Jeez Louise, where did that come from?"

"It's a gift from Benny the Skootch," I said.

"No kidding? I always liked him." My father went over and sat in the chair. "Oh man, this is great. I always wanted a chair like this." He put the footrest up and reclined the back. "Oh yeah," he said. "Heaven."

"It was Jimmy's chair," Grandma said.

My father got wide-eyed. "From the Mole Hole? No kidding?"

He brought the back up and the footrest down and ran his hand along the leather. "Wait until the guys at the lodge hear about this."

"It's a little lumpy looking," Grandma said.

"It just needs to be shook out," my father said. "The cushion can probably get turned around."

He picked the cushion up, and two long keys were lying on the seat bottom.

"It's the keys," I said.

Everyone went statue still and stared at the keys.

"Do you really think they're the keys?" Grandma asked.

I picked them up. I'd seen keys like this before. They were keys to a safe.

"They're engraved with six initials," I said. "These are the La-Z-Boys keys. No one thought to look in the most obvious place."

"We should call Joseph and turn them over to the police," my mother said.

"No way," Grandma said. "These are mine fair and square, and I'm going to find the treasure."

"How are you going to do that?" I asked. "You have no idea where the safe is located."

"You'll find it," Grandma said. "You're good at finding things."

"What about the two sicko killers that are still out there and want the keys?" I asked Grandma. "What about the three crazy sisters who want the keys? What about Barbara? Don't you think it would be a good idea to give the keys over to the police and get on with our lives in a sane, less stressful fashion?"

"Indiana Jones wouldn't do that," Grandma said.

"I'm not Indiana Jones!"

"You could be if you wanted to be. You could be anything."

I didn't have a comeback for this. Truth is, I wouldn't mind being Indiana Jones. He was brave and smart, and he could crack a whip and ride a horse. He didn't like snakes, but he was okay with spiders.

"Indy would have curiosity about the keys," Grandma said. "He'd want to go out there and see for himself, even if he had to hack his way through jungles and go into creepy caves and tombs."

My mother was looking at Grandma as if she had corn growing out of her ears. My father was laid back in his new chair, eyes closed and a smile on his face.

I was smiling too. "Fortune and glory, Grandma. Fortune and glory. Let's go find a treasure."

THE KEY IS ONLY THE BEGINNING...

FORTUNE AND GLORY

The twenty-seventh Stephanie Plum thriller, from No.1 *New York Times* bestselling author

JANET EVANOVICH

Available from Headline Review in autumn 2020

Join JANET EVANOVICH on social media!

JanetEvanovich

@janetevanovich

janetevanovich

Download the Janet Evanovich app!

Visit **EVANOVICH.COM** and sign up for Janet's e-newsletter!